Protecting Her

Copyright

Opening Quote

Chemicals rushing in. I know it's you that I belong to. I'm fighting like a cannonball in the air. Crashing into who I belong to.

I Know You by Skylar Grey

Chapter One

✕ Taylor ✕

(Twelve Years Ago)

I step out of my squad car and look around at the buildings. Most of them are abandoned in this part of the city. Chicago has a lot of sketchy neighborhoods, but this one ranks number one in my book.

It really is no wonder they assign rookies here. No other cop in his right mind would volunteer for this beat. No fucking way.

"This area is high as fuck drug activity. But be on the lookout because it's a high gun area, too," my partner, Rob Jones, says.

"Man, am I glad you decided to stay my partner after training was done," I tell him, relieved.

Rob has years of experience with the Chicago Police Department. He's about my height. Over six feet. I only have to look up slightly to look him in the eyes. He's muscular. Takes care of himself, unlike a lot of cops we work with. He understands we can't slack off in this job. Our physical health could mean our life or death or that of one of our partners.

"Training is never done, rookie. You should always be learning. We're all sponges when we train. Some get out here on their own and stop

being sponges. Think they know it all. That's what gets you killed out here. I don't want you to be a statistic, rookie. I see a lot of promise in you."

"I won't let you down, sir."

"Don't worry about not letting me down. Don't let yourself down."

We hear commotion coming from the alley ahead of us and cautiously approach it. Rob lowers his voice so only I can hear. "What was the call? Why are we here, rookie?"

"Woman screamed. Caller saw her get punched and knocked out," I whisper.

"Looks can be deceiving in this neighborhood. False calls just to get us out here. Always keep your guard up."

We both quickly and quietly look around the corner. What we see completely floors me. "What the fuck?" I breathe.

"Turn your radio down. We don't want to alert them."

I quickly turn my radio down and take a deep breath. Panicking will get me nowhere. Rob takes out his gun and crouches down, using the wall as cover. He motions me behind him, and I follow his lead, taking out my gun and crouching.

"What do we do? We can't take them on ourselves."

"We observe. We listen. We get backup. Text dispatch. Tell them we stumbled on a huge arms deal and need more cops. Code Three."

I do as I'm told. When I'm done, I put my phone away. The pounding of my heart is nearly deafening, but I force myself to calm down. To listen.

"Seems pretty brazen to do this here. Cops could drive by any second," an older male says. I can tell he's nervous by the slight shake in his vibrato.

"Those pigs don't dare come at me. I'd gun them all down," a young kid who has to be in his very, very early twenties says. He's got a mohawk colored purple and yellow. Who the fuck does that?

"Let's just get this done. Load 'em up. I want to get my shipment out tonight," the older dude I assume is the buyer says.

I glance across the street and see a person walking on the sidewalk. "Shit..." I tap Rob on the shoulder and give him a signal to look across the street. He does just as the person sees us.

"Fuck," Rob whispers. I pray the guy says nothing. I'm not that lucky.

5

"Hey, hey! Officers! Lovely night for a stroll!" the fucker yells. He's very obviously drunk.

"Dammit," Rob growls. We both shoot to a standing position as people come running out of the alley.

"What do we have here?" The young punk dealer raises his gun at the person across the street as Rob and I begin backing away. We both have our guns aimed at the dealer, but we have far more guns pointed back at us. The dealer shoots the person across the street without looking.

"Holy fuck." My heart rate spikes. Rob and I dive towards our squad, but we don't have a chance of getting into it. Too many bullets flying. We leap behind the squad and each take separate corners, using the rear of the car for cover.

"Fan out!" the arms dealer says. "Take out the pigs!"

His guys begin surrounding us.

"Where the hell is our backup?" I'm getting nervous and scared.

"Coming! Start shooting. Hold them back!"

I shoot one of the guys closest to me. Rob takes out another. I hear sirens in the distance and will them to hurry the fuck up.

"Fuck!" I yell. A bullet pings off the car near my head, but I force myself to hold my position as I take out another of the dealer's guys. A moving truck comes flying out of the alley and squeals away. "That's the shipment!"

"Focus on survival!" Rob screams at me. We each take out another guy as three more squads show up. Rob and I both run behind one of them further away from those surrounding us.

The gun fight seems to continue in slow motion. Our firepower doesn't come close to theirs, and we're quickly overwhelmed. I watch as each of my partners are executed, one after another, until Rob and I are all that's left once more. I glance at him just as a guy grabs him from behind and yanks him up. Fear crosses his face as he meets my eyes.

"No!" I take aim and shoot the guy in the head.

Rob drops to the ground to catch his breath, but he doesn't have long to recover. Another guy kicks him in the stomach. He hits the ground, but fights. I nearly reach him when I'm grabbed from behind.

I fight.

I kick; claw.

I land a few punches all in an attempt to get to my partner. To protect him.

Something hard hits me in the face and knocks me into a car. I run towards Rob. He's in far worse shape than me. He needs me. "I'm coming, Rob!"

But I'm not.

My feet are kicked out from underneath me, and I crash to the ground next to Rob. I quickly get up, pulling Rob with me as another shot rings out.

Blood splatters all over me. I know I'm screaming, but I can't hear myself. Rob goes limp in my arms, and I fall with him on top of me.

There's more shooting.

More guns.

Did other cops show up?

I struggle in my weakened state. Rob's dead weight is on top of me, but I finally roll him off. I scramble to my knees when a sharp force hits me in the side of the head. I hit the ground.

Hard.

I try to keep the guy off me, but my vision is blurring.

Stay awake. Fucking stay awake, Taylor. You're not dying today, *I think to myself.*

Blood oozes into my eye. I can barely hear anything anymore, and I can hardly see. But I can feel the guy's grip on my neck slacken before he falls on top of me.

"Stay with me, officer. I'll get you out of here. Don't give up on me," a deep male voice says to me. The ringing in my ears nearly drowns him out.

I try to get up.

I can't.

The pain in my head is overwhelming. "Nuuuhhhh...," I groan.

"Come on. Stay with me, officer."

I try to focus on the stranger's voice, but I'm losing it again. It's getting even more distant, and my vision is going dark.

"Hey! Don't you give up on me!" the stranger yells.

"I... can't..."

I get dizzy.

I collapse as everything goes dark.

XXX

(Present Day)

I launch up into a sitting position on the bed clutching my chest and stomach, feeling all over my upper body for any cuts or bruises or tender areas or blood. I'm gasping for air.

Air.

I need it. I can't get enough.

"Taylor? Babe?" I feel a hand on my back softly rubbing as I take deep gulping breaths. "Baby, you're sweating. Are you okay?"

I don't know where I am. What the fuck happened?

Arms wrap gently and hesitantly around my waist, and a warm body presses against mine. "Taylor. It's okay. It was a dream. You're okay. You're okay now." The soft, sweet voice is whispering in my ear as her body is pressing against my back.

Slowly, very slowly, I start coming back to myself. My breathing regulates, and I remember where I am.

"Fuck." I take another deep breath.

"It's okay, baby. I got you. You're okay now."

Nicole.

My beautiful fiancé of nearly six months.

Mother of my child.

I turn and wrap my arms around her, pulling her on top of me in bed. I'm sweating. Probably soaking her in it, but I don't give a shit. I need her. I need her to steady me.

"What happened?"

"Nothing, baby. Just a dream." I nuzzle my face against her hair and kiss her neck.

"You know I know you better than that." She does. Nicole knows me better than just about anyone.

"I just need you right now, Nic," I say into her hair. She wraps her arms around me and lets me hold her close. I know I have to tell her. She deserves to know. Before we get married. After a few minutes, I take a deep breath and hug Nicole closer. "I love you, Nicole."

8

"I love you, too." Her curves mold to me as she kisses my shoulder. I glance at the clock. Five-thirty in the morning. I wonder if Ryan will be up.

Ryan Crane is one of my best friends. Like a brother to me. He lives in New York but spends almost as much time here, in Chicago, as he does there.

Our friendship really shouldn't be. He's a mafia boss of one of the biggest in the world. I'm a Lieutenant with the Chicago Police Department. My taskforce is assigned to organized crime. My job is to take people like him down.

I gently move Nicole off me and sigh as I sit up. "I'm sorry I got you all sweaty."

"It's okay. It's nothing a shower can't fix."

I nod and lean down to kiss her. "Why don't you do that? I'm gonna go get some air."

She puts her hand on my arm and gives me a soft squeeze. "Okay." She smiles as I get up and walk out to the balcony. I hear her close the bathroom door. Standing here, I can also hear if our baby wakes up.

I take out my phone and call Ryan.

I'm shaky. I hate being shaky. Especially since I never fucking am.

"I'm on the way. I'm just grabbing Arianna's dress," he answers as he picks up.

"What?" I blink a few times trying to remember if I know an Arianna.

There's a pause on the other line. "You okay?" he asks. I sigh. "You're getting married today, but there's something off. What's up?"

"I swear. Between you and Chase, I can't just brood." I glare at my backyard.

"That's what brothers are for. Out with it."

"Who's Arianna?" I ask through narrowed eyes. He's never mentioned her before. He's mentioned a girl, but never a name. I'm sure of it.

"After you tell me what's going on. Cold feet?"

"Fuck no. I can't wait until Nicole becomes my wife."

"Then?"

I run my hand over my face and sit on a chair. "I had that dream again," I say quietly. Ryan is quiet. "I mean it's been twelve fucking years."

"Taylor. You watched your partner die in front of you. Several of them. You almost died yourself," Ryan says as I take a deep breath. I think of it like it was yesterday. "Have you told her?"

"No."

"Don't you think you should? She really should know. She's gonna be the one sleeping next to you the rest of your life. Probably would help her talk you down after you have these nightmares if she knew."

I sigh. "You're right. It's just been so long since I had it."

"Doesn't mean she shouldn't know. PTSD is a fucked up thing, man. She needs to be prepared to help you through it if you need her to."

I lean back in the chair and massage my temple. "I'm marrying her today. I don't want to upset her before the wedding."

"No time like the present, though. Keep putting it off, and it'll get harder."

We're both quiet a moment before I change the subject. "So…, who's Arianna?"

Ryan sighs. "She's a girl I know. Her dad is the leader of another mafia. It's a long story, but she's having some issues with him. She needs a break, so I'm taking her with me."

"Oh?" I bite my lip to hide the laugh.

I can hear it in his voice. Ryan enjoys women. A lot. He's one of the most eligible bachelors in the world. He's got a reputation for no woman being able to tie him down. Not to say many haven't tried, but he's never given any woman a second date. Let alone allowed his voice to show any type of emotion or admiration towards one.

I'm pretty sure this one is the same one he's mentioned before.

"And?" I finally ask when he says nothing.

"Stop it. It's not like that. I dated her mom a few years ago. Her mom got murdered by her ex."

"Wait. Dated? You don't date. And her ex? The mob boss? Arianna's dad? Why haven't you just taken him out? Doesn't seem like you to allow the guy to still be breathing after he took someone you cared about from you."

10

Ryan lets out a breath. "You're right. It isn't. But I haven't because of Arianna. I've mentioned her before. I care about her. I don't want her to get hurt, and she's seventeen. I can't exactly just keep her with me while I take care of him."

My eyes widen. No wonder he never told me her name. "Seventeen? Fuck me, Ryan. What the fuck are you thinking?"

"That this isn't what you think. I'm just helping her out."

"Dude. You can't just take her across state lines. He could come after you for that. Legally and otherwise."

"Taylor. Stop worrying about me. Get ready for your wedding and have a heart to heart with your girl. Arianna said she's going for school. And I made it look like that was exactly what was happening. He doesn't have any reason to think otherwise."

"This is not going to end well."

"I'm just helping her out, Taylor. Nothing else."

He can deny it all he wants, but I know him. He's in love with that girl.

I hear Nicole shut the water off, and I sigh. "I gotta go. Nic's getting out of the shower. I wanna get this over with before Tait wakes up."

"Good idea. And then focus on what you're doing today. I'll be there soon. I have a driver. We'll get ready on the plane and be there about an hour before the ceremony."

"You better know what you're getting into here."

"I'll see you later, Taylor." He clearly ignores my comment and hangs up.

I shake my head. I can't worry about it. Right now, I have to figure out a way to tell the woman who holds my heart that I killed my partner.

Chapter Two

✕ Nicole ✕

After my shower, Taylor is sitting on the edge of our bed. He looks like he's watching me, but I know he's not. His eyes are stormy. Like he's lost somewhere nowhere near me. Somewhere not in this universe. It frightens me because it isn't my Taylor.

I take a deep breath and turn to Taylor after getting dressed. "Taylor." I kneel in front of him and take his hands in mine. "I'm not going to lie to you. You're scaring me."

"I... don't mean to, baby."

There's so much pain in his eyes. I feel it straight through my heart. The pain is nearly blinding. Suffocating. "Please talk to me."

He looks in my eyes before turning his head and breathing deeply. He stands and reaches a hand down to pull me up. I take it, and he leads me outside.

As soon as we're outside, Taylor sits and pulls me into his lap. It takes my big, tough, badass cop a minute of hiding in my hair before he finally starts talking. I put my arms around him and lay my head on his shoulder.

"I joined Chicago PD thirteen years ago. After going through the academy and training with my Field Training Officer on the streets, I got lucky. My FTO, Rob Jones, decided he wanted to take a break from training. So, he requested me as a partner." Taylor takes another deep breath and kisses my forehead. His grip around my waist tightens.

I tighten my arms around him in response and start to soothingly run my fingers through his short dark hair as he relives this memory that has haunted him for so long. Something I know very little about because he's never been able to share everything.

"My... first day out, not in training, I was an actual rookie cop, we got a call. We'd had a few prior, and I breezed through them. Jones was proud as hell. So, we get this call. Woman screaming. Looked like she was being dragged somewhere after she'd been hit. Caller didn't have a lot of information for us. We show up. Streets are empty. It's a high drug area, and Jones warned me it was also a high gun area."

I feel his entire body tense, and I feel horrible that I can't make everything easier for him. That I can't protect him. Part of me wants to tell him to stop, that he doesn't have to tell me. But I also know that I need him to. I need to know. Only then will I understand and be able to help him to move on from whatever it is that gives him these night terrors.

"We came up to an alley and saw a huge arms deal going down. We crouched by a building wall and listened. I texted dispatch for backup. We didn't want to give away our positions, so we turned our radios down. Across the street, this drunk dude sees us. Screams his greeting across the street."

"Oh... no," I whisper, already knowing where this is heading.

"The arms dealer, buyer, and the dealer's guys obviously come running around the corner and see us. The dealer shoots the drunk guy. Jones and I take the distraction as a sign to move. And then the fight was on. It was just us for I don't know how long, but we held them off. Backup showed up just in the knick of time. But... it wasn't enough." He pauses again. His piercing blue eyes are nearly gray with pain.

I'm so near tears, but I'm trying so hard to be strong for him. I need to be the strong one right now. The one he can lean on.

"They slaughtered us. There were just too many. They outmaneuvered us. They outgunned us. Pretty soon, it was just me and Jones again. We fought like hell. Eventually, they caught us. We were out

13

of ammo. Jones was…" He inhales sharply. I hug him and kiss his neck. "He was gunned down. I... I couldn't get to him in time. I tried. I was fighting off guys to get to him. He needed me. He was shot just as I reached him. In the end I... I failed to save him. He died because of me. I couldn't -"

I reach up and turn his face to me. "Don't you dare. Don't you dare blame yourself, Taylor Reddick." He stares at me, lost. Like he's searching me for answers he needs and doesn't have. "You didn't pull the trigger. And I know you. If you couldn't get to him, if you couldn't save him, Taylor, then no one could've. No one." He buries his head in my hair again, seeking a comfort only I've ever been able to give. I feel his tears on my neck. "Baby…"

"I was beat up. Bad. I could barely move. I couldn't breathe. I was coughing up blood. I couldn't see. I'd been hit everywhere. Head, face, chest, stomach, ribs. I thought I was going to die. My first fucking day out of training."

"I'm so sorry." I run my fingers through his hair, tugging lightly.

"I wouldn't have survived if not for Ryan."

"Ryan? You met him that night?"

"He saved my life. I was lucky as hell that he was there. I was lucky as hell that he heard all the shooting. And I was lucky as hell he decided to help. He was just starting to... infiltrate, I guess is the word, Chicago. He got his guys moving quickly. He overpowered them, and he got me out. I woke up in the hospital."

"Thank God."

"Ryan had called out over my radio that officers were down. That we needed help. By the time more officers showed up, he had the situation under control and was gone. All I remembered was him yelling at me to stay with him. I had no idea who he was, or if I'd ever see him again. After a couple days in the hospital, though, Ryan showed up. Told me what happened. We kept in touch."

"It's more than that. You guys are really close."

"After that night, I had nightmares every night about what happened. I couldn't get over it, and I blamed myself. I guess I still do. As soon as we figured out what was happening, I wanted to get the fuck out of there. Wait for backup. I ignored my instincts. I didn't speak up, and we lost seven good cops, including my partner. It ate me up. I spent a lot of time drinking. Ryan kept checking in with me. Finally, he got me out of my stupor."

"Knocked some sense into you?" I smile teasingly.

He chuckles as he starts to run his fingers through my hair. I smile at being able to at least get him to do that. "Yeah. Forced me to talk to Chase about everything. Forced me to talk to the department psychologist. It took me three months to recover fully. Physically and mentally. I went back to work. And Ryan basically handed me the career I have on a golden platter. He gave me tips. I acted on them and got the credit for taking down some bad people. Ryan amassed more territory and cleaned up the bad neighborhoods."

"So…, the dream you had. It was about the shooting?"

He sighs. "I still have some serious guilt. Sometimes, I can't get over the thought that Jones being killed, all of them actually, was my fault."

"But it wasn't," I whisper. He doesn't say anything. He only continues running his fingers through my hair and staring out at the lake beyond our property. I look at him and bring his face to mine again. "You know all of that time you spend telling me how smart I am, and that what I say or how I feel isn't stupid?"

He smiles softly. "Yeah."

"Well. I will spend just as much time telling you this isn't your fault. And in your very own words, Lieutenant, maybe you'll start to believe me."

He grins his cocky grin, and just like that, my Taylor is back. "Is that so?"

I nod. "Damn right."

He kisses me. Hard. His hand snakes up my shirt to my breast, and he cups it. "Not wearing a bra?"

I shake my head. "Wedding dress. Remember?"

"Forget marrying the most beautiful woman in the universe? Hardly." He kisses me again and kneads both of my breasts, taking turns playing with each of the nipples until I moan into his mouth. "I can't wait to call you my wife."

"I can't wait to call you my husband." I wiggle against him, feeling his hard and large cock against my thigh. I reach down and squeeze it.

"Fuck, baby."

I turn and straddle him, tugging down his gray sweatpants and freeing his massive length. I lean back and take him in both of my hands. He groans and sighs softly as he looks down and watches me. I stroke him with both hands, squeezing lightly. I pinch his tip. His eyes glaze over with need and desire. I'm glad I can bring him at least a little peace through this action… And I can't say I mind having his incredible dick in my hands either.

I stroke faster, squeezing a little harder. My thumb flicks against his tip. I relish his fingers digging in my ass. I shiver when he moves one of them between my legs and squeezes.

"Oh!" I throw my head back and stroke him faster as his hand slides down my panties. Two of his long fingers find their way into my wet pussy. I grind against him, moaning at how close I am to coming for him already.

Tait decides to pick that moment to wake up and cry. Taylor groans, and I nearly whimper when I take my hand away from his massive bulge, and he takes his fingers slowly out of my pussy.

"Sorry. Guess this is to be continued?"

"I need to get used to being cockblocked by my damn kid."

I laugh and get up. As I walk through the sliding glass door into our bedroom, I call over my shoulder, "I promise I'll make it up to you, Lieutenant."

"Keep calling me Lieutenant, and I'll let Tait cry while I fuck you!"

"No you won't. You love that kid too much."

He grins as I head to the nursery next door to our room. I'm not sure I made him feel better, but I hope I did. I hate seeing him blame himself for something that he couldn't have prevented.

One thing I love, though, is how in just a few hours, I'm going to marry the most amazing man who I fall more and more in love with every day. I can't wait to officially be Mrs. Nicole Reddick.

XXX

I run my fingers along the chairs as I look at the final preparations for the ceremony. I want everything to be perfect. I want it aligned perfectly. I want everyone's focus to be on me and Taylor on our special day with the garden we're getting married in to surround them with peace and nature's natural harmony. Lord knows after all we've been through over the past year, we all truly need it.

The family I'm marrying into is incredibly busy and chaotic. But I've never been happier or felt more safe, protected and cherished as I do with them. And it's not just with Taylor. I feel just as safe and protected with his brother, Chase, or even Ryan. I'd trust them all with my life just as I would Taylor.

I make my way to the reception room and do a walk through. Everyone is bustling around, busy as can be making sure all of the decorations and colors are right. I smile as I make my way through, making tiny adjustments as I go. When I get to the head table, my mouth drops.

"No, no, no!" I've never been a bridezilla, but I refuse to allow the head table to look like… that. It's in disarray. The flowers aren't centered. The block candles that look like ice aren't evenly spaced between each couple's place setting.

I quickly fix everything before I take off for my dressing room satisfied that everything is going to be simply perfect.

Chapter Three

☒ Ryan ☒

It's been a long ass night, and I'm really looking forward to getting the fuck out of New York. Too bad my time away is going to be short lived. Too much shit going on for me to just disappear.

I lean my head back in the seat of my limo and close my eyes, feeling myself slightly smile.

Had Nicole not wanted a big wedding, I'm pretty sure Taylor would've married her in front of the Justice of the Peace. I couldn't be prouder of how far he's come, and of the woman he fell in love with. Those two are meant to be.

I feel a hand on my arm and open my eyes, glancing at the woman sitting next to me. "Sorry. Your phone is going off." She hands me the phone I had on silent sitting in the seat between us. I glance at the caller ID and sigh.

"Not answering." I lean my head back and close my eyes again.

"Thank you. For taking me away for a bit," she says softly.

"Anything for you, Aria."

She wraps her arms around mine and leans her head on my shoulder. My breath hitches, but I ignore it and clear my throat. "Why do you call me Aria? Or Ari? Instead of Arianna?"

I open my eyes and look down at her before leaning my head back on the seat. "Because."

"Ryan Nathaniel Crane. That isn't an answer."

I laugh and look down at her. "Did you just middle name me?"

She smiles up at me, resting her chin on my arm. Her golden eyes twinkle and dance every time she looks at me, and the fact that I know that pisses me right off. I shouldn't know that. Shouldn't be paying that close of attention.

"And last named you. I full named you."

I can't help but smile at her. She's the only woman I've ever been this comfortable with. Everything comes so easily and naturally to her, and it makes me feel even worse. She's seventeen. She's barely a woman at all.

I lean my head back on the seat and close my eyes again. She puts her head back on my shoulder. "I honestly don't know. I guess I just wanted to call you something that no one else does. Something just between us."

I started calling her Aria or Ari because I wanted to make her feel special. To show her how much I care about her. Something between us that no one else had. I'm not stupid. I may like her. A lot. But I know nothing can happen between us. So..., I'll take the little things I can get. And keep telling myself that I'm an idiot for reacting to her the way I do. Even though I would never act on it.

"Is something wrong? You seem so... I don't know." Of course she'd pick up on it. I've never been able to keep anything from her.

"It's fine, Aria. Just have a lot of stuff going on. I really just want to get on that plane and get out of here for a little while."

"I understand. You need to regroup."

"Exactly."

Arianna is far smarter than any person should be at her age. She can read people almost as well as I can.

The limo pulls up next to my private plane. The driver gets out and opens the door for us. I step out and help Arianna, then reach in to grab her dress and my tux. The staff grabs our luggage, and I follow Arianna up the stairs. My eyes drop to her perfect heart shaped ass. I mentally punch myself in the face and tear my eyes away.

"I've never been in a private jet before."

I smile. "Well, get used to it."

"Are you saying this is going to be a thing?"

Fuck. I shouldn't have said that. Too late to go back now. "I'm saying I'll take you anywhere you want to go. Just say the word."

"Australia. I've always wanted to see a kangaroo."

I laugh again. "Australia it is. I'll book it now!" I tease her with a wink.

Arianna boards the plane and stops in front of me. It's too late for me to do anything but collide into her back. Instinctively, I reach around her, my arm crossing her chest, to keep her from falling.

"Oh! I'm sorry!" she squeaks.

I haul her against my chest to steady her, my other arm still holding our clothes. It takes me a second to realize where my hand is on her, and I instantly pull it away. "Ari..., I -"

"It's okay! Really. I.... It's okay." She blushes a beautiful shade of pink.

I clear my throat. "Uh... I'll get these put in the bedroom. We can change after breakfast when we're in the air."

"Oh... O-okay." She can't meet my eyes. Which is fine because after just grabbing her very full tit, looking in her eyes is not a good idea. She'll see way too much emotion.

I quickly walk back to the bedroom, holding the clothes in front of me so she doesn't see how my dick is about to poke a very large hole in my jeans. I lay the clothes in the bed, then stand in the middle of the room a few minutes composing myself enough to face her.

Finally, I walk back out and take a seat across from her. She smiles at me. "I really am sorry. I didn't mean to grab you like that. You stopped so quickly, and when I ran into you I didn't want you to fall. I mean, I'm over a foot taller than you are." I'm six feet five inches. Arianna is just over five feet.

"It's really okay. I'm glad you kept me from falling, so thank you." Her smile is bright, and I relax a little. I don't think I could handle it if things became awkward because of me being ridiculous. "I was just taken aback. This plane is gorgeous."

I smile and glance around. "Thank you. The designer did a good job. I requested some pretty obnoxious things just to see if it could be done."

"Like that fireplace?" she teases, nodding towards it.

"Yeah. And the bedroom has a seventy inch TV mounted to the wall."

Arianna's mouth drops. "Seriously?"

"And a fairly luxurious shower." I smile, and Arianna laughs.

"That is absolutely you. All of this. Luxurious everything."

"I want only the best." I shrug and wink at her as the plane starts to taxi down the runway. Arianna takes a deep breath and squeezes her eyes shut as she grips the arms of her chair.

"Don't like taking off?"

"Actually... um... no. I've not only never been on a private plane, I've never been on a plane at all." She chews on her lip and looks down at her lap.

I shake my head in disbelief. "Really? I thought your dad took you to the Alps all the time."

"No. He goes. He's never offered to take me. That's his thing with whatever floozy he's dating at the time. I've always gone to my friend's, Renza's, house for the week."

I narrow my eyes. "How have I not known this? You know I keep a close eye on him."

"I don't know. I guess it's not really hard to assume I just go with him."

"I don't assume shit. You know that. Assumptions can get you killed." I'm kind of pissed that I did just that. I assumed she went with him when he took off to go.

"Now you know."

"Yeah." I glare at the window. The plane takes off and begins its ascent. Arianna whimpers and bites her lip. I force myself to look away. Damn.

After a few minutes in the air, the flight attendant comes by with breakfast. She hands me coffee and eggs, hash browns, bacon, and a waffle, and I raise an eyebrow. I hadn't ordered anything.

"I hope you don't mind. You were putting our stuff away, and she asked if I wanted to order. I ordered for you, too."

21

"I don't mind. Just a little surprised. I usually only get coffee, eggs, and maybe a bagel when I fly."

"Oh. Um... I d-didn't mean to overstep. I thought you might be hungry after the night you had." She bites her lip, and I look down. She stutters slightly when she's upset or scared. And bites her damn lip.

I take a deep breath before I look back up at her and smile. "It's okay. I'm not upset. Just surprised you knew what to order."

"It's what you eat almost every morning when you're home." She says it quietly as she looks down. Hmm… Interesting she's watched me enough to know that.

I clear my throat again because I don't know what else to do. "Quesadillas?"

She smiles as she takes a bite of her breakfast. "I love breakfast quesadillas. Bacon, eggs, cheese, mushrooms, black olives. Best. Breakfast. Ever."

I laugh as she devours her breakfast. She is definitely not typical. She isn't afraid to eat in front of a man. Most women her age, and even older, would shy away from eating in front of anyone. After we finish, Arianna sighs.

"What?" I ask.

She pushes some of her hair behind her ear. Her beautiful, dark, long hair. "Well, I... I told my dad. About college?"

"Yeah?"

"He said if I really want to go, I'm doing it on my own. He'll pay my tuition, but he isn't helping with applications or anything."

"Do you really need him to?" I question, a little confused. She's one of the smartest people I know. I can't imagine she'd need her father's help with anything.

"No. I've turned all of my applications in. And I made it to the second round of the college I really want to go to." She fiddles with her fingernails.

"Which is?"

"Promise not to make fun of me?"

"What possible reason would I have to do that?"

She hugs herself and looks out the window. "Juilliard."

"The school for music and arts?"

"Yes." She looks at me and her eyes light up. "It's such an amazing school. It's so hard to get into! Making it to the second round is such a huge accomplishment in itself!"

I laugh. "Well, you are certainly passionate! What's the second round?"

"Original music. I can record it. In a studio. But they really prefer a video recording so they can see how I'm playing. My emotions and evolution and everything. My dad won't hire anyone professional to help me, though. I tried to do it myself on my phone, but it turned out like shit. So I had Renza do it, but you can't really hear the music as clearly as I want. I want it to look professional so it looks like I care, you know?"

I smile. She plays the piano like a pro. She doesn't sing much, but when she does, she could rival any of the greats. Mariah Carey. Whitney Houston. She could hold her own against either of them. "Is Juilliard where you really want to go? Your first choice?"

Her eyes go wide. "Oh my God, yes! It's been my dream since I was little!"

"Then when we get home, I'll hire a production crew for you. You can do your second phase to Juilliard at my house."

"Ryan! Really?" She throws herself at me, crashing into my chest with such force it actually takes my breath away.

"Oof! Sweetheart, warn me next time, so I can brace for the hit."

She hugs me tightly, and I give in and hug her back. "Thank you! So much!"

I can tell how important Juilliard is to her just by the way she lights up when she talks about it. I'd give anything to keep that beautiful smile on her face. Especially since, lately, her dad can so easily wipe it away.

After a few minutes, yes minutes, she pulls away.

I reluctantly loosen my grip. "We should be landing soon. Why don't you get dressed?"

"Okay." I let her go. She gets up slowly, like she doesn't want to. I take a deep breath, immediately missing her against me. I give myself a mental kick to the nuts for missing the way she feels. We both head to the room to grab our clothes.

"You can change in here. You'll have privacy. I'll change out there." I quickly turn to leave the room; my tux slung over my shoulder.

"Ryan?"

I stop and turn back. "Yeah?"

"Thank you again. For everything. For the dress. For taking me away. For always being here for me. Everything."

I smile. "Anytime, Aria. I mean that."

She shines, literally shines, when she smiles. I give up. I don't care that she's so much younger. I won't let her dad take the light she radiates. Every time I see her, she's a little more sad. She loses a little more glow. I'll spend the rest of my life giving it back to her. I don't care what the hell I have to do.

Chapter Four

✗ Nicole ✗

"I'm getting married!" I spin around in a circle. Breetana is just taking my dress from the garment bag and laughs.

"You are! And you're going to make a beautiful bride!"

There's suddenly a light knock on the door, and I freeze. "I don't want anyone to see me in the dress," I hiss.

"Don't worry. I'll take care of it." Breetana opens the door a crack, and then squeals.

"What in the world, Tana?" I say, my eyes widening. She pulls Ryan and a rather scared looking young woman into the room.

"You made it!" She throws her arms around Ryan.

He laughs. "Miss me?"

"Yes!" Breetana laughs. "How was Paris?"

"Uh… Well, I had to work. Couldn't really enjoy the wonders of Paris." He takes out his phone and scrolls through it. He turns it to both of us with a big smile.

"Oh my God! How could you? You should've texted us this right away!" I grab his phone.

He laughs. The picture on his screen is of the Eiffel Tower all lit up at night. He knows Breetana and I have been dying to see Paris. Especially the Eiffel Tower.

"Where's the fun in that?" He swipes his phone back and quickly texts each of us the picture before putting the phone away and giving me a hug. "So where's the dress?"

"Hanging up. You can't see it."

"What? Why? I'm not the groom!"

"Because I want everyone to have the same reaction as I walk down the aisle! You'll see it soon enough anyway since you're walking me. Now out. Taylor is down the hall!"

Ryan laughs. "Alright, alright! But first…" He takes the hand of the young woman behind him and gently pulls her forward. "This is Arianna. Can I leave her with you? She doesn't know anyone so I don't want to leave her on her own. And I'm not bringing her into Taylor's room with me."

My eyes light up. "Of course! She can finish getting ready with us!"

Breetana smiles. "Happy to have her!"

"Good." Ryan turns to Arianna and leans down to kiss her head. "You need me, shoot a text, okay?"

"O-okay," she says quietly. Her eyes flick towards us, and she smiles nervously.

Ryan gently cups her cheek. "It'll be okay. They're like my little sisters. I promise you'll get along. I wouldn't leave you with them otherwise." She nods, but looks like she's about to cry. Ryan gives her a dazzling smile, and she visibly relaxes. Breetana and I share a look, both of us beaming. Ryan kisses her on top of the head again before squeezing her hand and leaving. "Take care of her!" He smiles and winks as he leaves and closes the door behind him.

"That was…," Breetana trails off.

"Interesting. Definitely interesting," I say.

We both look at Arianna. She's wringing her hands together. "W-what?" She focuses completely on her hands, not meeting our eyes.

"Is there... something going on between you two?" I ask carefully.

Her eyes go wide, and she looks at us like a deer in headlights. "N-no! No. O-of course not!" Breetana and I look at each other again. Arianna plops down in a chair. Tears burst from her eyes.

"Oh my goodness, sweetie!" Breetana says, surprised.

"What's wrong?" I ask. We both rush to her side and kneel next to her. She takes a few deep breaths but keeps her face hidden behind her hands. "Arianna, it's okay. What's happening? Are you okay? What did Ryan do? Breetana and I will go beat him up!"

"With no hesitation. Did he say something?"

She shakes her head as her tears subside. "It's not R-Ryan. Ryan i-is…" She takes another deep breath and wipes her eyes. The little bit of makeup she's wearing smears. "It's really s-stupid. It's so, s-so stupid!"

"Oh, sweetie." Breetana scoots in front of her.

"What's stupid? If we can help, we will."

Arianna looks at us, eyes watery, and bites her lip. "I... j-just…" She shakes her head and sniffles.

Breetana hugs her. "Whatever it is, Nikki and I are here for you."

Arianna hugs her tightly and pulls away after a moment. "It's j-just that... I-I'm seventeen." She looks down at her hands again.

Breetana's eyes widen. "Oh... Oh, sweetheart." Breetana hugs her again, but I'm confused.

"What?" I ask, shaking my head.

Arianna looks over at me and pulls away from Breetana again. "I r-really like h-him." It's barely a whisper.

It suddenly dawns on me. "Oh. I see."

She takes a deep breath and closes her eyes. When she opens them, she seems a lot more calm. "He's just so nice to me. And he isn't like that with anyone! I try not to bother him, but sometimes my dad is so mean to me that I just need someone to talk to. Ryan always drops everything for me. Even though I tell him not to. At first, I was just so happy to have a friend who actually liked me for me and cared about me. But then I just really started to like him. And now…"

"Now you really like him." She nods, and I hug her. I run my fingers through her hair. It's so obvious Ryan feels something for her. I can tell, but I don't know if it's my place to say anything. I look at Breetana. She smiles.

"You... you won't be seventeen forever," I say quietly.

27

"I know, but I don't… think he could ever feel the same way. I'm so much younger than him."

"I think you're wrong about that. Ryan feels something for you. I can tell." Breetana smiles and Arianna's eyes light up

"I think maybe you should just enjoy him for now," I suggest.

Arianna pulls away and wipes her eyes. "What do you mean?"

"Just enjoy his company. Don't worry about anything right now. If you let the tension and nerves get in between you, then it will just become awkward."

"It's pretty obvious he likes you, Arianna. But Ryan is…" Breetana pauses like she's trying to find the right words. "He's very moral. He won't act on how he feels right now."

"How come?" Arianna questions.

"Because of your age, sweetie. It might be completely legal in New York to be with you, but he's just not like that," I say. "Just… give it time. Use this time to really just… I don't know."

"To just be with him. Without stress," Breetana finishes.

Arianna nods and takes a breath. "Thank you. I'm really sorry I broke down like that. And I'm sorry for the stutter… I get it when I get nervous or upset."

"Are you kidding? It's fine!" I say comfortingly. "Breakdowns are totally normal. So are stutters."

"It's hard to have feelings for someone and not be able to tell them. But I promise you, in the end, it will all be worth it." My big sister always has had a way of being that comforting presence. It's heart-warming to see she has that same effect on Arianna as she has on me my whole life.

"Just be patient. And don't feel bad about it. You can't help how you feel. Age is only a number anyway." I shrug.

Arianna smiles, looking as if she feels a hundred times better. "Don't you have a wedding to get ready for?"

"Oh my Gosh! I'm so excited!" I stand and clap my hands together as I beam.

Breetana stands, grabs the dress off the hanger, and holds it up. My off-white spaghetti strap gown is simple. It's made of light fabric and lace that flows perfectly around my body to the floor. It hugs the top part of my body so perfectly it's like it was made just for me.

"Oh, wow. That dress is so pretty!" Arianna breathes.

"I know! I can't wait to get it on." I step out of my clothes, and Breetana helps me step into the dress. She starts to zip it, but struggles a bit.

"Arianna? Can you hold the back of her dress so I can zip it and tie it?"

"Sure." The two of them work together. Soon enough, I'm in my dress.

I look in the mirror and beam at my reflection. "I really feel like a bride."

"A beautiful bride... I r-really hope this dress is okay. It's almost w-white. Ryan got it for me," Arianna stutters adorably. Her strapless, light gray, satin dress just brushes her ankles and hugs every curve of her body.

"The dress is gorgeous! Nikki asked for the wedding to be black tie for the guys, and white, off white, or gray dresses for the women."

"It fits in with my theme."

"Good! I was worried. Ryan is wearing a gray tie to match me."

"Ryan has damn good taste," I gently tease. Arianna blushes and looks away. I smile brightly. "Let me just fix your makeup while Tana gets dressed." I take out my kit and get to work while Breetana gets her dress on.

"Thank you guys. For not judging me about Ryan. I don't know why I just spilled all of that. I guess I needed to get it out."

"We're definitely not ones to judge. Ryan really is amazing." I smile as I fix the little bit of make-up she's wearing.

"Honestly, I think we're both pretty happy about it," Breetana says.. Arianna blushes again as I finish fixing her makeup and hair. Breetana finishes getting dressed and stands at my side. "Awe! Perfect. Good as new."

"Wouldn't even know you'd been crying at all!" I fuss with her hair a little more before stepping back with a wide smile.

She blushes again and looks at Breetana. "That dress is so pretty, Breetana."

"Thank you!" She turns to the mirror, and the three of us put touch-ups on our hair and make-up.

"I think it's time!" Breetana grins.

"Not until Ryan gets here. He's supposed to walk me down the aisle."

29

"I can try and find him," Arianna says shyly.

"That would be nice. Thank you!" I smile. Arianna smiles back and leaves the room. "Okay. Not gonna lie. That girl is so cute. I don't even care that she's so young. I want her with Ryan."

Breetana laughs. "He won't. Not now. You know that."

I pout. "I know. But it's so obvious he likes her. And she likes him."

"He's too moral, Kiki. He won't do anything about it right now. And I know you, Miss Matchmaker. Leave it alone for now."

"You're no fun."

"I'm tons of fun. Also really smart."

I laugh. "Fine. He's too moral. But the day she turns eighteen, you have to help me. They need to be together."

"I agree. Now. Wedding! Let me adjust your dress so you look absolutely perfect."

Breetana spins me around with a laugh and starts fussing over my dress. I smile softly as I think of the man who will be waiting at the end of the aisle for me. I'm sure I could walk down there in a cardboard box, and he'd still think I'm beautiful. My smile widens as I think of how perfect he is. My soulmate.

XXX

Taylor

My hands are shaking. I've never been more nervous. Not even when I asked Nicole to marry me. My best friend and brother, Chase Shaw, is adjusting my tie because I can't do it. I've messed it up six times.

"Relax, dude."

"Easy for you to say," I grumble. "You're always so suave. Last time I wore a tux was at your wedding. And before that was prom."

Chase laughs as he finishes my tie. "Well, look at you." He looks me up and down. My black tux is tailored to me. Necessary because I'm around six feet three inches and muscular. I spend a lot of time in the gym. Nothing fits me. Most everything I wear, I need to get tailored. "You clean up pretty well." He shoots me a teasing grin.

I laugh. "I'd say you do, too, but you're almost always in a suit."

"I can't deny that!" Just then, there's a knock on the door. Chase pokes his head out, then opens it. "Bout damn time! Our boy's freaking out."

"I am not," I chuckle.

"Can't blame you if you are." Ryan walks in and gives me a hug. "You look good."

"So do you. Though, you wear tuxes a lot."

Ryan shrugs. "Part of the job."

"So? Where's this Arianna chick? I want to meet her," I say with a smirk.

"Arianna?" Chase narrows his eyes suspiciously. "Who's Arianna?"

"Stop. Both of you," Ryan growls.

I ignore him with a grin as I look over at Chase. "Yeah. Arianna. He brought a date."

"Date? You? Never thought I'd see the day. Now I have to meet her. See who tied down the famous Ryan Crane," Chase teases.

"Not a date." Ryan shakes his head.

"Yeah. Right. You should've heard him this morning." I grin wider as I continue to tease him.

"Enough. You both are assholes."

"Gushing?" Chase asks, ignoring Ryan.

"Like you do with Breetana."

"No shit?" Chase says, grinning.

"Guys! Enough," Ryan commands. "It's not a date. I'm helping her out. That's it. She's a lot younger than me. It's not happening."

"Age is just a number." Chase shrugs.

"Yeah. She'll be of age soon," I continue to tease.

"Fuck, Taylor. Shut up, would you?"

"Of age?" Chase asks.

"She's seventeen. Okay? I feel like a fucking pedophile." I watch my usually confident brother deflate and sink onto the couch with his head in his hands.

"Well, Jesus Christ. You got it bad, don't you?" I stop teasing when I see how torn up he is.

31

"Not having this conversation. Her and I are not a thing. It can't happen." He doesn't look up, and Chase and I look at each other.

Chase clears his throat. "So? When do we get to meet her? Where is she?"

Ryan looks up. "Do you two dickheads think I'm gonna subject her to your relentless teasing? Fuck you both. She's with Tana and Nikki."

I can't help myself. One more quip. I grin. "She's gotta be gorgeous in order to catch and hold your eye."

"I swear to God. Enough."

I hold up my hands in mock surrender. "Okay, okay! No more."

"Seriously, though. What are you going to do about it?" Chase asks.

"Nothing. Absolutely nothing. I'm going to continue to be her friend, and that's it. Anything more is immoral and, honestly, I'm not into sleeping with kids."

"Well, to be fair, she isn't a kid."

"I mean, just because she's not eighteen doesn't make her a kid. Yeah, it's immoral, but it's not illegal. At least, it's not in New York. There's such a thing as an age of consent." I shrug.

"I'm still not taking it further. She's dealing with a lot right now. Honestly, so am I. I won't sit here and deny that she's gorgeous, and I have some serious feelings for her, but I have *some* fucking morals." He stands and walks to the window, brooding. After a few moments, he turns to us. "Well? How do you feel?" He nods towards me.

"Nervous as fuck. I keep thinking that Nicole is going to see me at the end of the aisle and realize she can do far better than me."

"She can. But she loves the hell out of you." Chase smiles as he teases me.

"Asshole," I grunt. We all three laugh.

"Seriously, though. You really lucked out with her," Ryan says.

I beam with pride. "Don't I know it!"

"Hey, before I forget. I got the permits for Nicole's bakery," Ryan says, changing the subject completely.

I breathe a sigh of relief. "Good."

"We'll get the remodel going while you guys are in London," Chase says.

"Should be done by the time you get back."

"And it's in your territory, Ry?" I look over at him a little concerned. I don't want Nicole to ever go through what she went through in Silver Bay again. Having her bakery in Ryan's territory is my way of making sure she's always protected.

"Yep. It's a block away from Chase's office. I took over that area a few years ago, so she'll be safe. It's a good neighborhood now. Thriving. There's a couple good restaurants in the area. No bakeries for a few blocks, though, so she should be pretty busy."

"Man. I hope she likes it. She bakes all the time at home. I bring so much shit into the precinct for the guys that I think they're all in love with her."

"Bree said she was pretty heartbroken about losing her bakery," Chase mentions.

"And she has been talking a lot about opening one," Ryan chips in.

I rub my hands over my face. I'm a little nervous she won't want to open one again, but I listen to my brothers. "You're right. You're right. She'll love it."

"Ryan and I can vet a couple people while you're gone so she has a couple employees to help out."

"Perfect. Now, I'll have to convince her to look into daycares." I shake my head.

"Yeah... That's not happening," Ryan says.

"What? You don't think she'll go for it?" I raise an eyebrow.

He shrugs. "She might. I sure as fuck won't."

"Ry, she can't take him to the bakery every day," I tell him.

"There's a daycare for my employees on the floor underneath my office. Reese had that level redone when we did my office remodel. You can only access it with a security escort unless you have mine or Bree's access. Or yours or Nikki's. You can drop him there. That way you don't have to worry about finding a daycare and Ryan finding something wrong with every single one of them." He gestures to Ryan and smiles as he winks. "That good with you, Your Highness?"

We all laugh. Ryan nods to Chase. "Get me access so I can get to my nephew if I need to, and it's a deal."

"Done. I should've done it already, but you've been busy as hell. I'll take care of it while they're gone on their honeymoon."

I check my watch. "Well, fuck. Looks like it's time to head out and get all the final details tied up."

"Tell me what you need, and I'll have Chase get it done." Ryan smiles teasingly at Chase.

"The fuck I'm doing anything for you."

We all laugh again as we head out of the room. I'm excited as hell to marry my girl, but my nerves are killing me. My heart knows she'll become my wife, but my head is playing a twisted game with me. Any small chance that she'll get cold feet and run is too much of a chance.

"Dude. Get out of your head. She's not going anywhere," Ryan says.

"Except down that aisle to say 'I do'." Chase nudges me.

"You're right. Damn. My mind is just all over the place."

"She loves you, Taylor. All you have to do is take one look at her. She can't hide her feelings to save her life."

Ryan is right. My girl wears her heart on her sleeve.

And her heart belongs to me.

Chapter Five

✗ Nicole ✗

I laugh just as someone knocks on the door to my dressing room. Breetana jumps up and opens it. Ryan steps in.

He looks me up and down and smiles. "Wow. You definitely make a beautiful bride. I'm glad you made me wait to see the dress." He extends his arm as Breetana slips out the door. "Arianna said you might need an escort. Ready to get married?"

I take his arm. "More ready than I have ever been for anything in my life."

Ryan leads me out of the dressing room to the door leading into Crystal Gardens. I grip Ryan's arm tightly as he opens the door to the venue and slowly walks me down the aisle. My eyes are on Taylor's, and his never leave mine. No one else in the venue exists except him in that moment.

When we reach him, Ryan leans down and kisses my forehead as he takes my hand and places it in Taylor's. He shakes Taylor's hand and winks as he walks to his seat in the front. He puts his arm around the back of Arianna's chair, and Taylor and I share a knowing look.

As the officiant begins the ceremony, Taylor leans down slightly. "You're beautiful. That dress is…" He trails off. I reach up to wipe away a stray tear that falls from his eye as he smiles at me.

"You're so handsome in your tux." We hold each other's hands and look in each other's eyes as the officiant continues talking. Eventually, he asks us to exchange rings and say our vows. I take Taylor's ring and slip it on his finger. "From the very first moment I saw you, I knew I wasn't going to be able to walk away. I'd never be able to let you go. And I knew you felt the same when Ryan showed up in Minnesota. I knew all you wanted was safety for me and Tait, even though neither of us had officially met him yet. I knew right then that I was going to marry you. I didn't care that I'd only known you two days. I fell so far in love with you. So fast. And every day gets better and better. I can't wait to spend the rest of my life in your arms."

Taylor smiles and reaches up to wipe a tear from my eye, then slides a white gold wedding band with blue diamonds around the entire band. It matches the blue diamonds in my engagement ring's band perfectly.

"You took my breath away when you first walked into the room, baby girl. You take my breath away every day that I get the honor of waking up next to you. I never believed in love at first sight, but it happened when I saw you. I knew you were the only one I wanted. And when I felt Tait nuzzle into my hand when I touched your stomach, that was it for me. I knew he was mine. Just like I knew you were mine. I'll do anything to protect you. To show I love you. I can't wait to start our life together."

He squeezes my hands in his. I get lost in his blue eyes. When the officiant says he can kiss his bride, Taylor smiles widely and pulls me close. As soon as his lips meet mine, everything fades away. It's just me and him. His hands dip low on my back, and he slightly bends me backwards. After a few long glorious moments, Taylor reluctantly pulls away and gives me a cocky grin.

"I've been waiting the whole damn ceremony for that moment."

I smile softly as I blush. "I love you."

"I love you, too." He leans down to give me a sweet kiss as the officiant introduces us to our guests. There are hoots and hollers and whistles among the applause as we turn and look out at everyone.

XXX

Later at the reception, Taylor and I are dancing and mingling with our guests. I don't think either one of us has stopped touching one another in some way.

I lean my head on his chest as we sway to the music and catch sight of Ryan. He's smiling as he talks to Arianna. His hands are low on her back as he holds her close.

"Oh my God."

"What?" Taylor looks down at me quizzically.

"Look at them." I point as my smile grows wider. "He is so sweet with her."

"How did I know you'd be all for that?"

"Because I'm a romantic. Forbidden love. It's so... Jane Austen."

He kisses me with a chuckle. "He really likes her."

"I can see that."

"No, baby. I mean, he admitted it. He won't do anything about it right now, but he really likes her."

I smile so hard my face feels like it's cracking. "She feels the same way..."

"What? Really?" He looks over at Ryan and Arianna again. She blushes and leans into his hand as he pushes a strand of hair behind her ear. "Holy shit."

"See?"

He looks down at me. "I'm happy to see that, but I'm even more happy to call you my wife. You're so beautiful, baby." He leans down and kisses me.

"I'm having a really great time, but when do we get to leave? I'm really, really excited to see London."

"Well... Chase said his plane is gassed up and ready. Limo is waiting. They have Tait. Our bags are on the plane already..."

"So..., now?"

Taylor laughs. "Excited?" He tugs my hair.

"So excited."

"You know what I'm excited for?"

"What?"

"It's a long ass flight. And there's a damn nice bedroom."

"Taylor!"

He grins and leans down to lift me up. Bridal style, he carries me to the DJ booth. The DJ grins and holds the mic up to Taylor's lips. "Everyone! Thanks for coming. Venue is yours until they kick you out. Enjoy all the free shit. We'll see you in two weeks. We have a plane to catch!" Taylor carries me out to the waiting limo as everyone cheers and whistles.

When we are settled and the driver begins driving, I turn to Taylor. "Well, Mr. Reddick? You ready to do this?"

"You mean the rest of our lives, Mrs. Reddick? Fuck yes. Can't wait."

XXX

Taylor

After the plane is in the air, I pull Nicole into the bedroom in the back.

"It really is so nice of Chase to let us use his plane."

"Well. He has no meetings that would take him away. And if something does come up, Ryan will let him use his." As soon as we get to it, Nicole stops and stares in open-mouthed shock. I smile and laugh. "I mean, I know I'm gorgeous, baby, but staring at me like that is making me nervous."

She swats me playfully. I catch her wrist and kiss her palm. "Cop reflexes." She smiles teasingly.

"Charming, huh?" I pull her close and lean in to kiss her. She nips my bottom lip as she puts her arms around my neck, and I groan.

"This room. It's like a master bedroom."

"Ryan and Chase have extravagant tastes. You think this one is nice, you should see Ryan's."

"You've seen it?"

"I once had to fly to New York for a case. He took me because he was headed home anyway. This plane is nice, but you want to see something extravagant..."

"Well, I love it."

"So, I should get a private jet?"

"Definitely!"

I laugh and turn her around so her back is to me. I slowly undo each button and untie each tie. "I don't think I can afford this on my salary."

"Then I'll buy one for us when I become a famous baker!" I laugh again and lean down to kiss her neck as my fingers skim down her back. She shivers under my touch. "Mmm... I don't think I'll ever get tired of you touching me like that."

"Good."

I drag my tongue across her shoulder, then open-mouth kiss the trail I left as I finish undoing everything on the back of the dress. When I finish, I slip it down to her waist and hold it there as I kiss up her neck to her jaw.

"Taylor..."

She turns her face so that her lips meet mine. I let her dress fall the rest of the way as I run my hands up her stomach to her tits. I take one in each hand and slowly massage them, pinching her nipples and rolling them between my fingers until she moans. My tongue dances with hers. Her kiss becomes more needy and heated. She turns in my arms and pulls off my jacket as her lips meet mine again.

"God, you taste like Heaven," I rumble.

She undoes my tie and throws it aside as soon as she frees me from it. She starts working on the buttons of my shirt, but I've had enough. I pull it over my head and toss it to the floor. Her hands trail down my abs, and my breath hitches. I love when she touches me like this. Soft fingers with a touch of nail, just enough to make me quiver under her touch.

"So many muscles. I could trace the outline of them all day."

"You'd drive me insane." I catch her hands again and pull her to the bed.

She crawls in and sits on her knees. I smile as she beckons me closer with a crook of her finger. It's like my body moves on its own. As soon as my knees hit the bed, she grabs my waistband and undoes my belt.

She unbuttons my pants, then runs the back of her hand down the zipper against my cock before she unzips them. She pushes my pants and boxer briefs down. I step out of them. She takes my hand and pulls me into the bed.

"God, you're so big. I mean, I've only ever seen one other than you, but... damn, Taylor. I'll never get used to it."

I have no time to respond to her before she has me in her mouth. My fingers automatically entangle themselves in her hair. "Fuck, Nikki."

"Mmm..." She knows exactly how I like her to suck and touch me.

She takes me as far into her mouth as she can until I'm touching the back of her throat. She holds me there for a second before her hand starts pumping my length. She lightly grazes her teeth up my hard as hell dick, making me impossibly harder. She runs her tongue back down the path her teeth made and back up, swirling her tongue around my tip before taking me back in her mouth to suck. She repeats the motions several more times until I can't take anymore.

I tug her hair. "I'm going to come, babe." I feel her smile before she softly nips the spot just below my tip, then licks it as she pumps. I'm starting to pulse underneath her grip. I throw my head back. "Ah... God."

She gives me one last suck. I empty myself inside her warm mouth. She swallows everything I give her, then licks the rest up.

"I love the way you taste." She licks her lips. I growl and grab her hips, flipping her on her back. "Are you sure Chase will be okay with this?"

"Baby, I'm sure he expects it."

I tug her panties off and toss them somewhere. I spread her legs and settle myself between them. I run a finger down her already wet pussy.

"Oh... Taylor..."

I follow the path my fingers made with my tongue. She arches into me. "Talk about tasting good..." I dip my tongue inside her.

She gasps. "You're so, so good at this."

I smile against her and run my tongue back up to her clit. "Bet you I make you come within seconds with no fingers."

"You know it takes longer than that!" She grabs my hair and moves her hips in time to my tongue. I draw back. "Noooo!" Her whine is sexy as fuck.

"Yes. Here's my deal. I make you come in seconds using just my tongue, you let me go to the studios in London to see the Harry Potter stuff."

She rolls her eyes. The studios in London are one of the things we cut from our itinerary that we didn't think we could fit in. One of my secrets that no one knows except her and Chase is that I love the Harry Potter series.

I was one of those idiots that got the books the first day they came out and binged it. I even took the official quiz to be sorted into a Hogwarts House. Not that I'd ever admit that out loud. Only one person knows that I was Sorted into Gryffindor. And that's Chase. I know he would never reveal that secret to anyone. Not since I would reveal exactly where he was Sorted when he took the quiz. He would die of shame if anyone ever found out he was Sorted into Hufflepuff.

Nicole doesn't like Harry Potter, but she obliges me when I want to watch the movies anyway.

"And if you don't?"

I shrug. "Then I'll give in, and we can do the Palace Tour so you have a chance of meeting Prince William."

"You really think that's a good idea? If I see him, he'll fall in love with me, and I'll end up being a Princess."

Her teasing smile makes me laugh. "I'll fight him. He won't win."

"He has bodyguards! Are you planning on taking on the entire Royal Guard?"

"Yep. They don't stand a chance!"

"Okay, Superman. You're on. You have seconds."

I give her a dangerous smile. "It's on."

I practically dive into her. I flick my tongue furiously back and forth against her clit. She grips the sheets and arches her back, bringing herself closer to my mouth. I gently bite her clit, then suck on it before flicking it furiously with my tongue once more. Her legs start shaking, and I give her one last suck before she comes undone.

"Oh my God! Taylor!"

After licking up all of her sweetness, I look up at her and wipe the corner of my mouth as I smile sardonically. "Better than the prime rib we had for dinner."

"You are so cocky and totally cheated," she pouts

I laugh. "How did I cheat?"

"I don't know. But you did. And when I find out how, you're going to pay. Because you just kept me from the opportunity at being a real life princess."

I laugh again as I crawl up her, leaving a trail of kisses along her stomach, nipples, supple mounds, chest, collarbone, neck, and jawline. She rewards me with soft sighs and subtle arches into my mouth. When I finally meet her lips, I flick her bottom lip with my tongue. She laughs.

"Why would you want to be a Princess when you're already a Queen?"

"Your Queen." She pulls me down to her lips and gasps against my mouth.

I slide my cock inside her with a moan as she pulses around me.. "Couldn't wait anymore."

She wraps her legs around my waist and meets every one of my thrusts. What starts out slow and beautiful very quickly turns hard and needy. Our hot, sweat slicked bodies slide against each other with a familiar rhythm. Grunts and moans that come from her lips and low in her throat drive me mad.

"God, Nikki. It gets better and better every time with you."

"I can't get enough of you." Her nails rake down my back, not enough to leave marks or draw blood, but enough to make my thrusts inside her harder and deeper. I bury my face in her neck and kiss it while she bites my shoulder.

"Fuck, baby." I return the light bite. She throws her head back. I feel her walls tighten around me, and I nearly lose it.

"Taylor... Taylor, oh!"

I reach down between our bodies and rub her most sensitive spot. It's all it takes for her to fall off the cliff and drag me with her.

After a few moments of catching my breath, I roll off her and pull her to my side. She shivers in the cool, pressurized air. I pull the blanket over us. She yawns.

"Still got a few hours if you want to sleep for a bit." I gently rub her arm.

"I don't want to be sleeping when we land."

"The staff will wake us up with plenty of time to get dressed and get to our seats."

"Are you sure?"

"Positive. I went on a business trip with Chase once because I didn't feel comfortable with him going where he was without security. He hadn't slept. He had a ton of meetings. He flew right back here after but didn't get any rest because of the conference call he took while in the air. So when he landed and I boarded, the first thing I did was make him take a nap."

"I love how protective you are. Of all of us."

I kiss her hair. "Staff woke him up about an hour before landing so he had time to freshen up. We're in good hands, sweet girl."

"Mmhmm..."

I hug her a little tighter as she falls asleep in my arms. Not long after, I follow, content and more happy and at peace than I've ever been my entire life.

Chapter Six

✗ Arianna ✗

(One Week Later)

I'm sitting in my last class of the day waiting for it to end.

I really like school, but it isn't challenging to me anymore. I get straight A's with little effort. Even with all of the advanced classes I'm taking. Advanced History. Advanced Biology. Advanced Chemistry. Advanced Calculus. I don't even bother taking notes anymore. I don't need them.

My phone vibrates, and I discreetly look at it. There was a test today. I finished it a long time ago. I've been sitting here doodling ever since.

I smile and blush when I see Ryan's name.

Ryan: Hey. I'm outside.

I glance at the window but have no idea why. I can't see the parking lot from here.

Arianna: Okay. I'll play. Why are you outside?

Ryan: Because I have a surprise for you.

I smile and glance at the teacher. He's paying absolutely no attention to the class. I glance at the clock on the wall and sigh.

Arianna: I finished my test a long time ago, but I still can't leave for another twenty minutes.

Ryan: What class?

Arianna: Advanced Calc.

Ryan: Advanced? Fuck. I barely passed my regular math class. If it wasn't for Nick and Jason, I wouldn't have passed it at all. Though, I shouldn't really be surprised with you. You're ridiculously smart.

I blush and discreetly hide my burning cheeks.

Arianna: Stop making me blush.

Ryan: Just being truthful.

I glance back up at the teacher to make sure he still isn't paying attention. He isn't.

Arianna: So... What are you picking me up in? A limo?

Ryan: Left it in my garage.

I choke back a laugh. I wouldn't put it past him to have a limo sitting in his garage.

Arianna: Aww... So the chopper? Please say the chopper!

Ryan: Smart ass. You'll see.

Arianna: Fine. Keep your secrets. I have to stop by my locker, and then I'll be out.

Ryan: I'll be the one standing next to the car that everyone is gawking over.

Arianna: Cocky.

Ryan: Confident. Get out here.

Arianna: Coming.

The bell rings, and I make my way to my locker. I love when Ryan texts. It makes my day go so much faster. I grab my books for the classes I have homework in and zip my backpack. Just then, the door to my locker slams shut.

"Looking good, Arianna." I nearly curl into myself as Chad Ambrosio, my high school tormentor, crowds me against my locker. He's tall. Intimidating. He has a tattoo on his neck. He scares me so bad that I never cared to know what it was.

"Ch-Chad. W-what do you w-want?"

45

"That stutter. How the hell do you get anyone to glance at you a second time? Makes you sound fucking retarded." He takes my chin roughly in his hand and lifts my face to his. His face is so close, and his Axe body Spray is nauseating. "It's only a matter of time, you know. I'll have you one way or another."

"P-please go away."

"P-p-p-p-please go away," he sneers as he mocks me and laughs. He pushes his hips into me. I feel the tears sting my eyes. His hardness against me makes the bile in my stomach rise.

Chad is the son of one of my dad's friends. My dad has been pushing me to go on dates with him, but I refuse. Chad has been picking on me for the past two years, and it's only gotten worse. Over the past month, he's pushed me against my locker several times, and he once pushed me down a couple of stairs. It was only two, but when he pushed me, I fell. My books went sprawling, and I nearly broke my ankle. I had a really bad sprain.

Just as a tear falls, Chad is wrenched off me.

"What the fuck do you think you're doing? Didn't I tell you to leave her alone?" Robby. My best friend's boyfriend. Thank God. He's taller and far more built than Chad. His dark brown hair only serves to make his piercing blue eyes sharper and more intimidating. No one messes with Robby.

My best friend, Renza, pulls me close to her as I gulp in air. Renza is a little taller than me and just as petite. Her dishwater blonde hair hangs to her shoulders. I grip it and her like she's my lifeline.

"You have no idea who you're messing with," Chad growls.

"You don't scare me. Get the hell away from her and stay away. I'm not fucking around." Robby shoves Chad away. Chad storms down the hall.

"Are you okay, sweetie?" Renza asks. I nod, but I'm shaky.

"I'm sorry, Arianna. I tried to meet you here, but I got tied up," Robby apologizes.

"It's o-okay." I take several more deep breaths while I hug Renza.

"It's not. I'll be better about being here."

"We both will." Renza hugs me tighter, and Robby wraps his arms around both of us.

"Need a ride home today?" Robby asks.

46

"U-um.... No. Actually, R-Ryan is waiting for me."

"Good. At least we know you'll be safe," Renza says into my hair. Other than Ryan's two sisters, Nicole and Breetanan, the only other two people in the world who know how I feel about Ryan are Robby and Renza.

"I'll walk you out," Robby says.

I nod as they let go of me. "Thank you."

We walk out of the school and Ryan is standing against an amazingly gorgeous car with his arms crossed over his chest. Electric blue. I tilt my head. A Mustang, maybe?

Robby and Renza each give me a hug. I turn to Ryan when they leave. His expression is stormy. Almost angry. Maybe a little jealous? No. It can't be that.

"Who was that?"

I look up at him, still confused at his expression and the un-Ryan-like underlying edge to his voice. "Um... Robby?"

"The guy. Is that his name?"

"Y-yes. Um... He's a friend. He's R-Renza's boyfriend."

Ryan visibly relaxes and smiles down at me as he opens my door. I'm even more confused at his change in demeanor, but it's a welcome mystery to untangle. It saves me from thinking of Chad.

I sit in the car and wait for him to get in. As he begins driving, I look out the window. My mind goes back to Chad, even though I attempt to stop it. I try to hide my face from Ryan as tears sting my eyes, but he's too observant. He's always been able to see right through me.

"Ari, what happened? You look really upset."

I know if I tell him he'll take care of the problem, but I don't want him involved. He has enough going on. He doesn't need me to add onto it. If I tell him, he'll be involved in another conflict with another mafia. Chad's.

"I'm okay. It's... just been a hard day. That's all."

He looks at me as he stops for a red light. "Arianna." His eyes bore into me. I feel them. I don't even need to look at him. Arianna. He never calls me that. "You know you can tell me."

"I know." I refuse to look at him. I can't. If I do, I'll tell him everything.

"Then tell me. Whatever it is, I'll make it go away."

That's the problem. If he makes it go away, he causes more problems for himself. I won't let him do that. "It's okay. Really. Robby and Renza are helping me." I risk glancing at him as he turns back to the road. He doesn't look convinced.

The rest of the ride is spent in tense silence. I go back and forth with telling him, but I really don't know if I should. I hate causing more work for him above and beyond what he deals with already.

Finally, he pulls up to his house. He parks the car in the garage and shuts it off. I start to get out, but he puts a hand on my leg to stop me. I hold my breath. He has no idea how much I want to hold his hand. For his touch to never leave me.

"Aria. Whatever is going on, I hope you know you can trust me enough to tell me. I won't make you, but I care about you. I hate seeing you upset and distressed like this." He squeezes my thigh before taking his hand away. The spot on my leg where his hand was is instantaneously cold.

"I know. I do, Ryan. I promise I'll tell you if I need to. Okay?" I look at him and smile. He smiles back, but I can tell he's hurt, and it destroys me. I've never kept anything from him. It's hard to do it now, but I really believe it's for the best.

We both get out of the car, and I follow him into his house. His house is truly massive. It's two stories, but he has a home gym in the basement and another room he won't let me anywhere near. It's modern with all of the luxuries a billionaire like him could ever want. Including a pool and hot tub. He leads me down a hallway and stops outside a room. I look up at him as he turns to me.

"Close your eyes," he says with a half-smile.

"Um... Okay." I close my eyes. I feel him move behind me. He puts a hand over my eyes and one on my hip. He steers me around something, then stops and takes his hand away from my eyes. His chest against my back makes me feel safe and protected, and I have to fight to keep from melting into him.

"Ready?"

"Mmhmm."

"Open your eyes." Ryan's hands are lightly at my waist. I fight to breathe as I open my eyes.

The room is filled with cameras and audio equipment, and there are three people sitting in the room smiling at me. I barely see any of them, though. My complete attention is focused on the sleek, black, grand piano in the corner of the room. The one that was never there before.

"Oh... my... God." It's like I'm being pulled to the piano. My body moves on its own accord. The gorgeous lake glistening beyond the window and perfect amount of space Ryan's house sits on is a distant second to how beautiful the piano is.

I sit down and glide my fingers across the keys, closing my eyes and smiling. The music I bring forth sounds perfectly in tune. I smile wider as I feel Ryan's hand on my shoulder.

"What do you think?" he asks deeply.

"I can't believe you did this for me." I stand up and turn to hug him.

He hugs me tightly for a moment. "I said I'd help, but I didn't have a piano."

"So you bought one." I smile into his chest as he pulls away.

"You can't do this without one." He turns to the crew in the room. "This is Mike. He's the director."

"Hey, Arianna." Mike reaches out to shake my hand. I take it and give a nervous smile. "I may be the director, but you're the boss. My understanding is that you need this for a type of audition?"

"Um... Sort of? It's for the second step in the application process at Juilliard."

Mike whistles. "Well, alright then. Let's get you into Juilliard!" Mike starts giving his crew direction for the camera and audio set up, and I pull Ryan aside. He raises an eyebrow as I forcefully drag him to the other side of the room out of anyone else's earshot.

"You okay?"

"I know you're busy, but..." I bite my lip.

Ryan clears his throat. "Aria. I'm not too busy for you. What do you need?"

"Will you stay? Please? I'm just so nervous doing this with the cameras and everything and you... make me less nervous." I look down at the floor. Ryan reaches over and tugs my hair. I smile and look up at him. He always knows how to make me okay again.

"If that's what you want, I'll stay." I don't hesitate to hug him quickly before I take my place at the piano. Ryan stands on the other side of the room out of the view of the camera and out of the crew's way.

After a few minutes of audio checks and camera angle tweaks, I'm given the go ahead to play.

My first song is a haunting melody. It doesn't take me long to get lost in the music. The music transports me to another place. The heartbreaking months after my mother was killed is my inspiration for the song.

After it ends, and the director has yelled to cut, I glance at Ryan. He's wiping away a tear. I smile to myself. It's a beautiful feeling knowing my music can have such a profound effect on such a big, tough man like him.

My second song is a little more happy, and I intend to sing. The first one was just the music. Honestly, I'm terrified. Only four people have ever heard me sing. My mother. Robby and Renza. And Ryan. Doing this on camera is a huge step for me.

"Ready, Arianna?" Mike asks.

I take a deep breath. "Yep. I can do this."

I'm given the go ahead, and I begin to play.

Time stood still today when you looked in my eyes that way

I continue playing the familiar melody, once again getting lost in the music. I allow my voice to carry over the music, though it stays in perfect accompaniment and harmony. When I reach the hardest point in the song, I find Ryan standing against the floor to ceiling glass window watching me with a soft smile on his lips; his arms folded over his chest.

The crowd disappears
The room spins as you lead me across the floor
For just a moment, I'm okay

I turn back to the piano. I hope he understands the lyrics to the song are about him. I had written it after we had danced together at Taylor and Nicole's wedding.

50

The one I call when my world crumbles
The one who picks back up
The one who steadies me when I stumble
You're the one who picks me back up
The one who picks me back up

I end the song and Ryan is smiling proudly and widely. Adoringly? I really hope he understands. That song is literally my heart.

Chapter Seven

⚔ Taylor ⚔

(One Week Later)

I glance at my watch for the fiftieth time in five minutes and blow out a breath.

"She'll be here soon," Chase says next to me.

"You said that seven minutes ago."

"Dude. Calm the fuck down," Ryan says impatiently. Both Chase and I look at each other, then at Ryan. We're all leaning up against his SUV.

"Okay, spill it. You've been acting like an asshole since you got here last night." I fold my arms over my chest.

Ryan sighs and closes his eyes, rubbing his temples. After a few seconds, he opens them and focuses on the bakery in front of us. "Last week, I hired a production crew for Arianna. To help her with the second phase of her college application to Juilliard. Her fucking father wouldn't do it even though he could. He enjoys holding her back and treating her like shit. So…, I did it. I even bought her a piano so we could do it at my house."

I watch as Ryan smiles then glances at us once more before his face clouds over again. He doesn't continue. I press him. "Doesn't explain the attitude."

He growls but gives in. "The first song she did was a piano solo. It was so fucking good. Saddest thing I've ever heard, but it was really good, man. Actually brought tears to my eyes." He takes a deep breath and runs both hands through his hair as he groans. "The second song was about me."

"So…, was it bad?" Chase asks as confused as I am.

"No. And that's the problem."

"It was really good," I say as it finally dawns on me.

Ryan nods. "Arianna is an amazing singer. And when she plays the piano, it's like it's nothing more than an extension of her body. It comes that naturally."

I smile to myself. "So…, what's the problem?" I'm that much of a dick. I want him to say it.

"The problem is the song."

Chase and I glance at each other again. I know he's thinking exactly what I am. We know the two feel the same way for each other. He needs to say it. But I'll keep playing dumb for his sake.

"Okay. You're really going to have to start making sense because we don't see the problem," I say.

Chase shrugs. "Nope. If Breetana had written a song for me before we were together and played it for me, I'd be a fucking goner."

Ryan looks at both of us, and I see a confusion and a pain in his eyes that I've never seen before. Very suddenly, I understand why he doesn't want to say it. I know how he feels about her. And I know he'll need to say it a few times before he'll do anything about it. But he didn't know she felt the same way.

"You figured out she feels the same way. I knew that already, but you didn't."

"Yep." Ryan nods miserably.

"Makes it harder. Being she's so much younger than you and still a minor." Chase crosses his arms over his chest.

"Correct again," Ryan says.

It's my turn to shrug. "What do you have left? A couple of months?"

"Not that I'm counting, but six." Ryan pinches the bridge of his nose as Chase blows out a breath. "And I've admittedly been a complete dick this whole fucking time."

"Why?" I ask. This time I really am confused.

"Because I can't touch her right now, Taylor." He glares at me.

"So, you're being a dick?" Chase leans his back against the SUV and closes his eyes as he shakes his head with a chuckle.

"I thought it would be easier if she was mad at me."

"That never fucking works, Ry," I say. "Christ."

"You need to be honest." Chase opens his eyes and looks at Ryan.

"Honest? Tell her that I'm thirty-seven years old and in love with her? A seventeen-year-old? Yeah. That'll go over well." The fact that he just used the word 'love' throws me. "I really need to get a grip."

I shake my head. "No. Chase is right. She threw herself out there for you. You need to be honest with her. And you need to lay down your rules. Nothing until she's of age. Even though there's nothing illegal about it in New York, I know your morals."

"And tell her that she really needs to think about what she wants. She needs to really think hard about if she really wants to be with you," Chase throws in.

"Because it seems to me like you're all in," I finish. Ryan sighs as Breetana's Camaro pulls up behind the SUV. I smile when I see my beautiful wife blindfolded in the front seat. I turn to Ryan. "Talk to her." I pat his shoulder as I walk to the car and reach into the backseat to get Tait. I hoist him into my arms and kiss him on the cheek. He squeals and grabs my nose. I laugh.

"What's happening?" Nicole asks.

"Your husband is being really cute with your son," Breetana laughs.

"Awe... I'm missing it," Nicole pouts.

I put my arm around her waist and lead her to the front of the bakery. "Ready to see what we've been keeping from you?"

"Yes! I'm so excited!"

I look at Chase, and he unties Nicole's blindfold. We all watch as she takes everything in. I'm nervous as hell that she'll hate everything about it. The name. The design. The front. The inside. She's quiet for such a long time, I'm convinced she despises it.

I clear my throat. "Babe? Say something. Please?"

"I... can't believe you did this." She hasn't looked at me, and I can't figure out what she's thinking. Her face is a mixture of awe, fear, confusion, and a shit ton of other emotions I can't decipher. Which is unusual for me. I can usually read anyone easily. Especially her.

I bite my lip. "Beautiful, um... I didn't mean to upset you or -"

She throws herself in my arms, hugging me tightly. Tait babbles happily and grabs her hair. I hold her close with my free arm. "Thank you. So much."

Ryan smiles and plucks Tait from my arm so I can properly hug my wife. I tangle my fingers in her hair and breathe a sigh of relief. "You really like it?"

"I love it. So much!"

"We remembered you were talking about what you'd name it," Chase says softly.

"We sort of came up with a combination," Breetana continues.

"If you don't like the name, Ryan said he can get it changed," I say nervously.

"Exotic Sweets and Tasty Treats. What's not to love about that? I wanted to add things other than just bakery items. This gives me the opportunity!" Nicole looks up at me.

I smile. "There's my girl. All the emotions you just had on your face confused the hell out of me. I wasn't sure if you hated it or not."

"I don't. I love it. So much!"

"Then, how about we go in and you meet your staff?" Ryan asks.

"Staff?" Nicole blinks in confusion.

"Ryan and I hired a couple people to help you out," Chase explains.

"They both have experience, so they should be able to help with whatever you need." Ryan smiles down adoringly at Nicole. I can't help but love how they've taken to each other. Nicole really needs a big brother like him. Protective as fuck. Someone who'd do anything for her just like Chase and I would.

"You all are amazing. I don't know what I did to deserve you," Nicole says, teary. Breetana hugs Nicole. I take her hand and lead her into the bakery. Two girls are standing behind the counter smiling.

"Nicole. Meet Korie and Michelle," Ryan says.

"Hey! I'm Korie!" She waves and smiles cheerfully. Her chestnut hair is tied in a pretty messy bun. Her smile is just as bright as her bubbly personality. She's about average height. Small build. Almost fragile, unless you look closer. Korie has some incredible muscle tone. Underneath her happy attitude is a toughness I don't think I'd like to mess with.

"Korie has extensive experience in bakeries, and she has no problems working any position you put her in," Chase explains.

"And I'm Michelle!" She's a little taller than Korie. Also a pretty small build. Her long, dark-brown hair is braided neatly down the middle of her back.

"Michelle also has extensive experience, but she also can help you with that transition into other things," Ryan says.

"I'm a chocolatier, and I also have experience with sugar glass."

"Oh my God! Really? I've always wanted to use sugar glass as decorations!" Nicole says excitedly.

Ryan takes out his ringing phone and glances at it. A dark expression crosses his face as he puts it away. "Hey, sorry guys. I have to go."

I nod towards his phone. "What was that about?"

He looks at me before glancing around the bakery. Nicole is talking to her new employees, and Chase and Breetana are admiring the decorations. Ryan hands Tait to Breetana, then motions me outside. "It's Arianna."

"Is she okay?"

"I don't know." He leans against the SUV and rubs his temples. "She's keeping something from me. It has to do with school."

"How do you know?"

He raises an eyebrow. "You forget who I am?"

I chuckle. "No. I didn't forget who you are." The man knows how to find shit out in ways I will never understand. "Why do you think she's keeping something from you? And why do you think it has to do with school?"

"The day I picked her up to help with that second phase for college? Well, she came out with her friend and her friend's boyfriend. She looked upset but wouldn't tell me why. I've picked her up a couple of times since then, and her friend's boyfriend has escorted her to my car every single time."

"Escorted?"

"Yep. He won't leave her side until she's literally right next to me."

"Interesting."

"So, I've had Rico sitting at the school after to watch her as she leaves because I have a feeling something isn't right. Her friend is with her sometimes, but the guy is there all the time."

"You think she's getting bullied?"

"I have no doubt in my mind. I've seen how terrified she looks walking to my car. How she visibly relaxes when she's safely with me. Or near me." He holds up his phone. "Rico just texted. He said he decided to show up before school to see her walk in. Her friend and the boyfriend meet her in the morning, too. And he noticed this other kid there today that got into a fist fight with her friend's boyfriend."

"Hmm. You think this kid is messing with her?"

"There has to be a reason she has an escort."

I look at Ryan for a few moments. "I think you need to get the information from her before you do anything. I think something is going on, but this is different than you just doing what you do and storming in after having your guys do surveillance. This is high school, and I hate to say this, but this may be something you need to back off from."

"Not if she's getting hurt," he says dangerously.

"Agreed. But diplomacy, Ryan. You go storming in, you could cause more problems for her and yourself. Bullying is nothing to fuck with. Get the information from her first. And then talk to me. I have some experience with it. One of the guys on my taskforce used to be a school resource officer at the high school. I'll help you out, but this is a lot more delicate than the shit you're used to."

He closes his eyes and releases a breath. "Thank you."

"You need to go home? Or are you sticking around for her Grand Opening?"

"If she calls and needs me, I'll leave. If not, I'll be here."

I nod. "Good. We'll figure this out. Okay? I know you like doing shit on your own, but you have a lot of people who would do anything for that girl. Just like you would. Bree and Nikki already adopted her as a little sister. And Chase and I feel just as protective of her as you do of Bree and Nikki."

He looks at me, kind of surprised. "You've met her once."

I shrug. "How is that different from what you did when the cartel was after Breetana? You knew them for less than an hour, and you already felt protective of them."

"Because I knew how you felt about them."

"And I know how you feel about her. And how she feels about you. You're my brother, Ryan. Maybe not by blood, but by heart. That may be a stronger bond. I don't know. Either way, family protects family. End of story."

Ryan smiles. He nods and looks like a weight has been lifted off his shoulders. We walk back into the bakery, Ryan standing a little taller. We stand side by side as Nicole excitedly rattles off a list of everything that needs to be done before her Grand Opening in the morning. Chase and Ryan have already done a lot of marketing for it. I've already seen people walking by excitedly and trying to peer through the windows, which are blacked out and won't be opened up until tomorrow.

Chase joins us, and I glance at the two men standing next to me. No matter what is going on in our lives, I realize there is always one constant. The three of us are like a barrier. The dangers of the outside world can never penetrate the wall we created to protect those we love.

Chapter Eight

✖ Nicole ✖

(One Month Later)

It's been about a month since we opened my bakery, and I'm so pleased at how well it's doing already. We already have a nice customer base. Word of mouth is a very powerful tool. Especially in a business district like this one.

I'm so happy with the location. Not only is it in an area that Ryan cleaned up and controls, but the people are so incredibly nice and welcoming of a new business.

"Sanders Law Firm loved everything we brought!" I look up at Korie as she walks in and beams with pride.

"I knew they would!" I say cheerfully.

"Those cinnamon rolls melt in your mouth." Michelle licks her lips.

"Actually, they really loved the banana cinnamon donut. All of them! They actually want an order ready for them every morning." Korie bounces excitedly on her heels.

Michelle's eyes widen. "Really? Wow!"

"That's fantastic!" I smile widely.

"I wrote it down. Monday through Friday. And they'd like a coffee order as well."

I nod at Korie, then look over at Michelle. "I'm really glad you suggested the coffee, Michelle. Something other than just regular and decaf!"

"I'm happy people like it!" Michelle says.

"Korie, put the order up on the board so we can have it ready every morning, please."

"On it, boss!"

I never thought that having employees would be so much fun. I thought we would clash. Korie and Michelle are not only great employees, but are quickly becoming really good friends.

I look up as someone enters and smile at the tall, muscular blond coming through the door in his crisp Chicago Police Department Uniform. "Hey, Officer Richards! Usual today?"

"Please! I've begun craving those damn things."

I laugh and wrap up a vanilla bean toffee roll for him. "Coffee?"

"Caramel macchiato would be great."

"On it!" Michelle says, hurrying to make it.

"How the hell do you remember all of our orders all the time?" he asks me, smiling.

"Just a really good memory. That's all. You kind of have to have one if you're a chef or baker. Need to remember the recipes."

"Makes sense. Cops have to remember a lot of faces."

"Given time, you'd remember everyone's order, too!"

He laughs, and Michelle hands him his coffee and rings him up. "Okay. Coffee for you guys is on the house. So, I just need three-oh-six for the roll. Oh! Discount."

"You guys spoil us. You give us coffee for free. We don't need the discount, too." He gives a genuinely soft smile of gratitude.

"You guys deserve it. You all deal with a lot. Maybe I have a greater handle on it being a cop's wife, but I know what you guys go through out there. If I can make your day a little brighter with free coffee and a fifty-percent discount, I'll do it."

"Well, we really appreciate it, Nicole. Especially since you make such delicious stuff." He winks as he takes his bag and coffee.

"Have a good day!"

"Bound to now, gorgeous!" As Officer Richards walks out, a new person I hadn't seen yet comes in.

I smile brightly. "Hey! Welcome. Let me know when you're ready to order, okay?" I'm not sure what it is, but I keep an eye on the guy as he takes a seat at one of our tables and takes out his phone. I just seem to get a strange feeling from him.

After a few minutes of sitting there, the guy stands up and walks to the counter. He's really tall. Not quite Taylor's height, but enough to be intimidating. He has tattoos up his arms and neck

I swallow and smile. "Decide on something you might like?"

His eyes roam over my body, and I shiver. "Looks like it."

Michelle and Korie take notice of my discomfort. Korie comes to stand beside me. "So, can we get you anything or not?" Korie is a few inches taller than me and isn't afraid to face down anyone. She has nerves of steel.

"No need to get your panties in a bunch, honey. I'll just take a regular coffee to go."

Korie gives my hand a discreet squeeze to show she's here for me before going to pour the coffee. She pours a large, and I smile. He hadn't specified a size, so it's only fitting to give him the most expensive.

"So... um. Are you new around here?" I ask, trying to learn about him, more for my own peace of mind.

He glances around the bakery before looking at me again. "Just moved in a block down. Name's Chris. Nice place you got here."

"Thanks. We worked hard on it." I smile proudly.

He nods as he pays for his coffee with a hundred dollar bill. He winks at Michelle. "Keep the change." He turns to leave. "See you around... Nicole."

My breath catches in my throat. Korie is immediately at my side. "I..."

"I know." Korie hugs me.

Taylor walks in just as the guy walks out, whistling and smirking. Taylor raises an eyebrow and looks at me. "What the hell was that about?"

"He... knows my name."

61

Taylor looks to Korie and Michelle for an explanation. Korie speaks up. "We hadn't seen him before. He said his name was Chris, but none of us told him our name."

"And then he pays with a hundred dollar bill, doesn't take his change, then tells Nicole he'll see her around. Using her name. We were all really uncomfortable with his demeanor," Michelle says.

Taylor's expression darkens as he looks back towards the door. "I'll check it out. I'll have some additional patrol for you guys. A lot of the businesses around here know you guys by name. Wouldn't be hard for him to find out. In the meantime, ready to go, baby? Dinner tonight with the family."

I take a deep breath and look over at Michelle and Korie. "I actually forgot. Do you guys mind closing up alone?"

"We'll be fine. Go have dinner with the fam!" Michelle says with a smile.

I hug each of them and then take Taylor's hand as he leads me to his unmarked squad car and opens the door for me. I raise an eyebrow. "Did you break your truck?"

He laughs. "No. But Chase broke his car, so he's borrowing my truck."

"Do I want to know?"

He shakes his head. "You do not."

I laugh. "Is he okay at least?"

"He's fine. Can't say the same for his car."

We both get into the squad, and Taylor starts driving. My smile widens. "I have to know now."

"He thought the car was in park. It wasn't. So, he gets a call about an hour after he gets to his office saying to get to the parking garage. His car was not where he left it. It had sideswiped another car and somehow turned enough to roll backwards down the ramp. Landed at the bottom on top of another car." I stare at him in open-mouthed amusement, then start laughing. "You think the description is funny?" He points to his phone mounted on the dash. "Look at the pictures he sent."

I take his phone and find Chase's messages. Sure enough, his car is upside down at the bottom of the parking ramp for his building. I laugh again. "I'm just glad no one was hurt."

"Serves him right. That's what he gets for driving a manual transmission Italian import piece of shit."

"He'll just buy a new one. Not like he can't afford it."

"Probably. But maybe this time he'll buy a more sensible car. One that doesn't cost thirty years of my salary."

I laugh as he continues driving to his mom's house, but I can't shake the feeling that something about Chris isn't right. I don't know if what I feel is fear or apprehension, or if I'm being crazy, but something about him rubs me the wrong way.

Taylor

I sit next to Nicole and take her hand, bringing it to my lips to kiss it. She's been nervous about this dude at her bakery since she told me about him. She usually loves spending time with my mom, Chase, Breetana, Tait, and me. Tonight, though, she's been on edge.

"Baby. I'll look into it, okay? Just tell me if he comes back in and freaks you out again. And tell the girls to call me, too, if they need to."

She smiles at me and leans over to kiss my shoulder. "You're right. I won't let it get to me right now."

"That's my girl. Keep me informed. I'll check into it."

"Thank you, Taylor."

I kiss her palm as my mom sits down at the table. Chase follows with a platter of cut ham. My mouth waters. "Wow. Mom. Looks delicious."

Mom blushes. "Oh, stop. You've had my ham before."

"And it never ceases to be delicious." I lick my lips.

We all dish up, and Nicole takes a small bite of ham with mom's brown gravy. She closes her eyes and sighs happily. Breetana laughs.

"Mrs. Shaw. Seriously. Amazing," Nicole says, happily.

"You can call me mom, Nicole. Or Eve, if you like. You're married to one of my wonderful sons, after all. And you've been a part of the family now for six months. You don't need to be so formal, sweetheart."

63

Nicole blushes. "Okay. Thank you. I guess I still get kind of nervous." We eat in silence for a few moments before Nicole clears her throat. "So, I know Chase and Taylor are really close, but how did that come to be?"

I nearly drop my fork. I hadn't really gotten into my family history. She knew Chase and I were close, and she knew his mom had done a lot for me. But I haven't told her why.

Chase looks at me and clears his throat. "Taylor, uh... He didn't really have a great home life."

"My dad was a cop, and my mom was a nurse." I look down at my plate.

Nicole puts her hand lightly on my leg. "I'm sorry. I didn't mean to bring up a tough subject. We don't need to talk about it."

"It's okay, Nikki. You deserve to know. I should've told you long ago. I'm sorry. I guess it just never came up." I take a deep breath. "In a way, I'm glad you asked now. It's easier with family around."

Tait picks that moment to wake up and start crying. Nicole gives me a soft smile and stands up to get him.

"I didn't know you hadn't told her yet, sweetheart," mom says quietly.

"It's never really come up. Our love story is kind of a whirlwind. We've been pretty busy planning the wedding; taking care of Tait. And then the honeymoon, and her bakery. It's... just never come up."

"Well, it won't be easy, but we're here for you. If that counts for anything," Breetana says softly.

"More than you know, Bree." I attempt a smile, but my mind is racing.

A few minutes later, Nicole comes back into the room with Tait and a bottle. "Oh! May I?" My mom reaches for Tait.

Nicole smiles beautifully. "Of course you may."

She hands mom Tait and the bottle. Tait settles into my mom's arms and begins eating his dinner happily. I smile softly. He'll never have to go through the shit I did. Never.

"So... My family. I didn't have brothers or sisters. My parents didn't have siblings, and both of their parents died when I was pretty young. My dad got hired with Chicago PD after he got out of the military. He was an Army Ranger. We moved here when I was seven, I think. I was in second grade." I look down at my plate, and Nicole rests her hand on my leg again.

"Things weren't always bad," Chase begins. "Taylor and I became friends right away. His mom and my mom became fast friends."

"After a couple of years, though, when the kids were just going into middle school, I noticed Taylor's mother started coming to work less than eager. Then, I started noticing bruising," mom says.

I look up at my mom and Chase gratefully. My eyes are starting to get wet. "My parents started fighting a lot. Screaming and arguing. My dad would shove her around. I tried to get in between them, but... I was only twelve. Just going into sixth grade."

"Taylor stopped coming out to play near the end of the summer." Chase keeps his eyes on me. "One day, I guess I was kind of curious why. I went over to his house. I heard a bunch of yelling. I was just about to knock on the door when Taylor came out."

I shrug. "I had intended to run away. I had a backpack full of clothes. A couple sandwiches. I had been trying to protect my mom, but both my mom and dad told me to get away. So…, after a few explosive arguments, that's exactly what I did."

"My Chase talked Taylor into coming to our house and staying the night. We'd had him there a few times prior, so we were all used to each other. Those two were pretty much inseparable at that time."

"Taylor spent the rest of the week with us. His mom thought that's what was best."

"Things calmed down for a little while after that. But it didn't really last long. My mom stopped caring about anything. She quit her job. My dad's income was enough to cover our house payment and bills, but food and clothing? Nope." I wipe my eyes.

"Oh. Honey, I'm so sorry." Nicole rubs small circles on my leg, and I look at her. She's near tears, but she's trying to hold it together.

For me.

God, I love her.

"I started noticing that Taylor was only bringing an apple or a half a cheese sandwich or something to school for lunch. His clothes were starting to look beat up, and it was so un-Taylor-like. I went home and told my mom."

"I started making an extra lunch for him. When I took Chase shopping for school, I took Taylor with us. I sent Chase to school with breakfast for Taylor. And I made sure Taylor had dinner with us every night. Sometimes, if the fights were bad, he'd stay the night. One day, both of his parents came to the house with Taylor. Taylor looked upset. I invited them in, and they explained that things were hard. They appreciated all I had done for Taylor and asked a question that changed all of our lives."

"My dad had lost his job. He'd been caught drinking in his squad while on patrol and fucking some prostitute in the backseat. So my parents literally had no income, and my dad was in trouble." I feel a tear fall. Nicole reaches up to wipe it away.

"They hated each other, but they loved Taylor. They knew they wouldn't be able to take care of him. So they had some paperwork for me. Asking me to adopt him."

"We were just starting high school. Taylor and I had become as close as brothers by that time. He'd started calling my mom 'mom' because she pretty much was."

"And I had already grown to love him like my own son. I didn't hesitate for one second to sign those papers."

"The next day, Chase and I were packing up my stuff. My parents got into another fight. I think it had to do with the house being foreclosed on, and my dad having to go to court for, as it turns out, raping the prostitute. I don't know why he wasn't in jail, but he wasn't. Anyway. The fight started. Chase told me we should just grab my stuff for school and get out. So, we did."

"But when we got downstairs, the scene that greeted us was... It wasn't good."

I look at Nicole and will her to forgive me for what I'm about to say. I reach down and take her hand, bringing it to my lips and kissing it gently. "My dad was holding a gun to my mom's head."

"Oh..., Taylor." She squeezes her eyes shut as she squeezes my hand.

I choke back my own emotion and look at Chase for help. "I... can't. I can't say it."

Chase stands and walks around the table. He pats me on the back, then kneels in front of Nicole. "Taylor didn't think. Not for a second. He just acted. He speared his dad. Like a football tackle. He knocked him to the ground; wrestled with him for the gun. He thought he had control, but his mom stepped in and pulled him off his dad. His dad shot."

"Oh God. No." The dam bursts. Nicole starts sobbing, and I put my head in my hands. This is it. She's about to leave me and take my entire life with her.

Mom hands Breetana Tait and immediately comes to hug me. I'm doing my best to not fall apart, but as soon as she touches me, the tears start streaming from my eyes. "It's okay, baby. Shh..."

"His dad shot his mom. She was dead before she hit the ground. He turned the gun on me, but Taylor attacked him again. They were wrestling for it, and I heard a second shot. Taylor stood up with blood all over him." Chase's voice hitches. "I... thought it was Taylor that had been shot. But it wasn't. It was his dad. The gun went off while they were fighting for it. Taylor never had control of it. His dad was still holding it when he died."

"The police came. Taylor was never charged. It was ruled a murder/suicide," mom finishes.

My body is wracked with sobs at this point. I'm shaking. I'm overcome with the memories. It's almost like it just happened seconds ago. I'm even more terrified that Nicole is going to fear me and leave.

Suddenly, Nicole's arms are around my waist, and her head is pressed against my arm. I don't hesitate. I turn and pull her into my lap. I bury my head in her hair.

She buries hers in my shoulder. "I'm sorry. I'm so sorry you had to go through that, Taylor. Baby, I'm so, so sorry." She runs her fingers through my hair, soothingly.

I breathe in her familiar scent. It calms me. She calms me. Centers me. Makes me feel like I'll be okay. "I'm sorry I didn't tell you." My face is still buried in her hair, my lips against her head. My words are muffled. "It never came up, but I was glad because I didn't want you to hate me."

"Never. Taylor. I could never hate you. You didn't do anything wrong."

"I let him kill her." It's whispered. I know only she can hear me.

"You didn't. You did nothing wrong, my love. Nothing." Chase takes Breetana, Tait, and mom out of the room, leaving us alone. I hold her as tightly as I can without breaking her. "Do you really think you let him kill her?"

I shrug. "I don't know anymore. Most of the time I feel like I'm okay. I know it wasn't my fault. But I can't get over the fact that I let her pull me off. And I shouldn't have. I towered over her at that point. I was a lot stronger than her. I was stronger than him."

"Baby. Blaming yourself for what happened is like Bree and me blaming ourselves for the fire that killed our parents. It wasn't our fault. It was our uncle's. He set it. We couldn't prove it, but we knew. And now it's all come out, thanks to Ryan. The point is, you did what you could, Taylor. You're not the one who pulled the trigger. He did. Maybe if Bree and I had stayed home from school, he wouldn't have set it. Or maybe he would've set it another day. Maybe you could've stopped him only to have him do it after you left."

I kiss her neck and run my fingers through her hair. "I love you. Thank you for keeping me from falling apart."

"I love you, too." She kisses me long and passionately. "We're partners, Taylor. You always tell me that you aren't going anywhere. That you'll be here for me through everything. Well, I'm not going anywhere either. I love you. And I'll be here for you through everything, too."

I can't help but smile at her strength as she kisses me again. I feel all of my apprehension about my past lift as she kisses me and holds me close to her. It's backwards for me. I'm used to being the strong one. But I realize as she kisses me that I'm only strong because I have her and a strong family behind me. If I didn't, I don't know where I'd be.

Chapter Nine

☒ Ryan ☒

(One Week Later)

Whatever is going on with Arianna has been driving me crazy. I know she's getting bullied. I just wish she would come to me so I could figure out how to help her.

I put the steaks I've been marinating into the oven. It's been almost two months since Arianna played the song she wrote for me, and I still haven't figured out how to talk to her about it.

Thank fucking God things have gone back to normal for us, though. Despite the fact that I had changed the subject every time she brought it up. She stopped bringing it up, and we're okay again.

I know it isn't okay, though. I need to talk to her. I can't just let her think I don't feel anything for her at all. That's a good way to completely lose her.

I smile to myself and lean on my kitchen counter. If everything goes the way I want it to tonight, Arianna and I will be together in a few months. I invited her here so we can talk about it. Her dad's being an asshole today anyway so it works out to her advantage. And mine.

If I had my way, she'd be here with me now, but she had to go home for some reason first. I hate that she won't tell me why, and I think her keeping things from me may be another thing I bring up today.

I shake my head. I need to quit thinking. It's only going to piss me off, and that isn't the point of tonight. Instead, I take out my phone to text Nicole.

Arianna's eighteenth birthday is going to be a new beginning for her. Whether she chooses to be with me or not, it's still going to be a new beginning for her.

Away from her father. I'm taking his ass out as quickly as I can after she hits that magical age.

Ryan: Hey. I want a cake for Arianna's birthday.

Nicole: Oooohhh... When?

Ryan: A few months still, but I know you've gotten pretty busy.

Nicole: Are you still planning on bringing her here?

Ryan: That's the goal. At least for a little while. Get her the fuck out of here.

Nicole: What kind of cake?

Ryan: Well, I'll leave the design to you, but she likes vanilla and she likes strawberries. I thought maybe you could incorporate those.

Nicole: What about chocolate?

Ryan: She hates milk chocolate and dark chocolate, but she likes white chocolate.

Nicole: First of all, I love how you know that.

I shake my head and smile.

Ryan: Stop. You're just like your husband.

Nicole: It's just cute. That's all. As for her cake, I'm thinking vanilla bean with strawberry vanilla buttercream. And I think whole white chocolate covered strawberries on the outside of the cake.

Ryan: And that's what I pay you for. Thanks, honey.

Nicole: Anytime!

I put my phone down and check my watch. I still have a few minutes before I need to start my glaze and potatoes, but I open the red wine for the glaze anyway.

Just then, I hear my front door open and can't stop the smile that spreads across my face.

"Ryan!" Arianna calls.

"Kitchen!" I answer. Arianna runs into the kitchen and leaps into my arms, dropping her keys and some paperwork to the ground. "Whoa!"

She wraps her legs around my waist, and I suck in a breath. Instead of dropping her like I should, I run my hands down and grip her thighs, lifting her slightly higher. Her arms are wrapped tightly around my shoulders, and she buries her face in my shoulder and neck.

Holy fuck. Fuck, fuck, fuck.

She smells fucking amazing. I can't help myself. I turn my head slightly and breathe her in. "What is that? Your perfume."

"I'm not wearing any, but the body wash I use is Jasmine."

Fuck.

I take a deep breath and clear my throat. "So? What happened? Why are you so happy?"

"Thank you. For everything." She pulls away and looks at me with a huge smile. "I got to the last stage at Juilliard!"

"What? Aria, that's fantastic!"

"I couldn't have done it without you! They said that what I sent was incredibly professional and personal. They said it shows I care, and that I'm passionate. They loved my music."

"I'm proud of you, but you don't have to thank me. All I did was hire a crew. It's your music that inspired them to move you forward."

She hugs me again. I still haven't put her down, and the fact that I haven't is causing a serious battle to start raging inside of me.

Rico, my second in command, picks that moment to walk into my kitchen, I glare at him. He doesn't notice. He's too busy looking at his fucking phone.

"Hey, boss. That -" He cuts himself off as soon as he sees Arianna in my arms. "Sorry. I'll come back." He starts backing out of the kitchen.

I growl as I put Arianna down. "What, Rico?"

Arianna picks up the stuff she dropped and jumps up onto a barstool. Rico's eyes dart from her to me.

"Uh… that… situation you asked to be taken care of…"

"Just talk, Rico. Arianna knows everything I do." He breathes a visible sigh of relief. "What happened in L.A.?"

71

"We dealt with the small-time guy that popped up. Got some help from Josh and Alex. Situation has been resolved. You took care of the other guys earlier, so L.A. is stable again."

"Good. Thanks for the update."

"I did, however, want to tell you something else."

"What's that?"

"Chicago. There's a new gang I've been hearing about. They're causing problems all over the city. We can't pin down a territory they seem to be trying to control," he begins. I had just turned to the stove to start my potatoes, but I slowly turn back around and cross my arms over my chest. Waiting… "The last place they seemed to take interest in was... uh..."

I feel my glare turn darker. "Spit. It. Out."

"Halsted."

"Isn't that... where Nikki's bakery is?" Arianna asks softly.

My eyes don't leave Rico's. "Yes, baby... Rico. Find out a block. Find out who they are. And if anything happens to Nicole before you get me that information, it's on you."

"Yes, sir. I'm on it right now."

One thing I like about Rico is that I don't intimidate him. He does what I say. Most of the time, he's already doing exactly what I want before I even say it. Rico leaves the room, and I glance at the potatoes before turning back to Arianna. She's nervously biting her lip. Fuck. That damn lip.

"She'll be okay. Right?" She looks up at me through her long lashes. I have to force my fucking heart to quit racing.

"She'll be fine, Aria."

She gives me a soft smile as I turn my back to her and finish dinner. I don't want her or anyone to see my carefully crafted facade crumbling.

✕✕✕

Later, after dinner, I lead Arianna into my living room and sit down with her on the couch. I take a deep breath and let it out. "We have to talk."

"Oh. Um… Okay." She looks down at her hands.

I smile. "I don't think you have to be nervous, Ari. You've been pretty upfront with your feelings about me. It's me who hasn't been with you."

She doesn't look at me. She bites her lip, and I lean back on the couch so I don't see her do it. It's incredibly sexy.

I'm fighting myself on every breath to not kiss her.

"Aria. I have some very strong feelings for you. But you're a lot younger than me," I begin. She says nothing, but I see her reach up to her eye and wipe a tear away. Fuck. "We can't be together right now." Just those words break me, but I know they probably kill her. She nods and wipes another tear as she stands up and quickly starts walking towards the door. "Ari." I stand up and follow her.

"I know, Ryan. Okay? I-I'm sorry. I never should have p-played that song for you."

"Aria. I loved the song. I *love* that song."

She wipes away another tear as she reaches for the door. I grab her hand and pull her back to the living room with me. I don't say anything until we get there. "Ryan. I -"

"Let me finish. Sit." I sit down and wait for her to join me, but she doesn't. I didn't expect her to run before I got the rest of the words out, but she needs to listen. "Aria, if you don't sit, you're gonna end up in my lap."

She sniffles. "Really. It's okay that you don't feel the same." I grab her hand and pull her into my lap. "Ow! You're all muscle, aren't you?" She glares at me.

"I warned you." I can't help but smile. She looks down, but I gently tug her hair so she's looking at me. "I didn't say I had no feelings for you. I said I have strong feelings for you."

"And then you said we can't be together."

"Right now. I didn't say we couldn't ever be together." I let go of her hair as a small smile reaches the corner of her lips. "You're seventeen, Ari. I'm twenty years older than you. And the way I feel about you scares the hell out of me. I shouldn't feel the way I feel. But I do. I'm not going to lie to you because you don't deserve that. Especially after you put yourself out there for me." I take a deep breath. "Until you turn eighteen, I won't touch you. Not that I don't fight myself every day to keep from kissing you or... other things. I want to, but I won't. After you turn eighteen, you need to be the one to come to me. This entire thing needs to be at your pace. I won't force myself on you. I won't do anything you don't want. And that includes a relationship. If, after you turn eighteen, you decide you really don't want this, that's your choice. I won't like it, but it's your choice. Understand?"

She nods and then hugs me. I very hesitantly return her hug. Having her in my lap like this is crossing a line. The very one I drew in the sand myself. "What about when we're alone?"

"No. This right here is already crossing a line with me," I tell her. She sighs and pulls away, sadly crawling out of my lap and sitting next to me. Hating seeing her like that, I give in and pull her back in my lap, she smiles brightly. "I was honest with you. Your turn. What's happening at school?"

"Um..." She looks down again.

I grab her hair again and lightly tug it once more. "Tell me. Seeing you scared when you walk out of that school is killing me."

"It's just... this guy." She looks at me and takes a deep breath. "My dad has been pushing me to date him. He's the son of one of his friends. I don't like him, and I've refused to go anywhere with him. He doesn't like that very much so he's... he's really mean. At school. He's pushed me." My grip on her waist tightens. "He's shoved me against my locker. Robby and Renza started meeting me at my locker after school, so he started meeting me before. So, Robby started meeting me at school in the morning. He escorts me to all of my classes, and sometimes, Renza does, too. But Robby is more... intimidating. And he doesn't like when me and Renza are walking to class by ourselves."

"So, he walks with you?"

"Yes."

"And this guy? What's his name?"

She looks down. "Please don't. School is almost over, and he doesn't bother me now."

"Aria."

"I know you'll take care of it, but it'll just cause more problems. Please don't go after him."

I lean my head against the back of the couch and close my eyes. She shifts on my lap, and I groan. I'm instantly hard, and I pray she doesn't feel it. She slips her arms around my waist and lays her head on my shoulder.

"I'll make you deal."

"Okay."

"I won't go after him until you tell me to. But if it gets to a point where just getting an escort from your friend isn't enough, and he continues to bother you, tell me. Deal?"

"Deal." I sit with her on my lap a little while longer until she decides she should go home. She turns to me as we reach the door. "Ryan?"

"Aria?"

She smiles and pushes her hair behind her ear. "I... know it's a lot to ask, but..."

"But?" I reach over to push the rest of her hair behind her ear.

"The third phase. It's an interview."

"Okay?"

"Would you... come with me? I know it's not that far, but -"

I smile. "I'll take you, sweet girl. You don't even have to ask."

She hugs me again. We linger a bit too long before she pulls away and heads to her car. She rarely ever drives. She refuses to drive to school because she hates traffic. I had offered to pick her up today, but she wouldn't let me. She said if she was going to go to Juilliard, she needed to get over her fear of traffic.

I watch her taillights disappear down my driveway. As soon as I can't see her anymore, I turn and close the door.

This is going to be a long fucking five months.

Chapter Ten

⚔ Taylor ⚔

(Three Weeks Later)

I'm sitting at my desk in my precinct office. It's been nearly a month since Nicole first told me about the person in her bakery that freaked her out, and I can't find shit on him.

I scrub my hands over my face and look at my watch. It's nearly time to leave, and I couldn't be happier to get the hell out of here.

Just as I'm gathering my stuff, my door swings open. I sigh heavily and collapse in my chair.

"Lieutenant," a deep voice rumbles.

"Sergeant. What do you want?" I ask.

Dane Michaels is my right hand man and one of my closest friends. He's on my taskforce and is a Sergeant. He may be just as good as me at taking out Chicago's bad guys.

"I know you're about to head home, but you ain't gonna like what I found out."

I rub my temples and close my eyes. "Just tell me."

"I think I found out who this gang is."

"Okay. I'm game. Why would I not like that?"

"Because their headquarters is a block away from Nicole's bakery."

He's right. I don't like it. "So, who are they?"

"They're calling themselves the Halsted Crew. Looks like they've been shaking down businesses all over the city."

"Get surveillance on their headquarters."

"Already done."

"Why haven't we heard of these guys?"

"They're good at intimidation and covering their tracks."

"Never stopped us from getting info on gangs before."

"Damn right." He smirks. I chuckle and pop a couple aspirin. "Another headache?"

"Haven't been sleeping. Nicole's been worried, and I hate that I can't give her answers."

"Can't blame either one of you. At least we have a lead."

"Let's work on finding affected businesses. See if we can narrow down a territory."

"So far, we know none of the businesses near their HQ have been affected. Including Nikki's."

I sit back in my chair and cross my arms over my chest. "Why?"

"Good question. I hate to say I don't know, but I don't."

I look up as my door opens again. Mark Johnson, another person on my task force walks in. "We need to narrow down the territory. Priority."

"We may have done that." Mark tacks up several sheets of paper on my bulletin board, then grabs a handful of tacks from my desk. He starts sticking them to a map of Chicago I have on a second bulletin board. Another of my guys, Adam Temple, walks in while I'm standing up and leaning against my desk, watching Mark.

"It looks chaotic, but we think we found at least a motive," Adam says.

Following right behind him is Jesse Scott, another member of my team. He closes the door behind him. "Every picture up there is a business that we found out is being shaken down by these assholes."

"They're all small businesses. These ones in this cluster here?" Mark points to a cluster of six pins in the Northwest corner of the city.

"We think that's their actual territory. It's a six block radius," Jesse says.

I narrow my eyes. "Why would they hit businesses in the Southeast corner of the city? That's miles apart."

Adam nods. "Correct. We think they're expanding. We think they want as much territory as possible, like most gangs, so they're trying to find weak points in the city."

I shrug. "Makes sense. These are all areas where we haven't seen a lot of gang activity."

Dane furrows his brows. "But why is their HQ on Halsted?"

"We think they want as much territory as they can get before hitting their own home, so-to-speak, Mark says."

"Throw us off," Adam continues.

"We're pretty sure they have no idea we know where their HQ actually is," Jesse finishes.

I really do have a fuck of a team. "Not bad. Dane has surveillance set up at their HQ. I want interviews set up with those business owners. Plain clothes. Hide your badges and guns. Go in looking like a gang member. We don't want to tip anyone off that we might have any inclination of what the fuck they're doing."

"Let's get a few cars from impound. Nicer ones, but let's not go overboard," Dane commands.

"SUVs with tinted windows?" Mark asks.

Dane nods. "SUVs are fine. There's a Rolls Royce Taylor and I impounded last night."

"I don't want you guys in the souped-up street cars. Stay away from them. We aren't going after a streetcar gang," I add.

"We'll start in the morning. Where the fuck are Andrew and Zekeih?" Dane looks around.

"Zekeih went home an hour ago. Wifey needed him, She's pretty hormonal. He didn't want to piss her off." Jesse grins.

I laugh. "Nikki was the same way. One second she wanted to kill me. The next she wanted to fuck me. Thank God I didn't have to deal with that for long since she gave birth two weeks early."

Everyone laughs.

"My girlfriend was the same way. Maybe worse since she was two weeks late. She just wanted that little girl the hell out!" Adam shakes his head at the memory.

"What about Andrew?" I ask.

"Didn't feel well. He's been struggling all day, and I started to feel bad, so I told him we wouldn't miss him," Mark answers.

I nod. "I'll check in with him and Z. Dane, get us cars. Everyone else, I want you here at 8AM. We move out after the briefing."

"Yes, sir!" Mark says like I'm a drill sergeant.

I laugh. "Everyone out! I have shit to do." As soon as everyone leaves, I start making my phone calls.

"Hey, boss." Andrew sounds sicker than a dog when he answers the phone.

"Hey. I got word you ain't feeling hot."

"Nope. Pretty sure I got whatever the fuck my niece has."

"I'll need you to check in tomorrow morning with me. I need you guys on interviews for that new gang."

"I think I'll be okay. I'll let you know."

"Before 8AM."

"Sounds like a plan."

"Feel better. Okay?"

"Yes, sir!" He hangs up, and I call Zekeih.

"What's up, Lieutenant?"

"You think your girl will let you out to play?" My teasing tone makes him roar with laughter, and I smile.

"I don't know. She took my cuffs and handcuffed me to the bed. Don't look like I'll be able to play anytime soon!"

It's my turn to roar with laughter. There isn't a single member on my team that misses a beat when it comes to humor or sarcasm. Dirty or otherwise. It's one of the reasons we've been together as long as we have.

"Well, tell her I need you here at 8AM. If she has an issue, she can come talk to me."

"Yeah, right. You think I'm letting her anywhere near your office? I know how many girls you've had bent over your desk."

I laugh again. "While I can't deny that, I'm a happily married man now. No more easy fucks in my office with random women."

"Whoo. Nikki got you whipped, huh?"

"Don't be a dick. She's the best thing that ever happened to me."
We both laugh. He knows I'd never cheat on Nicole; that all of my colleagues' girls have always been off limits. My reputation, though, has always been a source of ridicule and entertainment for my team.

"8AM?"

"Yep."

"I'll try to be out from underneath her by then."

We both laugh and hang up as I get ready to go home.

✖✖✖

Early the next morning, I open my eyes to my phone ringing. It stops and starts again just as Nicole's starts going off.

"What the fuck?" I grumble as I reach for my phone. Nicole's stops ringing as I answer mine, not bothering to look at the caller ID, and then hers starts up again. Nicole, exhausted from a long day and a very, very fussy baby, doesn't move. I glance at the clock. "It's three in the fucking morning. What do you want?"

"Lieutenant Reddick? I'm Mike Kane. I work with patrol."

"What do you want, officer?" I grunt. Nicole's phone starts ringing again.

"Sir, we got a call of an alarm going off at Exotic Sweets and Tasty Treats. The alarm company tried to get a hold of the owner, but she isn't answering, so I looked it up and saw it's your wife."

Nicole's phone quits ringing, and then starts again. I gently nudge her. "Baby. Wake up."

"Mmm…," she sexily moans.

"Sir?"

"Hang on, Kane."

"Yes, sir."

I nudge Nicole again. "Nikki. Wake up, beautiful."

"Mmm..." She's sexy even when she's tired.

I reach over and grab her phone. "Baby. Get up. Come on."

"What?" she asks, disoriented. Nicole's phone goes off again. I hand it to her. Sleepily, she answers it. "Hello?"

"Are you at the bakery, Kane?" I say into my phone.

80

"Yes, sir."

"Have you looked around?"

"Yes, sir. We took a look inside and nothing is broken. The building is clear. Doesn't look like anything is missing, and there's no damage."

Nicole sits bolt upright in bed. "Are you kidding?" She starts to scramble out of the bed, but I grab her arm.

"I want you and your partner to stay there until I get there. No one gets in or out. Understand?"

"Yes, sir. We'll be here."

I hang up and turn to Nicole as she also hangs up. Her eyes are filled with fear. "Don't freak out. Officers are already there."

"Don't freak out? Taylor, my bakery was fucking broken into, and you're telling me not to freak out?"

I pull her close. "Officers are already there, baby. Nothing is damaged. Nothing was taken."

"I have to go there."

"I know. I'll call Chase."

"Why?"

"Because we aren't taking Tait to a crime scene."

"You're right. Of course. I'm sorry. I'm not thinking."

"Go get dressed," I tell her as I let her go. She gets up as I call Chase.

He answers, clearing his throat. "What?"

"The bakery got broken into. Can you and Bree get over here to watch Tait? Or I'll bring him there on the way."

"What? Yeah. Yeah. Bring him here. I'll get up."

"Sorry to wake you."

"It's fine. I'll get up." He hangs up, and I get up to get dressed.

"Why is this happening, Taylor?" Nicole asks.

"I don't know, baby. It could be random, but I'll find out."

She throws her arms around me. "I don't want the same thing to happen to my bakery as what happened in Silver Bay."

I can feel the fear in her body and hug her tighter. "It won't. I won't let it. You have all of Chicago PD on your side this time, baby. It's not the same."

I hug her even tighter, sensing she needs it. I feel some of the tension release from her, but I know she won't be completely okay until she sees nothing is missing or damaged. Besides me and Tait and our family, that bakery is the most important thing to her. Losing it would be devastating to her, and I refuse to let that happen to my wife.

Chapter Eleven

✗ Nicole ✗

I wait in Taylor's truck as he talks to the officers on scene. I hate that he made me wait in here, but I know he's doing it for my safety.

My bakery.

Other than my family, this is my life. I love this place. Over the past two months, I've worked my ass off to make it a success. Korie and Michelle have worked just as hard as me. To have something like this happen is awful. Taylor motions me to come out, and I nearly run to him.

"Was anything taken? Is the damage a lot? How much will it take to open again? Can I open today? I have people counting on me! What if -"

"Nicole. Stop. Calm down. Nothing was taken. There's no damage." He wraps an arm around me.

"We're done investigating, so you can open up as usual. Just need to replace the lock," an officer says.

I let out a breath I didn't know I was holding. "Thank God."

Taylor takes me in both of his arms and hugs me tightly. "I'll put extra patrol on again. It seemed to work before. And I'll have patrol officers in and out all day making their presence around here well known." I nod into his chest as he sways side to side with me. "I have a lead on the guy who freaked you out. I know you haven't seen him since, but I'm not stopping."

"Who is he?"

"I'll let you know when I get more information. Okay? I have some interviews set up for today. I should be able to have a lot more answers for you later."

"Promise?"

"I promise, Nikki." He kisses me on top of my head and then hugs me tighter.

"I love you."

"I love you, too, baby."

XXX

Later on that morning, I've nearly forgotten about the break-in entirely. True to his word, Taylor has sent in numerous patrol officers, and the police presence outside driving around is far greater than ever before. I definitely feel safe.

We all feel safe. I, of course, told Michelle and Korie what happened and they, while shocked, are true troopers. We've all been kicking ass today.

"Nikki?"

"Yeah, Michelle?"

"I'm going to head out for the day. Everything is done. I'll be in early to finish that chocolate order."

"Perfect! Thanks, Michelle."

"Of course!" She gives Korie and I both hugs and leaves. It's been busy all day. I am so thankful for the lull so we can restock.

"Korie, can you grab more peach custard muffins? Oh! And Raspberry cream cheese. We're out!"

"Sure thing, Nic!" Korie disappears into the back, and I start stocking cookies. I hear the door open and I turn with a big smile to greet my customer. The words, however, die on my tongue.

"Hey, Nicole. Long time no see. You by yourself?" The guy that's haunted my nightmares asks smoothly.

"Oh. Um. No. Not by myself." I try to fake a smile, but the guy instills fear in me.

"Korie and Michelle in the back?" Chris asks. I don't miss the fact that he used their names, and that he shouldn't even know them. Not unless he's asked around about us.

"Korie is just grabbing some things to restock."

"Looks like it's been busy today. Your display case is pretty bare."

"Y-yes. We've been busy."

He smiles. He doesn't leer at me, and he's being really nice. I clear my throat and meet his eyes. They portray a kindness I hadn't seen before, and I don't know what to think. "I'm glad to see you guys are doing well."

"Th-thank you."

"Hey, I think we got off on the wrong foot. I was a bit drunk when we met before. I probably freaked you out a bit."

I consider him for a moment. I can't see any insincerity in him at all. I take a deep breath and decide to be honest. "You kind of did. Yeah."

He chuckles. "I really didn't mean to. I apologize."

"I forgive you." I give him a genuine smile.

He smiles widely. "Good! Because that coffee is amazing, and I've kind of been afraid to come back in here to get it."

I can't help but laugh. "No need to be. So…, one black coffee?"

"Please! And I'd like to try that carrot cake cupcake, if I could."

"Sure thing," I glance at him as I take the cupcake out of the display case. It's weird, but I feel no apprehension towards him this time. I pour his coffee and ring him up. He pays and leaves a tip. "Oh! You really don't need to. And I've been meaning to ask. Why did you leave such a large tip last time? It was like ninety-seven dollars."

He grins and shrugs. "Your tip jar says it goes to the children's hospital here in Chicago. I like that you're helping out the kids." He winks and sips his coffee as he turns. I smile. "Later, Nicole."

"Have a good day, Chris."

I watch him as he leaves. He strolls out the door like he doesn't have a care in the world, and I don't know what to think. How can one of the most intimidating people I've ever met turn around and be so nice? And why does that make me feel slightly more confused about him?

XX XX XX

(Two Weeks Later)

"Hey, Chris! Coffee and a cupcake?" I ask brightly.

"You know me!"

It's been a couple of weeks since the break-in, and Chris has been coming in every single day. He never comes in at the same time, but he always orders the same thing. A large black coffee and a carrot cake cupcake. And then he sits down at a table by the window and looks at his phone.

Taylor told me he's a part of a gang that has been forcing small businesses to pay him for his protection. He doesn't know how he's getting them to agree, and he has no evidence of him actually doing anything wrong. Taylor said it's just the words of business owners against the word of the gang at this point. I can see how much it frustrates him, so I came up with an idea to help.

Ryan set up a CCTV system with both video and audio everywhere in this bakery. Every morning, it gets automatically downloaded to a computer program. I'm nowhere near tech savvy, so I don't know how it works, but it does. I tested it the day after the break-in.

I decided to be overly nice to Chris and allow my cameras to do their job. Watch and listen. Eventually, he would come after me and everything would be on camera for Taylor.

The problem is I know Taylor would never allow me to do this. So, I haven't told him. I also know that if I told him Chris is coming in every day, he would have one of his team members, or all of them, including himself, stationed throughout my bakery and all around it. Chris would never come in then, and Taylor would never catch him.

After Chris pays for his order and leaves his usual tip, he sits at his usual place and takes out his phone.

I'm just about to sit at the table with him when two people I've never seen walk in. They're both very rough looking and are acting obnoxious. They're shoving each other and laughing loudly.

I watch Chris look up as one of them shoves the other into my display case.

86

"Hey! Enough! You two idiots are going to break something. Order or get out," Korie growls. Chris sniggers and goes back to his phone. The two jerks glare at Korie.

"Maybe you should shut the fuck up, bitch," one of them says.

"Yeah. We're just messing around," the other finishes.

"You almost broke our display! Be responsible and respectful," Michelle says.

"Or leave," Korie says. She and Michelle both glare right back at the two guys.

I'm still near Chris's table, not behind the counter as Korie and Michelle are. I take a deep breath. "I won't tolerate that type of behavior here. You're welcome to order, but please. No more horsing around like that."

The two look at each other, and one of them stalks towards me while the other jumps over the counter, knocking everything, including the register, off it.

The guy who jumped it sneers. "What are you two going to do now? Huh? Not so tough now that I'm behind the counter, are you?"

He backs both Michelle and Korie against the wall, his hulking frame engulfing their petite ones. The guy who had been stalking towards me is so close to me now that I have to back away or his chest will be touching mine.

"W-what do you want?" I back up so far, I fall into a chair.

"Hmm... How about you, pretty girl? Wanna take me in the back and let me fuck that sexy ass?" he glowers.

I choke back a sob. The guy reaches for my hair and tugs. It's all it takes. The tears burst out. I can't stop them.

At that moment, the guy is thrown backwards and is sliding across the floor. The other guy looks over at his friend just as Chris leaps over the counter and punches him as he lands on the ground. The guy drops like a sack of bricks.

"I suggest both of you get the fuck out. I catch you here again, my fist will be the least of your worries." He's completely calm and collected, and I stare at him confused as hell. I had been convinced the two gang members were his.

The two guys scramble to their feet and run from my bakery. He checks on both Korie and Michelle and sends them in the back to gather themselves before he quickly crosses the bakery to me. I'm shaking and trying to catch my breath.

He kneels in front of me. "Hey. You're okay now. They're gone."

"Thanks to y-you!" I can't help it. I know he's the bad guy here. I know it with every fiber of my being. But had he not been here, I don't know what would've happened. I throw my arms around his neck. "Thank you. Thank you. So much."

"It's okay. Really. It was nothing."

"Are you kidding?" I pull back and wipe my eyes, regaining most of my composure. "You never have to pay for anything here again. Ever."

"Please. Nicole. It was nothing. Really." He tucks my hair behind my ear and stands. "I'll see you tomorrow."

I look at him completely dumbfounded. I expected him to try and make me pay for his protection. I even tried to lead him there with free stuff. "You're... just gonna leave?"

"Looks like you guys have some company. You'll be safe." He nods to the window as two squads pull up. He gives me a genuine smile and walks out as the officers walk in. I take a deep breath. "Afternoon, officers!" he says, nodding to them.

I shake my head. What in the blue fuck just happened? One of the officers glances at Chris as he leaves, then takes in the chaotic scene in front of him. There's a crack in the display case. Everything that had been on my counter is shattered on the floor. The register is broken. He looks at me, still sitting on the chair, and immediately crosses the floor to me. He kneels in front of me.

"Hey, sweetheart. Look at me. What the fuck happened?"

"Just some... some rowdy customers. They got out of hand."

The officer, I don't know his name, very obviously doesn't believe me. Michelle and Korie both come out of the backroom. "Should I ask them?"

The other officer looks between me and Michelle and Korie. I've told Michelle and Korie my plan. I felt like I needed to. My only hope is that they'll back me up right now.

"Looks like there was a fight," the other officer says.

"There... was." Michelle bites her lip.

"A couple customers were fighting." Korie to save the day. I close my eyes. Thank God.

I clear my throat and open my eyes. "I'm not sure I've met you yet." I stick out my hand to shake. The officer regards me for a moment, trying to decide if I'm lying. Finally, he shakes my hand.

"Reed Daniels. I work with your husband a lot. I'm with SWAT."

The other officer strides over and sticks his hand out as another customer comes in. "I'm Nicoli Sans. I work with your husband, too. I'm also SWAT." I shake their hands as Korie and Michelle take care of the customer. "Now, tell me the truth. What happened?"

"Just like we said. A couple customers got out of hand."

"Where are they now?" Reed asks.

"They left. Another customer, the one walking out when you guys walked in, broke it up." I hate lying. It's like acid in my throat. But I don't want them to ruin this for me. And they will. They'll go straight to Taylor if I tell them the truth. Then I won't be able to help him.

"What happened to the register?" Nicoli asks, nodding to the register.

"One of the guys shoved the other guy into it. It fell." I hate that the lie is coming so easily. It makes me physically sick.

Finally, Reed nods and stands and offers me a hand. I take it, and he pulls me up, but he doesn't let go of my hand. "You know if anything happens, you can tell us. We're here for you."

"Absolutely. All you need to do is say the word, and you'll have an entire army behind you." Nicoli smiles.

"I know. I do. I promise." I give them what I hope is a convincing smile.

Both of them give me a hug before Nicoli walks behind the counter and lifts the register off the ground. He puts it on the counter, and Korie gets to work fixing it.

"You need any other help? Cleaning up or anything?" Reed asks.

"I think we got it. Thank you for helping with the register," Michelle says.

"Anytime," Nicoli says.

Korie and Michelle get the officers their orders, which we refuse to charge them for. After they leave, we all look at each other and breathe a huge sigh of relief.

"I did not expect Chris to step in," Korie says.

"I thought it was set up by him," I say softly.

"Are you going to tell Taylor what happened?" Michelle asks.

"If I do, this whole thing stops. Taylor will send the entire force in here." I take a deep breath. "Obviously, this doesn't just affect me, though. I don't want you guys to feel unsafe working here. So, I want your opinions. If you don't want to do this anymore, I'll give Taylor what I have."

"If you give him what we have, it just shows Chris saving us. I'm in this until it doesn't make sense," Korie says.

"Me, too. This asshole needs to go down," Michelle agrees.

I smile. These girls are truly turning into the best friends I have ever had. I'm so grateful for them for so many reasons, but I know for sure I couldn't do this without them.

Chapter Twelve

✗ Taylor ✗

Nicole is not going to like walking into what I have going on in this house right now. It's a mess. She's such an organized neat freak that what is happening right now will drive her completely crazy.

Tait is on a blanket on the floor playing contentedly with... air? He's babbling happily. It's all I can ask for.

Spread across the table are files, papers, and pictures. I have a method. Everything on this table is completely organized. Nicole won't think so, though, and I have to laugh. Tait squeals at my sudden outburst.

I grin. "I completely agree, kid. Your mommy is beautifully hilarious."

Tait goes back to babbling contentedly, and Nicole finally walks through the front door. She's not going to like me very much in a minute. And not because of the mess I made in her house.

Her house.

This house became her house as soon as she walked through the door. I couldn't be happier.

"Oh. Wow. You... have a lot going on here."

"Organized chaos." I smile at her.

She laughs. "Or just chaos."

I lean back against the couch and look up at her. "So? How was your day?" It's very rare that I ever ask a question I don't already know the answer to. I just hope she's honest.

"It wasn't horrible. We were busy until later in the afternoon."

"Hmm. So... Nothing interesting happened?"

She raises an eyebrow and kneels next to Tait, picking him up and cuddling him. He grabs her hair as she kisses him. He squeals. I soften at the sight. She's so beautiful. The perfect mother. Perfect wife. She sets him back down. He grabs a toy, shaking it happily.

"There was a fight. Two customers kind of got into it. It ended pretty quickly. Another customer stopped it, but we were all kind of shaken up." I'm watching her for any of her tells. When she lies, she looks at everything but me. When she's hiding something, she grabs the hem of her shirt. When she's nervous, she plays with her thumb. "One of them cracked my display case. And my register got knocked off the counter. We thought it was broken, but it's actually fine." She licks her lower lip. Ah. Yes. There it is. The sign that tells me she's not telling me everything. I cross my arms over my chest and continue to watch her. "I have to get a new monitor, though." She frowns. "That definitely got shattered."

Interesting story. Now, let's find out everything that really happened. "Nicole."

"Yes?"

"I made Sergeant my second year on the force. My third year, I had my own task force. By my fifth, I became a Lieutenant." I haven't moved. She's still standing, looking at me. "I've turned down Captain five times and Assistant Chief twice." I stand and walk slowly towards her. She looks up at me when I stop in front of her. "I can read situations and people incredibly well. You've flat out called me a human lie detector. I know you aren't telling me everything." She looks down. "So, we can sit here all night long if you want, but you are going to tell me what happened."

"Taylor. Please. Just trust me." She looks up at me. Her eyes are pleading. I hold her gaze a few moments before sighing. "I promise I won't keep anything important from you. I'll tell you right away if something huge happens."

"Nicole. Whatever the hell is going on, I don't like it."

"I know. But if I tell you everything, I can't help you."

"Help me? What the hell are you talking about?" All at once, it hits me. "Son of a bitch." I turn and start pacing.

"Taylor?"

"No. No. You aren't doing this."

"Doing what?"

I turn to her, furious at her for the first time ever in our relationship. "Don't play stupid with me! I know exactly what you're doing, and I won't allow it!" I've never yelled at her, but I am now, and I can't control it. She immediately shrinks away. "You're putting yourself in danger! I'm not fucking letting this happen! It ends. Now!" I can see the fear and tears in Nicole's eyes, and I instantaneously calm down. I'd never hurt her, but the way I'm acting, there's no way she would know that. Not after what she's been through. I stop pacing and reach for her. "I'm sorry for yelling." She bites her lip and shakes her head as she swipes at her eyes and bends down to pick up Tait. "Nikki."

"Don't. Just don't. I need to be alone right now."

Fuck. What the hell did I just do? I watch her as she cuddles Tait into the crook of her neck and walks up the stairs. I can do nothing but watch her until she disappears around the corner at the top of the stairs. Dammit. Dammit. Dammit!

I force myself to take a deep breath as I drop into a chair. I take out my phone and dial the one person who I know might be able to talk me down. Chase and Breetana are on a business trip, and Ryan has been distracted with Arianna and the bullying she's been dealing with. That leaves me with one other person. He's not just my Sergeant. He's my friend.

"What's up, boss? You get an idea to crack this fucking case?" Dane. Always a voice of calm and reason in the chaos I sometimes call my life.

"Sort of, I guess. Pissed my wife off, though."

"Uh oh." I sigh heavily and put my head in my hands. Dane sighs. "What did you do?"

"Confronted her. She was hiding something. I know her. I know her tells."

He whistles. "You called her out."

"I figured out what she's keeping from me."

"This have something to do with what Daniels told us earlier?"

"Everything. Everything to do with that. She told me the same story she told him. I told her I knew she was keeping something from me. She admitted it, and then said she can't tell me because she won't be able to help me if she does."

"Help y-" He cuts himself off.

"Yeah."

"She's using herself as bait."

"Yep." That's what I like about him. He knows the way I think, and he can figure shit out just as quickly as me.

"She's using that CCTV system."

"Correct."

"Fuck. What did you say?"

"I told her I'm not allowing it. I... actually yelled at her."

"After everything that girl has been through, you yelled at her?"

"She looked at me like she was scared to death of me. Took Tait and walked up the stairs."

"She probably was scared to death of you."

"I know."

"Taylor. Listen. You're better than this. Your relationship is stronger than any I've ever seen. I think every cop I know has been divorced at least once because none of us have managed to find a girl like you found. She doesn't put up with your shit. She can hold her own against any of us. And the way she looks at you. Man. Any of us would give anything for what you have." He pauses. I hear him take a breath. "She's doing this because she loves you, you know."

"I know." I rub my temple as another headache develops.

"I'm sure she's seen what the stress this case is causing you. I bet you anything you're fighting a headache right now."

I look at the phone and stop rubbing my head. "Yeah. I am."

"And you think that doesn't affect her? She sees the same thing all of us do, dude."

I sigh. Of course he's right. "I know what she's trying to do, but I'm still not allowing it."

"I didn't say allow it. I wouldn't either. But there has to be a compromise. She needs to feel like she's doing something, man. Most women don't like feeling like a damsel in distress. And everything I know about you and your girl? No way she's just going to sit back and let you suffer when she knows she can help you."

"You're right."

"That surprises you? I usually am." We both chuckle. "Apologize for going off on her. Scaring her. And then figure out how she can feel like she's helping you without being put into danger. That's my unsolicited advice."

"Thanks, man. For talking me the fuck down."

"Anytime."

We hang up, and I stand. I pace downstairs trying to figure out how to talk to my wife. I just hope she forgives me for acting like my dick of a father.

✕✕✕

A little while after yelling at Nicole, I'm standing outside the nursery. The door is closed, but I can hear her sniffling. My heart shatters. I hate seeing and hearing my girl cry, but I hate the fact that I'm the cause of it even more.

I take a deep breath and open the door. Nicole is sitting in the rocking chair with her legs curled under her. Tait is sound asleep in his crib. Nicole's eyes are red and puffy. She refuses to meet my eyes.

I cross the room and take both of her hands in mine as I kneel in front her. "Nikki. Baby, I'm really sorry. I don't know what to say to you to make it better. Just that I'm sorry. I'm sorry I scared you. I'm sorry I acted like my fucking father. The one person in the world I hate. Even though he's dead." I bring her hands to my lips and kiss them. I then put my arms around her and rest my head on her stomach. "I'm sorry I acted like your ex and your uncle. I fucked up. I'm really sorry, Nikki."

She runs her fingers through my hair. "It's me who should be sorry. I should've been honest," she whispers.

"I shouldn't have yelled at you."

"You were scared for my safety."

"It's no excuse. I'm better than that."

"People do things that aren't like them when they're scared."

"I'm still better than that."

95

"People get angry, Taylor. I know you'd never hurt me. No matter how angry at me you get." Her touch gives me the comfort I hope I'm giving her.

I take a shaky breath. "Thank God. Thank God you know that. Thank you, baby. For not giving up on me."

"Oh, Taylor... Never. I'll never give up on you. On us." She leans down to kiss my head. "I just wanted to help. I thought I was doing the right thing."

I kiss her stomach and then pull away from her as I stand. I reach a hand down to help her up. She takes my hand, and I lead her to our bedroom, crossing to our balcony. The sun is just setting over the lake behind the house. Nicole loves watching it.

I sit in a chair, and she sits in my lap. My lap is her favorite place, and I love having her in it. "I think I may have figured out how to allow you to help while still maintaining your safety, which is all I care about."

She looks at me before laying her head on my shoulder. "How?"

"Jesse. Remember him?"

"I think so. He's on your taskforce, right?"

"Yes. He went to cooking school before he decided he wanted to be a cop instead. He's not as good as you or Korie and Michelle, but he can hold his own baking."

"You want to put a cop undercover in my bakery?"

"It provides extra security while still allowing you to help me. I'm thinking maybe do an interview with him, like you're looking to hire an extra baker, right in front of this Chris asshole. I know you didn't say it, but I'm assuming that Chris has been coming in, and that he was the customer who broke up the fight."

She nods slowly and sighs. "The theory is that he set up the fight so he could break it up and gain my trust."

"Not a bad theory. And I think you're right. All the more reason to have Jesse there." She runs her hand down my chest until she gets to the bottom of my shirt. I shiver. She pulls back slightly and starts lifting my shirt, not bothering with buttons. I smile slightly. "Want something?"

She continues lifting my shirt, her fingers graze against my skin, leaving heat in its wake. "Yes. You." She lifts my shirt over my head and tosses it to the ground.

"Hey, now. That's one of my nicer dress shirts, you know."

"Oh dear. Guess I'll have to buy you a new one." She smirks. I laugh as I run my hands over her breasts. She closes her eyes and moans.

"Yeah? You like that?"

She giggles. I lift her shirt over her head and toss it on top of mine. "So, when should we start Operation Take That Asshole Down?"

I laugh as I run my hand over her sexy black, silk bra, making her nipples hard for me. "I'll text the guys and tell them to be here in the morning. We'll hash out a plan."

"And I'll text the girls and tell them I'll be a little late." She closes her eyes and lets her head drop back as I lean forward and kiss the hollow of her neck. My gentle suck brings out a groan, and she spears my hair with her fingers. I flick the hooks on her bra and toss it. She spills out for me.

I smile. "God, you're the definition of beautiful." She tugs my hair so I'm looking at her and kisses me. Hard. I grin as I pull back. "So, it's gonna be like this, huh?"

There's a devilish glint in her eye as she nods. I shake my head as I laugh and stand with her in my arms. "I don't want to go inside."

"I have no intention of taking you inside." I put her down near the wall and kneel in front of her. I slowly run my hands up her legs until I reach her hips.

"Mmm..." She closes her eyes and melts into my touch. I run my hands across the front of her jeans. She slightly parts her legs so I can drop my hand between them. "Taylor."

She reaches out and runs her fingers through my hair as I unbutton her jeans with one hand and grab her core with the other. She gasps and moans as I start rubbing back and forth over her jeans.

"So hot."

"Oh, God...," she moans. I kiss and nip her over her jeans. "Taylor!"

"I love when you scream my name." I tug her jeans and panties down, toss them aside, and lean back to look at my wife in all her naked glory. "All mine."

She smiles at me. I push her back against the wall. Not hard, but forceful enough that she whimpers when she hits. I push her legs apart further and lick.

"Oh! My God..."

I follow my tongue with a nail, light enough to make her shiver, but hard enough to give her pleasure and make her moan. I run my teeth back up and circle my tongue around her clit before biting it.

She throws her head back. "Ah! Taylor!"

I thrust two fingers deeply inside her as I stand. She grabs my arms, digging her nails in. "Mmm... Baby," I rumble.

I continue my rough, deep thrusts as she runs her nails up my arms and across my shoulders. I bend to kiss her, my tongue finding its way in her mouth, as she wraps her arms around my neck. I set my thumb against her clit. She tightens instantly around my fingers.

"Taylor! Fuck! I'm -" She doesn't finish her sentence before I drag her orgasm from her with one hand as I unbutton my own jeans with my other.

She nibbles and sucks on my bottom lip as her legs nearly give out from under her. I grab my throbbing cock out of my jeans, then grip her thighs, lifting her. She wraps her legs around me as I position myself at her entrance.

"How bad do you want it?" I ask with a grin, holding my cock back from her.

"Taylor! Don't tease me...," she pouts adorably.

I grin and slowly kiss her, withholding myself from her as I push her harder against the wall. "I haven't even begun to tease you." I reach down and grab myself, holding her against the wall. I move my cock against her entrance but don't push in.

"Oh my God, Taylor. You're so mean! Please put it in..." She moves against me the best she can, which isn't a lot considering I have her pinned.

"You aren't getting relief until I want you to."

"Not fair."

"Hey, now. This is the way you wanted it, baby girl." I kiss her neck as I continue rubbing against her. I feel her get wetter and hotter against me. I bite her neck, soothing it with my tongue.

"Oh! Oh, Taylor. Please..."

I finally give in. Mostly because I can't stand to feel her against me without being inside her anymore. I grip her hips and drop her onto me. I plunge into her hard.

"Holy fuck…" I have to stay still for a second because I'm already close to coming. She feels better than she ever has. She always feels better than the last time.

She tightens her legs around my waist and her arms around my neck. "The anticipation is killing me..." Her tone is teasing.

I growl as I begin thrusting wildly into her and crash my lips against hers. My fingers dig into her ass as her back crashes against the wall hard enough to add to both of our pleasure, but not hard enough to hurt.

Her nails dig into my shoulders, and she buries her face in my neck. "Ah! Taylor... Taylor!"

"How do you feel better every time I fuck you, baby?"

"How do... you... feel bigger? Oh... Oh!" Her pussy is so wet. So warm. She's so tight.

I continue my hard, deep thrusts, growing harder and bigger by the second. "Fuck, Nikki. Goddamn. You're so tight. So wet, baby." I'm close, and I need her to be, too. I lick her neck, then open-mouthed kiss it as I reach between our bodies and start circling her clit with my thumb.

"Oh my God. Oh my God!"

"Come for me, Nicole. Right now."

Her legs weaken as she quakes. Her pussy tightens around me. I flick her clit. She shatters, screaming my name. "Taylor! Taylor... Mmm... Tay...lor... Mmm..." Her pussy pulses erratically around me squeezing my cock.

I thrust into her again before burying myself deep inside her. I come hard, filling her sweet pussy. "Nikki! Holy shit, baby."

Her limbs are like jelly. I hold her against the wall until we both recover. Leaving all of her clothes and my shirt on the ground, I pull out of her and carry her to bed. I strip the rest of the way and crawl in next to her. She curls into my side.

"We still have to make dinner. And call everyone."

"Later. Give me time to recover after that."

She smirks up at me. "Getting old, Lieutenant?"

I raise an eyebrow. "Bit sassy today?"

"Maybe a little..."

"You know you're not too old to put over my knee..." I give her a dangerous and challenging smile.

99

"Oooh... Promise?"

I spank her, then drag her on top of me, dropping her onto my already hard length. "You're being such a naughty girl."

"Maybe a little." She starts riding me. She bounces up and down on me until neither of us can hang on. We both break at the same time, screaming each other's names.

Breaking only for a few minutes to make the calls we need to, I make love to Nicole until we're both too exhausted to move. Skipping dinner, we finally fall asleep wrapped up in each other, me still buried inside my girl.

I sleep better than I have in weeks.

Chapter Thirteen

✗ Nicole ✗

The next afternoon, I'm sitting in my bakery doing paperwork in my small office in the back. Korie is running the front and Michelle is running the back baking cookies and other things we are low on. They both are under strict orders to let me know the moment Chris enters the bakery.

The plan we came up with this morning was rather good. Jesse would tap into his prior baking skills and help us out. He would also act as a bodyguard when Chris started pushing us to pay him. We knew it would be soon.

The rest of Taylor's team would go about business as usual, and the bakery would run as usual. We decided rather quickly that Chris was smart and could see if the bakery was being watched, so the team sitting around staking it out wasn't an option.

"Hey, sweetie. Chris just walked in." We had decided to keep the cupcakes he liked in the back, like we were out, so Korie had a reason to walk into the backroom to tell me he was here.

"Thanks. I'll text Jesse." I take out my phone and quickly text Jesse. He's in a building across the street waiting.

Nicole: He's here.

I stand and brush myself off. My phone vibrates.

Jesse: On the way.

I take a deep breath and walk out of my office. Michelle winks at me, and I smile.

"This will work," she whispers.

"It has to." I walk out of the backroom and plaster a winning smile on my face. "Chris! Hey!"

He smiles at me. "Hey, Nicole! Would you please tell Korie to let me pay?"

"Not a chance! After yesterday, I'm never charging you again."

"How about a discount instead?"

"Nope!" Korie shakes her head.

"We aren't charging you. But if you want to feel like you're paying, put the amount you usually would pay in the charity jar."

"Damn. You two make a hell of a team!" Chris says. Korie and I both laugh, then glance at each other as Jesse walks in.

Jesse is around six feet and has a killer smile. He has blonde, spiky hair. He's wearing jeans and a t-shirt, and I chuckle a little as Korie hands Chris his order. Jesse strides up to the counter as Chris turns and walks to his usual table.

"Hey! I'm Jesse. I'm here for an interview with Nicole Reddick?" He addresses the question to Korie and adds a bit of feminine flare. His cover is that he's gay. We thought Chris would feed into the stereotype of gay people and look at Jesse as weak and easy to intimidate.

Not that any of us think gay people are weak or easy to intimidate, but we're counting on Chris to look at Jesse as no competition. We don't want Chris to give Jesse a second glance.

"Hey, Jesse! I'm Nicole." I reach out a hand over the counter to shake his.

He takes it and winks. "Nice to meet you. Your bakery is lovely! So bright and inviting."

"Well, thank you! Why don't you head over there and have a seat?"

Jesse smiles and heads to a table near Chris. Chris is watching him intently. When Jesse sits, Chris gets up and walks up to me.

He speaks low and looks slightly concerned. "Hiring someone?"

I smile as I walk around the counter. I lay a hand on his arm and smile up at him. "I need another baker. I want Michelle to focus on the sugar decorating and chocolate stuff. And we've been getting a lot of special orders. I thought maybe if I could get someone else to help out, we could expand into weddings."

"Weddings? That's pretty huge."

I smile a little wider. "Cross your fingers." He walks with me and takes a seat at his table, taking out his phone. I can tell he's watching me, though, as I sit across from Jesse. "So. Jesse. Tell me about yourself."

"Well. I went to Kendall College of Culinary Arts here in Chicago. I fell in love with baking just as much as I fell in love with the guy teaching me how to do it."

"Aww... I'm such a sap when it comes to love stories."

Jesse laughs. "He's absolutely the most romantic man I've ever been with. On our first date, he picked me up and took me to a movie in the park. He presented me with a picnic dinner of the most fabulous fried chicken I've ever had. And for dessert, he made cupcakes. French Vanilla. The first flavor cupcake I ever tried to bake. I messed it up horribly, but I redeemed myself. I went home and didn't give up baking them until I got them right. Presented them to him the next day!"

"And then he made you the same cupcake? Oh my gosh, I may cry!" I smile widely. Jesse laughs. I see Chris smile, and I bite my lip, focusing on Jesse. I fed him that story, and he told it very convincingly. "Well, looking at your resume, you're definitely qualified." I make a show of looking at the resume I created for him based on the identity that Taylor gave him.

"Baking is definitely my passion."

"I see that. So, what can you bring here that will help us be better? I'd love to expand into weddings someday."

"I love weddings! They're so romantic. I'll be honest. Cakes are not my specialty. I can do anything else, but I don't do cakes. I can, however, decorate like no other."

"That's perfect! If you can take a little stress off me and help out with regular baking for the store, my time will be freed up to start expanding the wedding cake portion of this business."

"Hey! Just give me the opportunity, and I guarantee you'll be pleased with my work. I'm a people pleaser for sure! Anything to help you out!"

I look at Chris, who is outright staring. "Wow. If you don't hire him, I will," he says with a smirk.

I laugh and look back at Jesse. "You're hired."

"Great decision!" Jesse winks.

I laugh and stand to shake his hand. "When can you start?"

"Right now, if you need me."

"We'll be closing soon, but how about a tour? I can introduce you to the girls. And this guy here is Chris." I point to Chris. Chris grins and stands. The two shake hands. "Chris is sort of our resident bodyguard."

"Oh yeah? Be good to have a tough guy hanging around! I definitely hate fighting. Not one of my strong suits!"

Chris looks him up and down, just as I thought he would. It's almost like he's trying to size him up. "Really? Looks like you spend a lot of time in the gym."

"My husband has a gym in the basement. We like to... workout together." He winks again. "If you know what I mean."

Chris lets out a roar of a laugh. "Understood! Well, you won't have to worry about fighting anyone here. Nicole is in a good neighborhood."

"And we have a big, tough man to help us out!" Jesse says as femininely as he can.

Chris laughs again as he turns around to clean up his table. He walks to the door and throws us all a wink over his shoulder as he walks out. "See you guys tomorrow!"

"That went better than expected," Jesse says as we watch Chris leave.

"You play gay shockingly well." I look up at him.

Jesse laughs. "Cops are nothing more than actors. But truth be told, my cousin is gay. Nicest guy in the world. You wouldn't know it looking at him. But he's one of my closest confidants, and I sort of channeled him in that entire performance. Except the overly feminine part. I was playing into the stereotype." I lean against him, slightly deflating. He slips an arm around my waist. "Hey. We got this. Trust me. Trust my team. And trust your husband."

"I do. I just wish this could be over. I hate seeing Taylor so stressed. And I hate being scared of that guy. Or confused by him. He's so nice, but I know what he's doing. It's annoying. Truly."

Jesse gives my waist a light squeeze. "I get it. I do. Honestly, I think he'll make a move soon. You really stroked his ego with that bodyguard comment. I don't think he'll wait much longer."

I take a deep breath. "Alright, Officer Scott. Let's earn you that pay check!"

He laughs. I show him around the bakery. When we're alone in the back he pulls me aside and speaks low. "So... What's the deal with Korie?"

I raise an eyebrow. "You mean... is she available?" My inner romantic is leaping, but I keep her still as I look up into his piercing blue eyes.

"Yeah. She's..." He glances towards the door when Korie's laughter rings out. I bite my lip to keep from beaming as he looks down at me with a soft smile on his face. "She's beautiful. I know I've only seen her the few times I've been in here for my coffee and raspberry rose donut, but damn. I swear she gets more striking every time I see her."

"Well... she's not with anyone. I know from our conversations that she's tired of guys who only want to get into her panties." I also know he's exactly her type. I've noticed her blush every single time he's come in. I've seen how uncomfortable she gets when she tries to talk to him. It comes out as an adorable squeak or stutter.

"So, she's looking for something long term?"

I nod as I turn back towards the door leading to the front of the bakery. "She's only ever been with guys who sweet talk her. Make her think they have feelings for her. She's never just given it up to anyone. The couple of guys she has actually slept with she'd been with for awhile." I look up at him and shrug. "Not long after, they became assholes. She left them."

"I suppose that would make anyone a little jaded."

I shake my head. "Not jaded. Guarded. Korie isn't closed off to love. She's just... careful of who she chooses. If she gives up her heart, it's because she really likes you. She hasn't given it to anyone for the past few years. She's dated. But she's never felt that spark."

"It kills me that she's been hurt."

"It would take a lot to prove to her you aren't like the guys in her past. But… I think it would be worth every second."

He looks down at me. "You really like her, don't you?"

"She's an amazing woman. Truly one of a kind." I squeeze his arm before finishing the tour.

After I'm finished showing Jesse around, we all talk for a while as we clean up and close down. I can't help but notice that he can't keep his eyes off Korie. My heart soars when I see that she sneaks just as many glances at him as he does her. The matchmaker in me already has plans.

Having Jesse with us makes me feel more confident about our plan. I only hope that it works. I hope that we catch Chris so that he can't do this to anyone else.

And so my husband can sleep at night.

Chapter Fourteen

✗ Arianna ✗

I wipe a tear away and sniffle, trying to reign in my emotions. I'm angry. I'm sad. Maybe a little numb. I don't even know how to feel anymore. Chad has made my life a living hell without even touching or talking to me. So many rumors are going around about me now that everyone in the school is giving me the evil eye. All I have at this point are my grades and Robby and Renza, the only two people who haven't turned against me.

I hold my breath as some girls walk into the bathroom. I can see them through the crack in the stall door. I fight the sob that tries to escape. More of my recent tormentors. They used to be friends. At least I thought so.

"Adam is so hot, but he said that Arianna was such a prude that she wouldn't touch him," an exotically beautiful Asian girl named Mai says.

Adam.

It's true. I wouldn't touch him. But that's because he tried to force me before I was ready. I was only a Freshman. That was four years ago. Why are they even talking about this now?

"Chad said she can't keep her hands off him," another girl named Mandy says. Cheerleader. Captain. Blonde. Everyone wants her. Everyone wants to be her. Be her friend. Except me. I hate her now. I hate all of them.

"It's obvious she likes guys she can't have because Chad is totally yours." Krissa. Mandy's right-hand floozy. She's got perfect dark brown hair with blonde highlights that she loves flipping over her shoulder.

I fight the urge to throw up. It's Chad who can't keep his hands off me. Who won't leave me alone. If Robby wasn't always around, Chad would be all over me. He'd be touching me. Taunting me. Forcing himself on me. He'd be constantly shoving me and pushing me. Holding me against lockers. I have no doubt that if not for Robby, Chad would have dragged me into a dark corner somewhere and lived out whatever sick fantasy he has in his head involving the two of us.

"That slut will get what's coming to her," Mai sneers.

"I'm glad we're graduating in a few months. That way, that stupid bitch will keep her fat fingers off him. She won't see him every day. Maybe she'll forget about him and let me have what's rightfully mine." I can hear the hatred in Mandy's voice like acid in my ears.

"God. I swear she's retarded. Have you heard her stutter?" Krissa laughs.

"Oh my God, yes. I wonder why she never went to a speech therapist. Like, isn't that something people do?" Mai sneers.

"I don't even know how she gets anyone to pay attention to her." I don't need to see Krissa do it. The eye roll is in her voice.

"Oh my God, me either. She's so ugly and annoying." Mandy's disdain for me has never been more evident than it is now, and I wonder if she ever really liked me at all.

She used to be one of my closest friends. I'm not really sure what happened to make her hate me the way she does, but I've always thought it had to do with Adam. She had a serious crush on him. When I broke it off, she was on him like a bee to a withering rose. He nearly destroyed her life just as he had nearly destroyed mine.

"And fat." Krissa makes a gagging noise.

"Her ass is so big." Mai joins in the gagging noise, and they all laugh.

It's getting harder and harder to hold back the tears. My hands tremble as I take out my phone and order a Lyft. I can't finish the rest of my day. Between Mai, Krissa, Mandy, and my locker being vandalized this morning, I can't be here anymore.

"Ugh. I don't want to talk about her. If I see her, I'll probably slap her. Chad said she pushed him into the guys bathroom this morning and tried to kiss him." Mandy growls low in her throat.

"Ugh. Gross." I watch Mai shiver.

I put my hand over my mouth to stop the gasp. The three of them leave, and a few moments later, I'm throwing up. I hear the bell ring signaling the end of lunch, but I don't move. After throwing up my guts, I pick up my backpack and quickly leave, making my way through the crowd of students to the front of the school. My Lyft is still a few minutes away. I hope he hurries.

I can't fight the tears anymore. They start to fall freely. I don't think as I start texting Ryan.

Arianna: Hey. Are you home?

My Lyft pulls up. I quickly get in the back. I had put in my address, but going home makes me even more upset. I wipe my eyes as my phone vibrates.

Ryan: No. I have some things I need to take care of. Why?

The tears start falling again.

Arianna: I just... didn't have a good day. I wanted to see you.

Moments later, my phone is ringing, Ryan's face fills the screen. I take a deep breath, trying to stop crying as I answer. "Hi."

"Baby, what's wrong? Are you crying?" he asks soothingly with a hint of edge and concern. A sob escapes. I try to hold it back, but I can't. "Hey. Hey. What happened? Tell me."

"Not over the phone. Please." I sniffle and try to stop crying.

"Okay. Where are you? It sounds like you're driving."

"I was going home, but I... don't... want to," I sob.

"Okay, sweetheart. Shh.... It's okay." His voice is so calm and soothing. "Go to Jason's office. He has a key to my house. I'll be home in a little while, okay?"

"O-okay."

"Aria, it'll be okay. I promise. Whatever happened, sweetheart, I'm here for you."

"Okay." I hang up and tell the driver the new address, giving him cash for the change and still paying for the original ride. When we arrive, I thank him and hurry into the building, going straight to the security desk.

"Hey, Arianna. What's up?" Nick Crane, Ryan's brother and Jason's head of security asks with a smile.

"Um... Is Jason here?"

"Yeah. He's in his office. Want me to escort you up?"

"If it's... not too much." I look down and fiddle with the strap on my backpack. I can feel Nick, looking at me with an intense as hell, dark gaze. I nearly wilt and spill everything to him. He comes around the edge of the security booth and leads me to the elevator.

"Did something happen? You look upset."

"Just... not a good day." I refuse to look at him. The Crane brothers are notorious for getting information. Their dark, intimidating look is only part of the reason why. The rest? It has everything to do with how protective they are of those they love or are close to. It's how much they care that makes their loved ones want to talk to them. I can feel how much Nick cares, even though I barely know him.

Everyone else? Well, they're also ruthless. People don't mess with them. Those who are stupid enough to try end up regretting it. Many end up as fish food.

Nick scans his key card and pushes the button for the top floor. "I'm here if you need anything, you know."

"I know. Ryan said I could always count on you and anyone in his family." I take a deep breath.

"You can. We're all pretty close knit, sweetheart."

"Thank you." I pause and look up at him. "I may need you sooner than you think."

"Just say the word." He gives me a quick side hug as the elevator doors open. He leads me to Jason's office and knocks on the door before walking in. "Jas? Visitor."

"Hey, Arianna. Ryan just texted. You need a key?" Jason asks. I glance at him. He's sitting behind his desk, but he seems so big. Larger than life almost. He looks a lot like Ryan. Tall, dark. Incredibly handsome, but to me he's so much more intimidating than Ryan.

"He said you have one," I say quietly. Nick leaves, and I stand in front of Jason's desk. He smiles warmly. I relax a little.

"So? Skipping school?" he teases.

I try to smile, but my lip quivers. Before I know what's happening, I'm in tears again, sinking into a chair in front of his desk and covering my face with my hands.

Jason is immediately at my side. "Hey. I was just kidding. Ry said something happened. I was just trying to make you feel better."

I shake my head and sob. I wouldn't be able to use words if I tried.

Jason pulls me up and wraps me in his arms. "Shh... I got you, Arianna. Whatever happened, you're safe now," he whispers soothingly. I nod into his chest. He holds me tightly. "I'm free for the rest of the afternoon. What do you say we get you to Ryan's?"

"I just want to hide." My voice is muffled. I can barely hear myself, but Jason does.

"I can tell. All the more reason to get you to Ryan's." He hugs me a few moments longer. "You okay if I let you go now?"

I nod. He pulls away, slowly, and then leans down to grab my backpack. He takes my hand and leads me back to the elevator. He pushes the button for the parking garage.

"Will Jessa be upset with me?" I ask, referring to his wife.

"Why would Jessa be upset with you?"

"For taking you away from work?"

"Sweetheart. No. Jessa won't be upset at all. I texted her right after I got Ryan's text. She's in a meeting, or she'd be here, too."

I look down at the floor. "I'm really sorry. About your shirt."

He looks down at his shirt and shakes his head. I bite my lip. His shirt is wet with my tears and stained with the little bit of makeup that I wear.

"Arianna. If I cared at all about my shirts, I would be pissed off a lot at my wife. She's stained a lot of them with her tears and makeup. My job is to comfort her. Not be pissed off at her when she's upset for ruining my shirt. Just like..." He tugs my hand and draws me to his side. "... it's my job as your big brother to comfort you when you're upset. And knowing my brother, I have a feeling over the coming years I'll be comforting you a lot!"

I can't help but laugh a little as he hugs me. My big brother. He called himself my big brother. Like I'm already Ryan's. I feel so stupid, but

111

that's all I want. I already feel like I'm part of Ryan's family. That Jason and Nick and Jessa are really my big brothers and sister.

It's only now I realize just how much I want this. Not just him. But this. This sense of security. Of safety. Of... family. Of trusting family above and beyond everything. Of knowing I can count on them to protect me. To defend me. I want Ryan more than anything. But also, more than anything, I want all of this.

Jason helps me into his car and climbs into the driver's side. He pulls out and starts driving across Manhattan to Ryan's home. I curl into myself as I stare at the traffic and buildings as they blur with my tears that refuse to stop falling. I sniffle and feel Jason's hand gently rubbing my arm.

"I don't know what happened, but I know that whatever it is can be fixed," Jason says softly.

I nod. I want to believe him, but it's difficult because I know things. Things I refuse to discuss. I know how powerful Ryan and his family are. I know that if I told him who Chad is, he'd take care of the problem and be fine.

But I also know the other things he's dealing with. I know how tense he is. How stretched thin he is. He doesn't need another battle. Especially not one that's caused by me. I won't do that to him. I love him far too much to cause him more trouble.

Chapter Fifteen

☒ Ryan ☒

For the entire afternoon, ever since Arianna called me, I've been trying to get to her. I know she needs me. I don't know what happened, but she sounded broken. Defeated. I don't like that. I may refuse to touch her right now, but that doesn't mean she isn't mine. No one, and I mean no-fucking-one, fucks with what's mine.

I'm sitting in the back of a limo finally heading home. I may be a dangerous as all hell mob boss, but I also own legit businesses and companies that I sometimes have to tend to. Like today. I had several meetings with several people to make sure things were and continue to run smoothly. I don't run illegal activities. I'm not into the drug trade or illegal arms trade. My money and my power comes from the legal business I own and the smaller ones I partner with all around the world.

The single reason that I'm so intertwined with law enforcement agencies and government law enforcement agencies, like the FBI and even Interpol, is because I hate seeing the scum of the Earth trying to control it. I do what I can to help them clean up the streets because I want the world to be a better place.

My father didn't agree with me. He hates that I turned his beloved mafia legal, but even he can't argue with my methods. I've grown much more powerful than even he could dream. He's on board with me now.

Being legit doesn't mean I'm afraid to get my hands dirty if I have to. It's what makes me so dangerous. If I have to kill, I do it, and I move on. I don't feel uncomfortable with it, and I don't allow emotions to enter the equation. Sometimes, it's an essential part of my job.

My limo pulls into my driveway. I step out, pulling my keys out of my pocket as I walk to my door. I unlock it and am immediately greeted by the sweet sound of music coming from the piano I bought for Arianna. I hadn't heard her play since the day the production crew was here. I didn't know until this moment how much I not only missed it, but also how much I need it. How much I need to hear her play out her emotions.

I make my way to her piano room. It became hers as soon as I walked her into that room and she opened her eyes. The door is open, and I silently step inside, I lean against the wall with my arms crossed over my chest.

The music that flows out of her is haunting. I can feel her sadness and her anger; her heartbreak and betrayal. It's the heartbreak and betrayal that gets me.

Your heart is hollow
And it weighs heavily on me
How could you hurt me
And be so mean?
You lied when you pretended to be my friend.
Left me alone in the end.

She launches into a piano solo, then stops abruptly, dropping her head into her arms on the keys. Her body starts shaking with gut-wrenching sobs. My heart shatters into so many pieces for her, I don't know if I'll ever recover from it. I waste no time crossing the room, sitting on the bench next to her, and pulling her close to me. She turns and buries her head in my shoulder and arm, bunching my shirt into her fist as she shakes and cries.

I can do nothing but run my fingers through her hair; my hands up and down her back. With my lips against her ear, I start whispering anything I can think of to make her okay again.

"Shh... It's okay, Aria. Whatever happened, I'm here now... I promise I'm not going anywhere." I don't know how long I sit there with her until she finally begins to calm, but I don't care. I'll sit like this forever if she needs me to. "You're okay now, honey. I won't let anything happen to you."

"I can't wait until school is done. I hate it."

"Aria, I hate that what's going on makes you hate school. You love school." I hug her even tighter. She sniffles and hugs me as tightly as she can. "Baby, please let me help you. Let me stop this."

"No. Please, Ryan. It's almost over. I just have a couple more months."

"A couple more months of this? Aria, I'm having a really, really hard time staying out of this. Seeing you like this is killing me, baby girl."

She looks up at me. Her eyes are puffy and red. Her mascara, the little bit she wears, is smeared. She reaches up to wipe her eyes, but I grab her wrists. I fight to keep from kissing her tears away.

Instead, I reach up and wipe them away myself. "Please let me help you."

She shakes her head. "You'll make it worse."

"What? How? When have I ever made anything worse?"

"Ryan. This is high school. You can't just walk in and break an arm and threaten them. They're high school students." She reaches up and puts both of her hands on each side of my face. "Please just trust me when I say if you try to fix this, you'll only make things worse. For both of us."

Something else is going on, but I can't figure it out. This is bigger than just her being bullied by a few people. The issue is that unless she allows me to do anything, I can't get close enough to do any kind of investigation into the people responsible for her torment. And I won't force her to tell me unless I feel like she has no other option.

I sigh. "I'll trust you. For now. But please just promise me if you can't handle this anymore, you come to me."

"I promise."

I search her eyes a moment before finally standing and offering her my hand to help her up. She takes it, but after she's up, I refuse to let go. I lead her to the living room before turning to her.

"I know I'm a little late getting home, but do you have time for a movie? I can order something for dinner. Have it delivered."

"I really don't want to go home. My dad is going out of town this weekend, and I hate being there with the guards. They all look at me like they want to fuck me." She sits on the couch and sighs.

The protectiveness I have towards her fights to escape. "Yeah. That's not fucking happening. No one touches you but me. Stay here," I tell her. She looks up at me. Shocked. I'm shocked the words even came out of my mouth, but the thought of another man touching her makes my blood run fucking cold. I sit next to her and take her hand in mine. "I won't do anything with you right now. I have a guest bedroom. Well, I have nine guest bedrooms. You can pick one. I have some women's clothing. Please don't ask me why. I don't know if any of them would fit you since you're so small, but you can look."

"I would love to. You know I hate leaving here, but what would I tell him?"

"Tell him you're staying at Renza's. She'll cover for you, right?" I see her thinking about it and know I've already won, but I have one last ace up my sleeve. "I'll even clear my weekend so it'll be just you and me. Strictly G-rated, but still just us."

She smiles and looks up at me shyly. "PG-13?"

I lean closer to her, my lips nearly on hers. She closes her eyes. Fuck, I shouldn't have done that. Pulling away and not kissing her is going to be pure fucking torture. I tuck her hair behind her ear and kiss her forehead.

"PG."

She opens her eyes and smiles, squeezing my hand. "If we're watching a movie, and I'm staying here the whole weekend, I need something more comfortable then this dress."

My eyes wander over her, stopping on her thighs and imagining my head between them. I groan as I force my eyes back to hers and stand up, pulling her with me.

"Sweats and a t-shirt. Anything else will make this weekend complete hell for me." My cock instantly hardens when she giggles. "Fuck me, Aria. Your eighteenth birthday cannot come fast enough."

"You're telling me," she mumbles.

I stop outside the guest room across from my master bedroom. "I'm going to put something more comfortable on myself, then I'll order something for us. There's some stuff in the drawers in the dresser in there. Make your arrangements to stay here. Clean up. Wear what you want."

"What I want?"

I look at her for a moment. She bites her lip, and I have to bite my tongue. "Within reason, Ari. Please don't challenge me. My resolve is precariously thin."

I touch her cheek before turning to my room. I wait for her to close the door to the room across from mine before I quietly close mine. I quickly change into gray sweats and a t-shirt, then order Chinese from Arianna's favorite Chinese restaurant.

After a few more minutes, I hear Arianna knocking on my now open door. I glance at her and suck in a breath. She's wearing a pair of tiny purple shorts and a matching tank top. She isn't wearing a bra and just looking at where the shorts are riding up, I also know she isn't wearing panties. I try to look away as she approaches, but I physically can't.

"Um... There weren't any sweats. Or t-shirts. Actually, this was by far the most... um... conservative thing I found."

I should've known. Old Ryan loved when the women I fucked the night before wore sexy shit like that. New Ryan? I still fucking love it. She looks sexy as hell. But if she wears that, the last of my resolve is gone.

I clear my suddenly very dry throat as she stops near me. Within reach.

Fuck.

Me.

Before I know what I'm doing, I reach out and trail my fingertips along the lace running along her hip. She shivers under my touch. I force myself to pull back and look away. I stand and walk to my dresser.

"You can't wear that, baby. I won't be able to keep my hands off you." I pull one of my t-shirts out and hand it to her. She'll drown in it. And hopefully it won't show her peaked nipples because I'm fighting hard not to lick them right now.

117

She smiles nervously up at me, then puts the t-shirt on. Thank fucking God.

I lead her back downstairs just as our dinner arrives. I have her pick out a movie while I get plates and drinks.

After dinner is done and we've finished cleaning up, Arianna curls up into my side as I turn the movie we had paused back on. She shivers.

"Cold?" I ask, feeling like an idiot. Obviously she's cold. She wouldn't be rubbing her arms like she is if she weren't.

"A little."

I know she wants my arm around her, but if I do that, it would be another line I crossed today with her. Being like this is everything I want, but I have to be the strong one here. We have to do this the right way.

I stand up, and she watches me cross the room. I feel her eyes on me as I round the corner into the hallway, disappearing from her view. I grab a comforter from the bed of one of the many rooms in this house and return to her. Her eyes light up.

I smile. "I know how you love wrapping yourself up."

She looks at me as I sit and hand her the blanket. "I'd love it even more if you laid down and wrapped yourself up with me, too."

I cough. "Aria, honey. No. We can't do that."

"You said PG."

"And I meant it. Do you have any idea how quickly that would turn to rated X?" My voice is a little higher than normal. She continues looking at me and not saying a word. "Ari." A small smile starts to turn the corners of her mouth up. She knows she's winning this fight. I can't hold out when she looks at me like that. "This is a truly horrible fucking idea."

"I trust you."

"At least one of us does." I sigh and stand up, motioning her up, too. I take the blanket and arrange it neatly on the couch, taking extra time to control my raging fucking hormones. I feel like a teenage boy. After a few extra moments, I lay down and wait for her to crawl in next to me. I cover us both with the blanket, and she snuggles into me. "You're going to kill me. This is fucking excruciating."

"It's still PG. Think of it as we just started dating, and we're just enjoying being with each other. That's pretty much what this is."

"Except I've known you for four years."

"As friends. Not like this. I don't care what you say about it. I'm close enough to eighteen. I know what I want, and I know it's you."

"Ari -"

She cuts me off and fuck if that doesn't turn me on. "So, for all intents and purposes, I am considering you my boyfriend. You don't have to consider me your girlfriend yet if you don't want to, but that's how I'm getting through this."

I put my hand on her hip and pull her back further into me. I'm having a hard time caring about any of my morals right now. I bury my face in her hair and kiss the back of her neck as I wrap my arm around her waist. The other she's using as a pillow.

"Is that what you want? For me to consider you my girlfriend?"

"More than anything, Ryan. But I know the position that puts you in."

"If that's what you want, then that's what you get. But I'm still not touching you. No further than this. Understand me?"

"I understand."

"Good girl."

I hold her close as we finish the movie and start another one. Before the second one finishes, we're both fast asleep.

XXX

(Two Days Later)

The weekend flew by. I'm far more disappointed than I should be that I'm about to have to send Arianna home. If I had my way, she'd just stay here. I know her dad has begun being far worse than he had in the past. Instead of spending his time yelling at her, she's told me he's started not caring at all. Not ignoring her. Just not caring.

If she tells him she did well on a test or something, he shrugs and tells her she can do better. She was excited about Juilliard and the third stage. He barely acknowledged how difficult it is to even get to that point with a school like that.

Arianna has her own style. She hates sexy clothing. It makes her feel self-conscious. She's more of a jeans and t-shirt kind of girl. She loves her sweaters and her hoodies. She'll wear shorts if they aren't too short, and she'll wear tank tops, but tank tops are where she draws the line. Halter tops and all that other shit girls her age wear is completely out of the question for her. The dress I bought her for Taylor and Nicole's wedding was even a bit hard for her to wear. Showed too much of her curves.

Her father enjoys trash talking her outfits every single morning. He thinks she never wears enough makeup or dresses sexy enough. Which is baffling to me. Who the fuck would want their daughter to go to school dressed like a fucking slut? With short as hell shorts with their ass sticking out and shirts that can't even be considered shirts?

I take a sip of my coffee and push my newspaper aside. Not like I'll be able to concentrate on anything in there with Arianna walking down the stairs anyway. I smile into my coffee as she walks into the kitchen. She slips her arms around me from behind, kisses the back of my shoulder, then presses herself against my back, hugging me tightly.

"You know, it's way too easy to get used to this," I say.

"I don't want to go home. This has been the best weekend of my life."

"The best? Really?" I set my coffee down and untangle myself from her arms so I can swivel the barstool around to face her.

She steps back as I turn, then looks at me shyly when I'm facing her. I grab her hand and gently pull her until she's standing between my legs. She places both of her hands on my legs and looks down at the new semi-intimate position, a soft smile on her lips. I reach up, push her hair behind her ear, and gently raise her chin so she's looking at me.

"Do you know what my new goal is going to be?" I ask. She shakes her head. "To make you feel like every day of the rest of your life is better than the day before."

She smiles and leans forward, wrapping her arms around my waist and resting her head on my shoulder. I hold her close. "Would you mind if I made breakfast today?"

"Promise not to burn our house down?"

She pulls back abruptly and looks up at me. "O-ours?"

I smile and kiss her on the forehead. "See that small box on the counter behind me?"

She looks and her eyes widen. "Um... Y-yes?"

I push her gently back so I can turn back around. "Open it."

120

I watch her over the rim of my coffee I've picked back up as she hesitantly walks around the counter and picks up the box. She looks at me again as she slowly starts unwrapping it. I see her take a deep breath as she takes the top off revealing a key.

"Is this...?"

"A key to the front door. Actually, it'll open the one in the garage that leads inside, too." She takes out the key and looks at the piece of paper underneath it. "First number is the gate code. Second is the alarm code. Please just memorize them and throw that away. I don't want that getting into the wrong hands."

She looks at the paper for a few moments, then tears it up and throws it away. I smile. My girl has a photographic memory. I knew that paper wouldn't leave our house. "Are you... sure about this?"

"Why wouldn't I be?"

"The only people who have a key to your house other than you are Jason and Nick. Not even your parents have one. Or Taylor."

"Sweetheart. Do you want to be with me?"

She doesn't hesitate. "More than anything."

"Good girl. Then you need a key to the house. If I'm not here and you need to get away, you can come here. And it's probably a good idea if you have a key to what's going to soon be your home anyway."

She plays with the key and focuses all of her attention on it. "What if I lose it?"

"Then you tell me, and I change the locks, baby. Quit worrying. Give me your phone."

"It's upstairs." She gestures to my t-shirt and smirks at me. "Not really any place to put it."

I laugh "Fair enough. Before you leave, I need it. I need to put a few numbers in it."

"Whose?"

"Well, Jessa for sure. Jason. I want Nick's in there. My parents. And probably Rico. If I'm out of town and you need immediate help, any of them can get it for you. Rico can get you guards."

She smiles. "It's starting to sound like I'm already yours."

"You are. You told me Friday night that you're considering me your boyfriend. Unless you tell me otherwise, that's what I am. Which means you're my girlfriend. Mine."

"I really like the sound of that."

She puts the key back in the box and turns to the refrigerator, gathering ingredients to cook with. When she bends for the eggs, my t-shirt slips up, revealing nothing but purple lace panties.

"Fuck, Aria. What the hell happened to the shorts?"

She quickly stands and tugs the t-shirt down. "I'm really sorry! I completely forgot to put them on since I don't sleep in -"

"Stop. Please. Stop. I already have images of you sleeping in nothing but those panties. Don't you dare tell me what you slept in last night, or you'll kill me. It's hard enough keeping my hands off you."

She stops talking and bites her lip. I groan and stand up. She lets out a giggle as I take the stairs two at a time. I walk into the room she's staying in to find a pair of shorts for her to wear. She was right the other day when she said there's nothing in here that could be considered conservative. I need to fix that. Immediately. She can't walk around looking like that, or I won't be able to wait until she turns eighteen.

✗ ✗ ✗

Later that afternoon, I sink into my indoor hot tub. Hot tubs are imperative in New York in the winter. It's unfortunate that not everyone can afford them. I lean my head back and rest it on the edge of the hot tub as Arianna slowly drops in.

"Wow. It's so hot."

"That's kind of the point." I close my eyes and chuckle. Arianna is sitting across from me. "You're too far away."

"What? I'm literally right across from you. I can touch you." I feel her toes slide from my foot up my calf and back down.

"Mmm..." I don't even have to look at her to know she's enjoying everything she's doing to me. I still don't open my eyes, but I crook a finger at her, beckoning her to me. She swims over, sliding her body up my legs and sitting next to me. "Oh no you don't." I grab her around the waist and pull her between my legs. I sit up fully and wrap my arms around her. I lean in so my lips are against her ear. "This is hard, baby."

"I know."

I chuckle and hug her tighter. "It's torture."

She sighs as she nods. "The truth is, I've never really allowed anyone to touch me. I've never wanted them to. But you? I want everything with you. I'm sorry for making it hard."

"I get it, Aria. I do. But you know my reasons. I know it's legal for us to be together. It's just not... who I am. I want this done right. I already feel pretty bad about the age difference between us. It's hard because I don't want to do anything to influence your decision. Just hugging you like this can be considered -"

"Ry, first, I know where you're going with that. And it's nothing like that. You've never acted like a predator or a pedophile. I know you. I know that's what you're thinking. You're not grooming me. You've done nothing but be kind when I had no one. And second, we discussed things. We're doing things that we're okay with. I feel like things are just naturally progressing."

I kiss the back of her head and tighten my grip around her. "Thank you for saying that. I didn't realize I needed to hear it." She wraps her arms around mine. I hold her close for a few minutes with my face buried in her hair. "Can I ask you something?"

"Anything."

"What happened? On Friday? Why were you so upset?"

I feel her hold her breath. After a few moments, she lets it out and tries to move away. I hold her tighter. "Ryan..."

"Just tell me. I promised to stay out of it, but I at least deserve to know what's happening to you."

"If I tell you, you have to swear to me you won't step in, Ryan. I mean it." She turns her head to look at me.

"I won't step in unless there is no other option."

"Ryan -"

"That's the best you're getting from me, Arianna."

She sighs and turns her head to look across the room. "The guy who was messing with me? He started spreading rumors. And now? People I thought were friends are proving not to be." I hug her tighter, sensing she needs it, as she takes a deep breath. "Friday, my locker was spray-painted. With a penis. It said cock-licker."

"Aria. What the fuck?"

"The school resource officer took care of it really fast. He found out who did it and suspended them. But all day long, people constantly

123

teased me. And called me... that. I hid in the bathroom at lunch. And when I was in there, a few girls who I used to hang out with came in. They didn't know I was there, but they were talking about me." She takes a deep breath. "One of them is dating the guy that started this. She said that he told her I pushed him into a bathroom and tried to kiss him. They accused me of wanting guys I can't have. Which is stupid but also kind of true since all I want is you."

"No. Not the same. You already have me. I'm not someone you can't have. We just have to wait a little bit, baby. That's all. You have me." I feel some of her tension release.

"They were really mean. They called me a bunch of names. Said I was ugly and fat. I have a huge ass. And they made fun of my stutter. I usually ignore it all, but it just... got to me. I couldn't take it anymore. I ordered a Lyft, told Renza and Robby I was leaving, then left." She turns in my arms enough to reposition herself so she's sitting on my lap and looking at me.

I keep my arms wrapped around her. "You aren't ugly. You definitely aren't fat. Your stutter rarely ever happens unless you're upset about something. And it's adorable as hell. And as for your ass? Trust me when I tell you it isn't huge. It's one of your best features."

"You have to say stuff like that. It's part of the boyfriend code." She smiles.

I laugh. "Is that really a thing?"

"Most definitely. It's your job to always make me feel good about myself. Even if you have to lie."

"Well, thank God I don't have to lie when I tell you how beautiful you are. And how great you are. And how talented and smart you are."

She beams at me and rests her head back on my shoulder. I kiss her forehead, enjoying my last bit of time with her today before I'm forced to send her back to her own personal hell. I need to figure out a way to make this better for her. I don't know how, but seeing my girl upset like this is absolutely not something I'm capable of dealing with.

Chapter Sixteen

✕ Taylor ✕

(One Month Later)

I roll over and groan. The sun hasn't come up yet, and Nicole's alarm is going off. I got home pretty late because I had a lead I needed to follow up on for another case I was working. After I got home, Tait was being extremely fussy, and Nicole was about to cry.

My poor girl is so stressed out. That Chris fucker hasn't made a move, and it's been a month since I put Jesse in undercover at her bakery.

We're all starting to think Chris is onto us. It's the only thing that makes sense. We'd given him a prime opportunity to swoop in, and he didn't rise to the bait. Jesse has started referring to him as "bodyguard" every time he shows up. Nicole and both girls are being flirtatious. I hate it, but Jesse thinks it's a good idea. I trust my team.

"Baby, I love you. But if you don't shut your alarm off, I'll break your fucking phone." She doesn't answer. "Nicole." I'm talking into my pillow and laying on my stomach. "Nicole. Please? My head is killing me."

"I'm so sorry, baby. I was taking a shower and getting ready to go to work." She shuts the alarm off and crawls into bed. She straddles me and starts rubbing my back, my neck, and my head.

"Mmm... Fuck that feels good." Her fingers dig into my neck and head with just enough pressure to make me whimper in delight. She's hitting every place that hurts and massaging it until the pain disappears "Where did you learn this? It feels amazing."

"Breetana's migraines would put her out for days. So, I did some research on pressure points and massage therapy for migraines. Whenever she got them, I would do this and make it better. Or at least tolerable. Yours are more... tension related. Now stop talking and let me work."

I smile and chuckle. "Yes ma'am."

She continues to work for a good while longer until Tait starts crying. I groan, and she sighs, climbing off me. "Just lay still for a few minutes. I'll be right back."

"Yes, ma'am." I'm pretty sure I doze off. When I wake back up, Nicole is kissing me and running her fingers through my hair.

"Feel any better, my love?"

My headache has subsided considerably. "If I say no, will you go back to pampering me?"

She laughs softly and kisses me again. "I left some water and two tension headache pills for you. I promise they'll work."

"I can think of other things that will make it better." I turn and grab her around her waist. I pull her on top of me as I roll onto my back. I crash my lips onto hers, and she melts into me. I run my hands down to her ass and grab it, pushing her down harder on me as I grind into her.

"Mmm. Taylor..."

"That towel needs to go away," I command. She sits up and slowly removes the towel. My eyes never leave her. As soon as she's free, I grab her tits. She takes my hands in hers and grinds down again, sliding herself against my hard cock. "Ohh... Damn, you feel good." I run my thumbs along her nipples. She reaches down to pull my boxer briefs off. I kick out of them the rest of the way, then plunge into her.

"Oh my... God." She closes her eyes and starts moving against me. I grip her hips as I thrust up into her.

"See? Sex. Cure for everything."

126

She laughs and leans down, pressing herself against my chest and wrapping her arms around me. She kisses me, slowly and deeply. Reading her, I slow my pace and give her long, slow, deep thrusts. "Mmm... Yes..."

"So good, Nic. So tight for me."

"Taylor..." Her tits rubbing back and forth against my chest as I slide in and out of her add to my pleasure. I grip her ass a little firmer and move her against me a little harder. She moans as she breathes against my neck.

She wraps herself around me tighter. Her pussy pulses and gets wetter as my cock throbs inside her, begging me to thrust deeper. I oblige but only because it's what Nicole is asking for. Her thighs tremble, but she clenches them around me just as tight as her pussy is squeezing my dick.

I grip her ass a little harder as I thrust into her wet heat. Her entire body starts to tremble.

"Baby..." I feel her tighten around me even more, gripping me like a vice.

"Oh... Taylor..." She slides herself harder against me. Seconds later, both of our releases hit.

I hold her for a little while after our quaking stops. She loves the after sex cuddling, and I love being the lucky one who gets to provide the sense of closeness she desires.

XXX

Hours later, I'm sitting at my desk when my phone rings. I glance at it and see Chase's number. I raise an eyebrow as I pick it up. "Chase? What's up?"

"You aren't going to like it."

I sigh and immediately feel a headache starting. I take out the tension headache bottle Nicole gave me and pop two pills. "Just tell me."

"Reese was just in my office. One of his guys just told him that two people dressed in suits came in demanding to talk to me. When he asked if they had an appointment, they said it had to do with the safety of my business, and that it was imperative they talk to me. My security refused. They said we'd regret it."

"Tell Reese to email me the video."

"He already did. But here's the thing. I watched the video."

"And?"

"One of them looks like the guy you gave us a picture of. Reese is pretty sure it's him, too."

I pinch the bridge of my nose and open my email. I find the email from Reese and open it. "That's what I was afraid of."

"I thought you said you didn't think he'd go after big businesses?"

"I didn't think he would. It's totally the opposite of everything he's done so far. He's gone after small businesses. I have no evidence of him going after corporate offices or large companies, but I feared he would get fucking brave and try it."

"Well. You have the evidence now."

"It doesn't make any sense. You guys have your own security. Everyone on your block has their own -" It hits me. I suck in a breath. "Fuck."

"What?"

"Holy shit. I just figured it out."

"What?"

"Hang on." I quickly get up and cross the room to my door. I fling it open looking for Dane. "Dane!" I wave him over. Seeing my expression, he hurries to my office. I put Chase on speaker.

"What's up, boss?"

"Get in here. Close the door." He does. Dane is the only one on my taskforce that knows not only my relationship with Ryan, but how closely we work together. "Chase, you're on speaker. I got Dane in here with me."

"Okay." He sounds confused as hell.

"Dane, you got the map of Ryan Crane's territories?"

"Um... Yeah? Where are you going with this? This isn't him."

"I know. Get the map," I command. Dane quickly leaves.

"What are you thinking?" Chase asks.

"I need that map. And then I'll tell you."

"You show him the video?"

"I will," I say firmly. Dane comes back with the map and closes the door. We stick it up to my bulletin board next to the map of all the businesses hit up by this gang. I grab my phone and turn on video. "I sent you a video chat invite, Chase."

"I got it. Can you see me?"

"Yep. Can you see the maps?"

"Yep." It only takes him seconds to see what I do. "Holy shit."

"How did we not see this before?" Dane asks when he sees what I do.

"We weren't looking. I realized it today after I was sent this by Chase's security team." I motion Dane over to my desk and push play on the video. Like Nicole, Chase has video and audio, so we hear everything.

"He's going after businesses in Crane's territories." Dane shakes his head in disbelief.

"Not only that," Chase begins.

"He's hitting Crane's territories because he wants to bring chaos back to the streets Crane helped clean up," I finish.

"Doesn't explain my street," Chase says. "These are all corporate businesses. Looks like he's trying to gain Ryan's territory and expand."

"He isn't trying to expand." I take my phone over to the map of Ryan's territories and turn it so Chase can see where I'm pointing. "All of this is under Ryan's protection. I say protection because he's not only cleaned those areas up, but he's also worked closely with us to keep it that way."

"He can do shit we can't, and he cleans up after himself nicely," Dane says.

"Yeah." I point to Chase's block. "See that?"

"I didn't know I was within his territory," Chase says as soon as he sees his block is in Ryan's area.

"The business right next to you is one of his that he owns. He has three in the city. Here, here, and here." Dane points to three separate areas on the map.

"I just thought he had the one. Near the lake in the corporate district. The one where his penthouse is." Chase lets out a breath. Not sure if it's relief or exasperation, though.

"The other two are businesses he partners with," I tell him.

"So, he's specifically targeting Ryan?" Chase asks, shaking his head.

"Looks that way," Dane answers.

"Ryan is powerful. He's always in some kind of turf war." I shrug.

"He just has so many people involved in his mafia, that he really doesn't have to deal with many of them." Dane interlocks his fingers behind his head as he looks at the map.

"So, we call Ryan," Chase says.

I shake my head. "No. We handle this. Ryan doesn't need to be involved."

"Not unless he has to be. We don't ever call him in unless things get too fucked up for us." Dane doesn't turn around. Instead, he continues staring at the map.

"Who's to say he doesn't already know?" Chase wonders.

"He may. But we can handle this. Now that we know what the hell is happening."

"I trust your judgment, bro, but I think you need to give him a heads up."

"I'll give him a heads up."

"We always do," Dane chips in.

Dane and I say goodbye to Chase, then launch into a discussion and plan about this case. I feel better about it than I have in months.

Chapter Seventeen

☒ Nicole ☒

(Three Days Later)

I'm driving to work early a few mornings after Taylor figured out Chris's plan. It still doesn't make sense to me. Chris has literally been the perfect gentleman, and I don't get what the game is. We all know what he wants. We know what he's trying to do. He has taken over the entire block rather quickly. Mine is the last business. I just don't understand why.

After the first incident with the gang members, I expected things to escalate. We all did. That's why we have Jesse. So why? Why not my business? I pull up next to Jesse's car parked in our small parking lot. He gets out and glances around. I get out and raise an eyebrow.

"I'm glad you came in the back. Prepare yourself."

"What? What happened?" I shiver against the chilly April air as he leads me around to the front of the building.

"I already called this in." He turns and reaches out a hand.

"What's going on?"

"Trust me. You'll want my hand."

I glare at him but take his hand. "Your lack of answers is starting to piss me off."

"Because you have to see what I'm about to show you, sweetheart. It's better to just see it." He leads me around the corner of the building. As soon as my eyes take in the destruction, my legs buckle. I collapse and Jesse pulls me to him. "Told you you'd want my hand."

"Not again. How is this happening again?" The front of my store is completely ruined. It's graffitied. I don't even know what it says.

"The graffiti is one thing, Nic. Did you see the door?"

I wipe my eyes as I take in the door. "It's... open?" Odd. The windows aren't broken. Nothing is smashed in. It's just the graffiti.

"Yep. And I didn't do it." I immediately run towards the building, but Jesse catches me and hauls me against his chest with such force and speed that my feet are lifted off the ground.

"No! Michelle and Korie could be in there!" I fight against him. It's no use. His hold on me is firm.

"Stop. Nic! Stop. Do you see their cars here? I already did a sweep before you got here anyway. They aren't here."

I gasp out a sob. He puts me down as Taylor's truck pulls up. He just closes his door when I'm launching myself at him.

"Hey, baby. It's okay. We expected shit like this." He's whispering against my ear. "He's just trying to scare you."

"He got in. Bypassed the alarm," I sob into his chest.

He hugs me tightly. "I know. Dane filled me in already."

"Dane?" I look up at him, confused.

"Yes. Jesse called Dane. Dane called me. Everyone should be here shortly."

"Everyone? Taylor, what if he's watching?"

"Let him. Pretty sure he knows your husband is a cop. And if he knows that, he knows who I am. He thinks that he's smarter than my taskforce because he thinks he's been able to elude us for four months. I want him to see us here in force. Stroke his ego."

My eyes dart around as Taylor's team starts showing up. "Jesse's cover could be blown!" I hiss worriedly.

We're both keeping our voices low. I'm in a sudden panic about not having Jesse here anymore because of this. "He's under strict orders not to break his cover. The other guys know. Don't worry, beautiful."

"Where do you need us, boss?" Mark, one of Taylor's team members asks him.

Everyone gathers around us. Jesse stays near the front entrance, away from us. Taylor is nearly whispering to his team. "Andrew and Zekeih. Cameras. Mark and Adam. Bugs. Dane. With me. Nicole. Out here with Jesse. I know he did a sweep, but I don't want you in there until we make sure this fuck didn't put any of his own shit in there to spy on you."

"Would he do that?" I ask in disbelief.

Taylor shrugs. "I would. Look. Baby, he knows I'm a cop, but I know he doesn't know Jesse is."

"We hid his personnel files. There's no record of him being a cop. We know Chris looked for him, but he won't find anything we don't want him to," Adam explains. I breathe a sigh of relief, even though I'm terrified.

"You five. Go," Dane commands. Taylor's team leaves us and cautiously enters the bakery, guns drawn. "We know he's going after Ryan's territory, but we don't think he knows yours or Taylor's relationship with him."

I shake my head. "I still don't understand. Why has he not come after me?"

"Because of me, baby," Taylor says simply.

"Our team is really good at what we do. We're the best. If he knows, and we think he does, he'll want to really make it look like you need him."

"Like we can't protect you," Taylor says.

I nibble my lip. "So, maybe I should have him overhear me talking about how I don't think you can protect me. Since he walked through the security system."

Taylor beams at me and then kisses me. "Couldn't have said it better."

Dane nods with a grin. "We want you to play up Taylor and us setting up your security system."

"I'm going to up the police presence, but it's going to be my team. We'll hide well. He won't know we're around."

"So, you'll be near?" I ask.

Taylor nods. "Yes."

Dane looks towards the bakery. "I want hidden cameras."

133

"Already have them per Ryan. If he compromised the CCTV, the hidden ones still run to a backup file source on my computer," Taylor explains.

Dane smiles. "Smart."

I shake my head. "I didn't know that."

Taylor nods. "Ryan's a smart man. He wanted all bases covered. And he wanted no outside access to the hidden ones on your business computer."

"Also smart," Dane says again. "Can't find them that way, then."

"I don't understand any of that stuff but if it works..." I bite my lip.

"Trust me, babe," Taylor says, kissing my cheek and running his thumb over my lower lip

"You were right." I jump a little and turn as Zekeih approaches. Taylor looks at him as Dane heads towards the building. He says a few words to Jesse. Jesse walks towards us.

"He cut CCTV?" Taylor asks.

"Yep. It would take a couple days to repair, so he'll probably up his game," Zekeih says.

"Up his game?" I look up at Taylor. I'm starting to become terrified. My lip is quivering. He takes my face in his large hands and bends down to kiss me.

"You're safe. I promise. You have all eight of us solely focused on this, beautiful girl." He takes my hand and turns to open the truck door. "I want you and Jesse in here until we finish up."

"It'll look like I'm just as scared as you and they're just protecting another employee," Jesse says.

"But really, his job doesn't change. He's in there to protect you," Zekeih clarifies.

Taylor helps me into his truck, then leans in to kiss me. "I love you, baby."

"I love you, too." I can't help the overwhelming sense of fear that overtakes me as Taylor closes the door and walks back to the building with Zekeih.

What if someone is hiding that they missed? What if someone opens fire on them? What if there's a bomb and someone trips it? I sniffle and hug myself.

Just then, Jesse leans forward and puts a hand on my shoulder. "Given the circumstances, I don't think the Lieutenant would be too upset if you crawled back here with me."

"Thank you, but you can't stop the endless images I have running through my head."

"Maybe not. But I can hug you and help ease some of that fear."

I think for a moment. Images of Taylor getting shoved into my display case and having glass shards sticking out of his head make my decision for me. I climb into the back and Jesse wraps me up in a hug. He rests his chin on my head and tightens his grip.

"Taylor is incredible at what he does. He's never been in a fight he hasn't won. Dane is like a bloodhound when it comes to explosives. But he'll call in his buddy to have his dog sniff around. If there's any explosives, we'll know."

"How did you know that's what I was thinking?"

"I've been around you every single day for how long? I know how your mind works."

I take a deep breath and settle in for what I think is going to be a long wait. I feel like we're being watched. And with how tense Jesse feels and how many times Taylor and everyone on his team has stood outside the front door to the bakery looking around, I know they all feel it, too.

I shudder. "I hate feeling like someone is watching me. Like they're waiting to pounce."

"There's a reason the whole team is here. All of our eyes are better than one or two of us. It's the reason they're all taking turns looking around. I have my eyes open, too."

"It just feels like we're a herd of sheep and there's a snake out there waiting to strike each of us. Take us down."

He chuckles. "Interesting analogy. What about a fox waiting to get into the chicken coop of chickens?"

I smile and shake my head. "Foxes are too cute. And we aren't chickens. What about a terminator trying to take out the pack of wolves?"

"There we go. I like wolves. And terminators may be difficult, but they aren't indestructible. We can take that fucker and his entire band of terminator wannabees out with a good plan and fucking team work."

"Yes! I'm so excited about this. Now. What's the plan?" I look up at Jesse.

He grins. "Well, first, it's imperative that we stick together. A wolf pack always sticks together no matter what. So, we lure the fuckers in."

My eyes light up as he works to distract me. "How?"

"Easy. Wolves put their weakest members up front. Many don't understand why that is. They think they should be in the middle or something. Protected. But wolves are smart. They put them in front so they can set the pace for the rest of the pack. So, the pack can all have their backs. They do it to lure in potential predators. Wouldn't you go after something you thought was weak before you would go for something you thought was strong?"

I nod. "For sure."

"What the potential predators don't know is even though the weakest are up front, the strongest are behind to protect. And quite often, the weak aren't as weak as they're thought to be. The leader is always in the back looking out for everyone."

I think of Ryan. Though me and the girls aren't weak, we are deemed that way by Chris. Easy targets. We're a bakery run by three women and a gay guy who doesn't like conflict. He would prey on that. Behind us, is Taylor's team. Chris feels like he can take out the weak before the warriors get to him. He's cocky. Too confident. Overly conceited.

And behind Taylor's team is Ryan. The one who looks out for any danger. The one who protects all of us. A silent threat hidden in the shadows. Ready to attack at any moment.

Dangerous.

Treacherous.

Vicious.

Savage.

Willing to do anything to protect his pack.

Us.

Chapter Eighteen

✗ Arianna ✗

"Arianna, please don't do this. You should tell him," Renza says as she kneels next to me in the bathroom stall.

"I can't. I can't. You don't understand."

Renza is holding my hair back as I throw up. Again. Sobs wrack my body. "What don't I understand? Chad is torturing you. Every single day. Even with Robby escorting you everywhere, he's still getting to you. We can't stop the rumors."

Just the word rumor makes me throw up again. The newest rumor is that I slept with the entire basketball team. It wasn't Chad that pinned me against my locker today. It was some random person from the football team wanting the same treatment as the basketball team got from me.

"Ryan can help you, Arianna. He's one of the most powerful people in the world. And he's your boyfriend, right? At least in most every sense of the word. If not every."

"I can't tell him. You don't understand what would happen to him."

"He can handle a fight with Chad's crew. Ryan can handle himself. You don't need to protect him."

"I don't want him involved."

"If you don't talk to him, I will. He needs to come get you. Right now."

"He's picking me up after school. I can finish the day." I start heaving again, and it makes me cry. Which makes me throw up even more. Which makes me cry more. It's a torturous, vicious fucking cycle.

"I'm not arguing with you about this, Arianna. I'm texting Ryan to come get you."

"Please, Renza. Don't." I wipe my mouth and grab for my phone, but I can see she's already had an entire conversation. She must have done it when I was puking.

Arianna: Hey. This is Renza. Arianna's friend. Something awful happened and Arianna needs you.

Ryan: WHAT?! What happened? Is she okay?!

Arianna: This is what's on Arianna's locker.

Renza had sent him a picture we took of this week's graffiti spray painted on my locker. Words like 'whore' and 'slut' are all over it. Someone drew a girl on her knees sucking the penis of someone drawn in a basketball players uniform.

Arianna: This one was all over her Chemistry textbook.

She had sent the picture we took of a woman sucking on a penis that someone drew on my textbook.

Ryan: I'm leaving a meeting. I'm on my way. Tell me she's okay, Renza.

Arianna: Physically? Yes. Anything else? She's been throwing up for an hour. We both missed our history test.

Ryan: Text me your number. I'll be there soon.

"Renza. He's going to be so mad at me. I wish you wouldn't have bothered him."

"Bullshit. He loves you."

I start throwing up again. I hear people come into the bathroom after class is out, and I whimper, trying to keep from continuing the vicious, gut-wrenching heaves that are tearing me apart. It doesn't work.

"Oh my God. Arianna? Is that you? I can totally tell by your ugly shoes." Mandy's voice doesn't help me at all.

"Back off, Mandy," Renza growls.

Mandy ignores her. "Are you pregnant?"

Oh no. No. No. No. Another rumor is about to be spread. I can feel it. Mandy and her posse of gutter whores start laughing.

"Have you not done enough? If you start any more rumors about her, you'll regret it, you stupid bitch!" Renza is vibrating with anger as she smooths back my hair.

"We didn't start any of those rumors, Renza," Mai says.

"Yeah. Don't be as stupid as her," Krissa agrees.

"Why are you still even friends with her? You could be with us and be cool." I can hear the smirk in Mandy's sickening voice.

"Like hell," Renza growls.

"It's your funeral." Mai laughs.

Renza hugs me tightly as the bell signaling the next class rings. Mandy, Mai, and Krissa all leave the bathroom cackling like the evil witches they are.

Renza's phone vibrates. "Robby is waiting outside. Are you okay to get up?"

I nod, and she helps me stand. She leads me to the sink and hands me a toothbrush and toothpaste. I can't help but laugh, even though it's soft and half-hearted. "Always so prepared."

"Who else is going to take care of you?"

I brush my teeth and Renza puts everything away again. She leads me out and Robby hugs me.

"You okay?" he asks.

I shake my head. "Not really."

"Ryan's coming," Renza announces.

"Good. Did you finally tell him?" Robby questions, looking down at me.

"I did," Renza says.

"He's going to be really mad," I whisper, shaking my head.

"Stop it, Arianna. He is not," Robby says to me.

"Oh! He's here. He wants us to meet him at the administration office."

I nearly choke. "No! Tell him no. Tell him I just want to leave. Please!"

"Arianna. No. This is for the best. He's helping." Robby gives me a stern look.

I feel the nausea again, but I fight it and start crying instead. Robby picks me up and carries me. "He's only going to make this worse for me. Robby, please." I'll beg and plead if I have to, but Ryan can't be involved.

Robby puts me down when we get to the administration office. He has to drag me inside. Ryan is standing with his arms crossed over his chest, talking to the school resource officer, Officer Grant.

"I understand, Mr. Crane, but without the student's approval, I can't tell you anything."

Ryan glares. "Let's try this again. And this time, give me the right answer. Because I'm growing fucking tired of the run around. Tell me what the fuck you're doing to curb this, or I go to your Chief."

"Mr. Crane. I understand you're upset, but I can't help you without _"

"My consent?" I ask weakly from behind Ryan.

"Arianna..." He breathes a sigh of relief and rushes to my side, pulling me into his arms. I let him hug me for a moment before gently pushing him away.

"Officer Grant. It's okay. You can tell him." I only agree because I know this isn't going away. Now that Renza has told him, Ryan won't give in to me this time.

Robby pats my back and Renza gives me a hug before they both leave.

"Very well. Shall we?" Officer Grant gestures to his office as Ryan shoots fire through his eyes at him.

Once we're all settled, Ryan becomes the all intimidating mafia boss. "This is getting out of hand. This is the second time she's had her locker vandalized."

"Um..." I trail off, not wanting to admit I've been keeping things from him.

"Actually, it's the sixth," Officer Grant mercifully says for me. I look down at my hands.

I can feel Ryan turn his intense dark eyes on me. "Six."

"Yes, Mr. Crane. She has more than one bully. She has several people who are tormenting her."

"And what the fuck are you doing to stop this?" He turns the viciousness back to Officer Grant.

"We've found out who has been behind each instance with her locker. And each person has been punished with a three day suspension."

"Three days? Are you kidding?"

"It's the school's policy."

Ryan shakes his head, bewildered. "The school's policy? You're going to sit here and tell me that the school's policy is to allow students who torment other students to come back here after three days and do it again? While the student being tormented goes from absolutely loving school to hating the fact that she even has to get up to go?"

"Well -"

"Did I say I was done talking?"

"No, sir."

I hide a smile behind my hand. Despite the fact that I'm upset and hurt by everything going on, seeing my boyfriend be such a bad ass is kind of hot.

"There are three weeks of school left. Despite the fact that she's being tormented every damn day, lost a lot of weight, and has become quiet as hell, Arianna is getting straight A's. What's to stop her from just not showing up?"

"Well, sir. Uh... If she gets more than three unexcused absences, she'll be expelled."

"What? You... For Christ sake. Knowing what's going on, you'll expel the victim? I can't..." Ryan pinches the bridge of his nose and closes his eyes. "You have until the end of the weekend to fix this situation."

He opens his eyes and glares at Officer Grant. He stands and offers me a hand. I take it, wiping my eyes. Despite how hot I think Ryan is when he's in protective mode doesn't help the fact that I'm still really upset. And sick to my stomach.

"If I have to step in, Officer Grant, you won't like it. I'll see to it Chief Ramsay personally hands you your pink slip. You can't begin to imagine how fucking serious I am." Officer Grant chokes down a swallow and can't meet Ryan's eyes. Ryan leads me to the door, but stops, turning back around. "She's leaving for the rest of the day. Excuse her," he growls dangerously.

"Y-yes, sir. I'll take care of it."

Ryan pulls me in front of him and guides me out of the office. I take a deep breath. As soon as we get into the hall, I see the guy who shoved me against my locker. A strangled sob escapes. I turn from Ryan and run.

"Arianna?"

"No…" My stomach is starting to recoil. "Please, no…" I run outside to the parking lot and search for Ryan's car.

Ryan catches up to me and grabs my arm. "Aria."

I twist my arm free as soon as I see his car and sprint for it. He's parked close to the door and, thankfully, near a bush.

As soon as I reach his car, I drop to my knees and throw up into the bush.

"Oh my God, baby." He pulls my hair back and rubs my back while I throw my guts out. I start crying again, and, like usual, it forces me to throw up more. Ryan waits patiently until I'm done. I collapse back against him. He holds me tightly. "Shh... I'm here now. You're okay, Aria."

"I'm so s-sorry."

"Don't. None of this is your fault."

"I'm n-not a sl-slut. I d-didn't sl-sleep with the entire b-basketball t-team," I cry. I don't know why I feel the need to say that, but I do. I need him to know.

"Who the fuck started that rumor?"

I bury my head in his shoulder and breathe in his comforting, spicy scent. "I d-don't kn-know. I r-really d-don't. I'm n-not ly-lying."

"Baby. Come on. I've never accused you of lying." He kisses me on the head and helps me up. He helps me into the car, then gets in himself.

"I sh-should've t-told you." The words are nearly a whisper. I hiccup from the tears.

Ryan starts the car and begins driving before he reaches over and takes my hand. He brings it to his lips and tenderly, sweetly kisses my palm.

"I know now. That's all that matters."

"Pl-please don't t-take me h-home."

He twines his fingers with mine and holds my hand in his lap. "I'm taking you home, but not to your dad's house. You know as well as I do that isn't your home anymore. Renza's taking care of it with him. Give me your phone."

I do as he says. Driving with one hand, he flips through a few settings on my phone. "Are y-you t-turning m-my GPS off a-again?"

"I don't think he has any reason to question you, but I'd rather be safe, sweetheart. It's risky for you to be with me."

He hands me my phone back, and we drive in silence.

Home.

I haven't felt at home since my mother died. Was killed, actually. I haven't felt home since her.

Until now.

Ryan

I didn't sleep at all. I've been up all night staring at my ceiling. I sat with Arianna last night until she fell asleep. Then I swam a hundred laps in my pool. It didn't wear me out or calm me down, so I swam a hundred more. I did a hundred push-ups, two hundred sit-ups, a hundred pull-ups, and five miles on the treadmill. By three in the morning, I gave up trying to exhaust myself and went to my bedroom... after checking on my girl.

It's now six in the morning, and I not only haven't slept, but I'm also far more pissed off. How the fuck does a school let this happen? How does a school punish the victim more than the fucking bully?

I growl and reach for my phone. Taylor might be one of the only people who can talk me down right now because all I want to do is kill everyone.

"Five in the fucking morning. You do remember there's a one hour difference between Manhattan and Chicago," he says crankily.

"You gonna tell me you ain't up?"

"No. I'm up. Apparently bakers think it's fun to be up before fucking sunrise."

"How's my district, by the way?"

"District? Not sister?"

"Oh, I know she's okay. What I don't know, since some dick beat cop doesn't think it's necessary for me to show up, is if my territory is okay."

"Beat cop? Fuck you. I haven't been a beat cop in ten years," he growls. I laugh. I was right to call him. "Your district is fine. We're handling it. What's up? I know you didn't just call me to bust my balls."

"Arianna. The bullying is... It's fucking bad, Taylor." I send him the pictures Renza sent from Arianna's phone. "Her friend texted me yesterday and told me I needed to get to the school. She'd been throwing up for an hour. Just sent you a couple pictures."

"Her locker and where's the other one? Bathroom?"

"Her Chemistry textbook."

"What? That looks like a wall. How the fuck did they get to her books?"

"Apparently she went to the bathroom during class. When she got back, that's what she found. They took a picture of both instances. The book has a protective cover on it. School requirement."

"Did you talk to the school? What are they doing?"

"Fuck. Nothing. They suspended the people who did it for three fucking days. She's had this happen six times."

"Six?"

"Yeah. Six. They just keep doing it. And that's not even the worst part. The rumors are fucking awful. The latest is that she slept with the entire basketball team. Three girls were in the bathroom and heard her throwing up. Recognized her shoes."

"So, there will be a new one about her being pregnant."

"I think so. Probably be all over the school by Monday morning."

"Fuck."

"Not even fucking all. The school isn't doing anything about the violence. She got shoved against her locker yesterday by a football player that I want to fucking kill."

"Calm down, killer. I'll take care of this one."

"I gave the school resource officer until the end of the weekend."

"I only need an hour. Maybe two."

"Confident."

He chuckles. "Go be with your girl. He'll be in custody before noon."

"Name's Brentwood Nolen."

"I'm on it. Take care of Arianna. She probably needs you more than ever right now."

"Yeah. Already on it."

"And Ry?"

"What?"

"I mean it. Take care of your girl. Fuck the age bullshit. She needs you." He hangs up. He knows me far too well. He knows I'm holding onto every little bit of resolve I have to not take things further with Arianna until she's eighteen.

But fuck all of that right now. He's right. She needs me.

𝗫 𝗫 𝗫

It's nearly noon when Arianna makes her way downstairs. I had fallen asleep on the couch and wake up to her crawling onto it next to me. She lifts my arm and wraps herself up with it. She's wearing nothing but one of my t-shirts and a pair of panties.

I don't have the heart to make her put something on. I asked her for her sizes and went out and bought her stuff she could wear when she is here. Saves her from having to bring anything when she stays. Which has become every weekend.

"Morning, Sleeping Beauty," I mumble into her hair.

"Sorry. I didn't mean to wake you up."

I kiss the back of her head and pull her close. "Never be sorry for that."

"I'm sorry I didn't tell you."

"Didn't we talk about this last night?" I ask. She doesn't say anything. She takes a deep breath instead. "I can't do this anymore. Turn around, Arianna. Look at me."

Her breathing shutters as she slowly turns to me. She doesn't look at me. She looks down and bunches my shirt in her fist. "Ryan -"

"Stop. Stop, baby. I know how your mind works. And I'm not going to say what you think I am. Look at me." Her hand starts shaking, but she does as I say.

"I'm only asking you this one time. My reaction is going to depend on your answer... Do you want me? Do you want to be with me?"

"Yes. Ryan, yes. More than anything." No hesitation.

I force myself to hold back from crushing her, but only slightly. I gently cup her cheek. She leans into my hand and closes her eyes. I lean into her and run my hand to the back of her head, tangling my fingers in her silky hair. She smiles softly and opens her eyes just as my lips meet hers.

I can feel how surprised she is, but it doesn't take her long to close her eyes and give in. Her mouth moves with mine. The more she allows herself to feel, the more open she becomes to me.

I run my hand down to her hip and pull her closer to me as I run my tongue against her lower lip. I pull back slowly. She whimpers. I smile as she opens her eyes. She reaches up to run her thumb along my lower lip. I kiss it. She giggles.

"That lip gloss tastes amazing." I lick my lips with a soft smile.

She puts her arm around my waist and smiles shyly. "It's vanilla bean." She's nearly whispering. I lean in and kiss her again.

"It's uniquely Arianna." I can't get enough of her now that I've gotten a taste.

I lean in and kiss her again. After a few moments, she moans and tries to push herself closer to me. She rubs her leg against mine, and I drop my hand to her ass. This is such a fucking mistake. I knew as soon as I kissed her that would be it. I wouldn't be able to stop kissing her or touching her.

She runs her hand up my arm and to my hair. She runs her fingers through it. Her body flush against mine makes me hard as hell.

The kiss grows far more intense the longer it goes on. Her moving against me the way she is makes me harder than I think I've ever been in my life. I pull back, but only enough to keep her from rubbing against me. To keep us both from losing control.

I kiss her neck and work my way up her jaw back to her lips. "God, Aria. You're making it difficult for me to care about not taking this further."

I kiss her, deep and long, as she moans and gives me soft sighs. I run my tongue along her lips again, forcing my way in. She gasps as our tongues collide. She lifts my shirt so her hands are against my bare back.

"Mmm..." I growl into her neck as I toss my shirt. She pulls herself closer. Her nails lightly rake down my back. Everything in me is telling me to pull back, but I can't. "Had I known your lips tasted this good, I wouldn't have held out." I smile teasingly

She laughs. "Liar. Though, why? I thought you wanted PG until I'm eighteen."

"I did. But I guess I don't feel like kissing should be off-limits. Do you?" I run my fingers through her hair as she shakes her head.

"No. I understand why there can't be more. I…" She looks down at my chest. Her fingers follow, and she starts to lightly brush her nails across my chest.

I tug her hair lightly when I reach the end of it. "What?"

"I've… never… I mean…"

I smile softly and lift her chin with one finger. She looks at me shyly. "Never…?"

Her cheeks flush a beautiful shade of pink. "Never been with… anyone. Like that, I mean."

My heart expands exponentially when I realize what she's trying to tell me. I lean down and kiss her forehead. "I'm happy to be your first. But not now. Not only is it crossing lines with me, but you aren't ready."

I feel her collapse against me in relief. "I'm really not ready. I mean, I guess the making out was fine, but… I… didn't want to come off like I wasn't…," she trails off.

"Like you weren't to my level?"

I can see the moment the hesitation in her eyes turns to gratefulness. "Yeah."

"You never have to worry about me forcing you to do anything you aren't ready for, Aria. You know that. Don't you?" I search her eyes as she nods. I'm relieved to see she understands.

"I understand. I guess… I was a little worried that you would lose interest or something."

I run the back of my hand along her cheek. "Never, honey."

She smiles. I lean down to kiss her once more before she turns her back to me and cuddles into me. She puts her favorite movie on, and I'm out like a light in minutes with her safely wrapped in my arms.

Chapter Nineteen

⚔ Nicole ⚔

(Two Days Later)

I'm restocking my bakery case while Korie and Michelle work on a wedding cake for the weekend. Jesse is leaning on the counter doing some of my paperwork. It's been unusually quiet the last couple of days, since we had been vandalized, and it makes me uneasy.

Since that day, my CCTV has remained down. Taylor and his team looked at the hidden camera footage since nothing could be seen on the regular ones after they took out my CCTV. The hidden camera footage showed Chris with the same two gang members that had caused issues previously with us. So, we have proof that he was involved in the first attack. Though it's all pretty weak. We need more. Taylor thought using just the hidden cameras would be beneficial and allow us to say CCTV still doesn't work.

Korie comes out from the back with Michelle following close behind. They both start stocking the bakery case.

Korie shakes her head. "This is completely ridiculous. This is one of our busiest times of the day. I mean, I get that Chris is probably fucking around with the customer base or something somehow. There's really no other explanation, but this?" She gestures out to the front of the empty bakery. "All we've had for customers is Chicago's finest."

Michelle chuckles softly. "Not that I'm complaining. My entire day is made when that really cute SWAT cop comes in."

Jesse looks over at her. "I didn't know you had a thing for Reed. Should I tell him?" He gives her a teasing grin as her eyes widen.

She furiously shakes her head. "Don't you dare! I'm perfectly happy admiring him from afar!"

Korie laughs. "I wouldn't mind being the one to break the news. I bet you look as hot as Jesse does when he blushes."

Jesse's cheeks flush to a soft red as he looks away. "Fuck, Korie. You gotta go and spill all my damn secrets?" He smiles softly as his eyes light up. They haven't officially said it, but I'm pretty sure they're a couple. One of the most adorable couples I have the pleasure of knowing.

She reaches up and pinches one of his cheeks. "But it's so incredibly sexy."

He grabs her wrists and grins brighter. "Should I spill all your secrets? Like how you can't sleep without your -"

She immediately puts a hand over his mouth. "Don't you dare!"

I crack up. "Without your what?"

"Yeah! Don't hold out on us!" Michelle says.

Korie lowers her eyes. "My Pootie Bear. He's a koala I got when I was a baby."

Michelle and I squeal as Jesse laughs. "That's adorable! Korie and her little Pootie Bear!" I give her a toothy smile as she looks at me. She tries to pout, but I can see her lip quiver. Jesse reaches over and taps her pout. It's all it takes for her to start laughing with the rest of us.

After a few minutes of joking around with each other, Korie and Michelle go back into the backroom to grab the rest of the items we need to stock up. The goal is to make it at least look full. The four of us have been grazing the bakery case all day, so all we're replacing is what we've eaten. The stocking at least gives us something to do other than clean the already spotless interior. I've cleaned the counter so much today that I can see my reflection.

I look up as Chris walks in and dramatically sigh. Jesse frowns as he looks up and puts the paperwork away.

"Well, that sounded a bit melancholy. What's up?" Chris asks.

"Ever since we got vandalized, people seem a bit freaked out to come in." Jesse frowns and lets his lip quiver. I hide a smile. We had decided to really play up our vulnerability.

"My CCTV is still out." I wipe away a forced tear.

Jesse hugs me. "We'll be okay." He rubs my back, and I fake a strangled sob. Korie and Michelle both walk out when they hear Chris and our conversation.

"It's okay. Didn't your husband say he was looking into it?" Korie asks.

"Yeah. He said he'd take care of it." Michelle leans her head on my shoulder.

I shake my head, continuing on with our plan. I make a show of wiping my eyes. "He's been saying that since those gang people came in. And they cut our cameras this time... Taylor has nothing to go on."

"We'll figure it out. You've come so far since you opened," Jesse says.

"Yeah. Don't give up." Korie shakes her head vigorously.

"What if I said I could help you guys out?" Chris asks, playing right into our plan.

I smile softly. I'm sure he thinks it's because I appreciate the offer, but really, it's because we just got him, and he has no idea. "You've already done so much, Chris. This is our problem. Well. Mine. I'm the owner." I look down, feigning self-dejection.

"Well, didn't you say your CCTV isn't fixed? I know someone who can help." Chris shrugs.

I sigh. "I can't afford it. Things are going well, but expanding and taking on another employee is taking its toll." I'm completely lying, and everyone but Chris knows it. We're doing really well. Despite having no customers this week.

"He owes me a favor. And I also think I can help you out with protection."

Jesse smiles softly. "By staying here all day? I can't say I'd mind the eye candy, but not even I would ask you to stay all day long."

Chris laughs at Jesse's flirtation, and Jesse hides a fake blush. We're all getting too good at this. "Not exactly, handsome."

Michelle snort-laughs and covers her mouth. "Sorry!"

Chris winks at her. "Your problem is happening at night. Or early morning when no one is here, right? Not counting those guys that were in here being stupid."

I nod. "The break in and this. Yeah. At night or early morning. When no one is here. Thank God for that."

Chris nods thoughtfully. Jesse turns from the counter and pours Chris's coffee while Korie gets his cupcake. "Well, I don't know. If you really want help, I could get some people to hang out at night and keep your building safe." Jesse hands him his coffee and Korie hands him his cupcake.

"I don't know about you guys, but I'm for it. I'm terrified to come in early," Michelle says with a shiver.

"Me too. I don't know if someone is going to be waiting here for me," Korie agrees.

"I'm for it, too, honestly. I know I'm the new guy and my opinion doesn't matter much, but I hate coming in early. My husband wants me to have a police officer with me until you guys get here," Jesse says. Korie bites her lip and leans her head on Jesse's arm. I'm standing on the other side of him and rest my hand on his arm.

"Your opinion matters, Jesse. You're one of us. And I do really like the idea of extra security." I chew on my bottom lip, pretending to think. "What would we have to pay you for that, though? I'm sure you don't work for free."

"And we really are stretched thin financially. With no customers these past few days..." Jesse frowns dejectedly. I look down, pretending to be as vulnerable as possible.

Chris holds up a hand and shrugs. "Hey. I would do it for free. I like you guys a lot. But I do have to pay those that watch out for you."

"I understand. I probably can't afford it, though." I let my lip quiver as I sniffle.

"Nicole, don't cry. Come on." Chris takes my hand, which I had resting on the counter. Jesse stiffens next to me and watches him, stepping slightly closer, but not enough that Chris notices or cares. "I usually charge a thousand a week, but I like you guys a lot. And you've made me kind of feel like one of you. All the bodyguard talk. Makes me feel protective of you all. And you've taken care of me with the coffee and cupcakes. I'll give you a discount. What do you think you can do?"

I look up at Jesse, biting my lip. Jesse shrugs. "I think we could swing seven fifty? If I got a good grasp on the books, I think that would be okay." He tries to project being unsure, vulnerable, and a little scared, and he pulls it off like a pro. I look back at Chris.

He smiles at me. "How about seven even, sweetheart? We can renegotiate later when things start picking up again."

Korie bites her lip and looks at him through her lashes. "You'd really do that for us?"

"I can't believe you're so nice," Michelle whispers.

"Guys. Honestly. I really want to help you out." He's still holding my hand. "What do you think? Want some time to think about it?"

"Would you mind? Maybe just until tomorrow?" I ask quietly.

He lets go of my hand and gives me a sweet grin. "I'm absolutely okay with that." He takes his cupcake and coffee and turns to leave. Near the door, he turns back. "Just one thing." Here we go. Chris looks directly at me. Jesse stands close. "It might not be a good idea to tell your husband. Keep this between us. Men hate when they think they can't get the job done. I'd hate for your husband to get jealous and upset with you for going outside of him and his team for help."

"Of course. I understand. He definitely wouldn't approve of me paying an outside firm for security he thinks he can provide for me." I make a show of rubbing my arm like there's a bruise there.

Michelle nods and puts her hand gently on my other arm. "I totally agree. He wouldn't like that."

Korie looks at me. "I'd hate for him to be upset with you... Again..."

"I don't really know him well, but I kind of agree with them. He seems to think he can handle it," Jesse agrees. "And I... don't want to see you..." He looks down at my arm. "You know."

Chris seems to brighten as he picks up on our hinting. The idea that he could possibly think Taylor could hurt me is truly disgusting. "Then it's settled. I'll be in tomorrow to get your answer. Sleep well, ya'll." Chris leaves, and I let out a low growl.

"I hate that I have to talk about Taylor like I'm afraid he'll be violent with me, don't trust him, and have no faith in him. I trust him with my life and have all the faith in the world in him. And I definitely don't fear him. He'd never touch me like that. Ugh. This is so sickening."

Everyone surrounds me in a group hug. The stress momentarily melts away. "You guys are the best friends ever."

"We are pretty great!" Korie says cockily. We all laugh, stopping abruptly when we hear the door chime. We all look over and see Reed Daniels. Michelle turns a bright red and flees into the back room.

Reed watches her disappear with an unreadable expression before he turns to us. "What could possibly have you guys laughing so hard?" He perches his sunglasses on top of his head and gives us all an easy smile.

"Korie made us laugh," I say, smiling.

His eyes flick towards the back room as he nods. "Taylor wanted to make sure you have us checking in all day. With Chris just leaving, I wanted to make sure you all are good."

I nod and lean against Jesse, feeling a little worn out. "We're okay."

Jesse kisses my forehead. "Why don't you call Taylor? You'll feel better. And he'll want to know what happened."

"You're probably right." I smile up at him and Reed. I squeeze Korie's arm on my way through the doors. Michelle isn't in the backroom. I'm assuming she's trying to calm herself by gulping in air outside. I beeline for my office and sit, taking out my phone. This entire thing is really starting to weigh on me. I need to call Taylor to tell him what happened, but really, I just need to hear his voice.

Chapter Twenty

⚔ Taylor ⚔

Spending the past couple days in my car while my wife is as stressed as she is has been killing me. I want to be with her more than anything, but I know that I can't be. At least not more than a normal stop in. If Chris knows who I am, it could put Nicole and her employees in more danger than they are.

My phone rings as I'm taking a bite of my sandwich. Seeing Nicole's face, I put my sandwich down and answer immediately. "Hey, baby."

"Hi." She sounds stressed to the max and more down than I've ever heard.

"What's wrong? Are you okay?"

"I love you. I just needed to hear your voice."

"I love you, too, but, Nic, what's going on? You sound like you're crying."

"Not crying yet."

"Baby, what is going on? What happened? I know Chris just left there. Do you need me or the team?"

"No... Well, maybe you. Chris did just leave, and I was going to tell you what happened on the phone, but maybe you could just come here instead?" Her voice sounds weak and tired. She's speaking so quietly I have to strain to hear.

"Is that what you want?"

"Yes."

"Then I'll be right there, Nikki. All you have to do is say the words." I put my unmarked car in gear and start heading towards the bakery.

"Okay. I'm in the office."

"I'll be right there, beautiful. Just sit tight."

"See you soon." She hangs up, and I grab my radio.

"Bravo One to all Bravo. I'm heading into the bakery. Sector one is unoccupied."

"Bravo Three. I'm on it." Adam is Bravo Three.

"Bravo Six, I got mine and Bravo Three's sectors." Zekeih says.

"Ten-four." I park outside the bakery and glance around as I walk in.

"Hey, Lieutenant. Nikki's in her office," Jesse says as I walk in.

I nod and make my way into the back. Nicole is sitting at her desk wiping her eyes. She gives me a watery smile when she looks up at me. "Baby. Come here, sweetheart." I close the door, and she stands up. I pull her into my arms and bend to kiss her neck.

She sniffles into my chest. "I just needed to see you. I needed a hug."

"Anytime, Nicole. Whenever you need it." I hold her close to me until she pulls away. She looks up at me, and I bend to kiss her. "Feel a little better?"

"I do."

"So, what happened, gorgeous?"

Nicole smiles and sits on her desk, gesturing to her chair for me. I sit, and she places both of her feet on the chair on either side of my legs. "Chris came in and finally offered his services."

"Well. That's a good thing." I give her a soft smile. Nicole looks down. "Baby. Come here."

She takes a deep breath and moves to sit in my lap. I put my arms around her waist. "I just have a bad feeling."

155

"Okay. Why?"

"Because of the way he was acting."

"How about you start from the beginning? What did he say? How did he approach it? Walk me through."

"We played our plan perfectly. He finally took the bait. I told him CCTV was still out, so he said he had a person who could fix it."

"Did you talk about your financial situation?"

"Yes. I said I couldn't afford to have it fixed, and he said the guy owes him."

"I think it's the tech business down the block. Did you accept?"

"Kind of? He talked about protection and stuff. I told him I didn't think I could afford his help. He offered a discount. What we could afford."

"Did Jesse negotiate?"

"Chris said he charges a thousand a week, but then told us that he would give us a discount because of how we treat him. With the free stuff and calling him our bodyguard. He said he felt like one of us and would do it for free, but he had to pay his guys. So, he asked what we could afford. Jesse said seven fifty. Chris offered seven hundred until we get back on our feet after the loss of business and moving into weddings and hiring Jesse."

"Good. That's good. Did you accept?"

"No. He said he would be in tomorrow for an answer. But he was so respectful and nice. He was acting like he really wanted to help us. I have a horrible feeling that the reason, though, is because he's planning to do something."

"I think you have good instincts. I have a feeling you're right."

"And I think he's responsible for it being so slow since the vandalism."

"Also agree. I think he's threatening them to stay away from you until you agree to pay him for his protection. You're the only business on this block not under his control. I have some guys questioning some of the area businesses to confirm the theory."

"Are you sure we shouldn't talk to Ryan? It's not that I don't think you can handle it, but I just really have a bad feeling."

"Nikki. I know how scared you are." I push her hair behind her ear. "But this is a really small time gang, baby. It's not worth Ryan's time."

"I really am scared." She sighs and buries her head in my chest. I kiss her forehead. "So, what do I do?"

"You accept the offer. And at the end of the week when he comes to collect, you aren't going to have it. I want to push him."

"Taylor, I hate that idea."

"He won't hurt you. You have Jesse and you have my entire team."

She slowly stands up and walks towards her door, hugging herself. When she looks back at me, my heart breaks. Tears are streaming down her face.

"I can't do this anymore. Taylor, what if we need you, and we can't call you?"

I stand and walk towards her. "There it is." I smile. She looks at me confused. "It's getting more intense and dangerous. I have that hidden feed going directly to my laptop in my office. How about instead of keeping it in my office, I keep it with me? That way we have eyes on the outside and the inside at all times. You don't really need to call because we'll be able to see you."

She exhales loudly. "Do you mean it?"

I take her face in my hands. "Will it make you feel safe?"

She nods. "Much safer."

"Then that's what we'll do. I hadn't done that because from our vantage point we can see inside the bakery. But if you would feel safer that way, I'll do it."

She leaps into my arms and wraps her legs around my waist, leaving kisses all over my face. I don't like that she's involved in this, but those bastards are going down. No one fucks with my family. I don't care what I have to do to make her feel safe, how many lines I have to cross. I'll do it. Anything to protect her.

(Five Days later)

A few days later after Nicole accepted Chris's offer, I'm driving her to the bakery in my truck as I had started doing every morning. Given we have to be there so early, we started dropping Tait off with Breetana and Chase every morning. Turning the corner to Nicole's bakery, my heart drops as I see lights and sirens. I hadn't turned my radio on yet so I hadn't heard the call, and I know I'm the first one of my team here because no one has checked in with me yet.

"Taylor? What the hell is happening?"

"I don't know. I don't have my radio on yet. No one called me."

"Why is there an ambulance?" She grabs my arm as I pull up behind a squad.

At the end of the week, which was just a couple days after Nicole agreed to his deal, Chris had come to collect his money. Nicole told him she didn't have it all. She only had half because the week had been so slow and it wasn't a full week of his protection. It was only two days. Her only customers were Chris and area cops. Since she gave us discounts and didn't charge him, she told him she couldn't quite afford to pay him everything. He gave her to the end of the weekend.

Today.

"I don't know, Nicole."

"Michelle was supposed to be here!" She starts to get out as soon as I stop, but I grab her arm. "She could be in there!"

"You know the rule, Nicole. My only fucking rule. Me first. Your safety is all I care about. Now, stay in the damn truck." I start to open the door on my side and look at her. She looks like she wants to cry. I lean over and kiss her. "I promise I will find out what happened." I open the door the rest of the way and jump down. I look at her before I close the door. "Make sure the door is locked. I'll be in your line of sight the whole time. You need me, honk." She nods. I close the door and wait as she locks it. I walk over to the officers near the ambulance.

"Lieutenant Reddick," Officer Kane greets me.

"Officer Kane. What happened?"

"Not exactly sure, sir. I heard the call come out and rushed over when I heard about an injury. I thought it was your wife. I got here about a minute before you."

"One of the employees got hurt," Reed Daniels, a SWAT officer I've worked with a lot, says to me.

My eyes widen. "How? And who?"

"Michelle." His voice cracks. "Broken leg. She's unconscious."

"Unconscious. From a broken leg."

158

"Seems far-fetched," Reed finishes for me. "I thought so, too."

"What's SWAT doing here, Daniels?" I ask.

"OT shift, sir."

I look up as the paramedics bring Michelle out on a stretcher. I swallow. Hard. Nicole and I have become close to these girls. "Fuck. Daniels, go stand by my truck. No one gets in there but me or my team."

"Yes, sir."

"Kane, with me."

"Yes, sir." He follows as I walk over to the stretcher while the paramedics bring her out.

"She conscious yet?" I ask the paramedic.

"Just woke up. We need to go. You got any questions, ask now."

I grab Michelle's hand just as my team members start showing up.

"What the fuck is happening?" Adam asks when he reaches my side.

"Adam, get to Nicole. I want you in my truck with her. I want Daniels to stay outside. Go."

"Yes, sir." I hand him my keys as Dane walks up. I lean down to Michelle and squeeze her hand. Her face is bruised. She has a gash on her head.

"Michelle? Sweetheart, what happened?" I ask. Her eyes flutter open, and she weakly squeezes my hand. Her voice is barely above a whisper. I can't hear her so I lean further down.

"Who did this, Michelle? Do you know? Did you see anything?" Dane asks, following my lead and leaning down.

"Chris... and someone... else." I see her eyes moistening as she closes them again.

"I'm sorry, Lieutenant. We gotta go. You coming?" the paramedic asks.

"No. Kane!" I call over to Officer Kane, who's talking to the other paramedic.

He jogs over. "Sir?"

"I want you with her. Get her statement. Find out what happened. Report back to me immediately. In the ambulance. Go. Daniels will follow."

"Yes, sir." He scrambles after the paramedics into the ambulance.

"You do not leave her side under any circumstances!"

159

"Yes, sir!" He closes the door. The ambulance takes off.

Dane and I turn back towards my truck. My entire team is standing guard and Adam is inside in the driver seat. I love that I don't have to give any of them the order to guard Nicole. They know she's top priority.

"Didn't he give her until the end of the day to come up with her payment?" Dane asks.

"Yep. He's sending her a message. Do what he wants, or it will be worse next time."

"What do we do?"

"Pay him and back out on the deal. No more of his help. That was the plan. And we stick to it." We reach my team. "Daniels. I want you with Michelle and Kane. Neither of you leave her side. Get her statement. Report to me. I gave the same orders to Kane."

"Yes, sir." He starts to leave.

"Wait. I want you both in her room. If anyone tries to visit her, approve it with me. I have a feeling this gang is going to try and go after her again."

"No one in or out. Got it."

"I'll reassign both of you for the time being, but until this ends, you're both on bodyguard duty. Top priority. No other assignments."

"Yes, sir. Understood."

"You need anything, you tell me. I'll get it."

"Understood, sir."

He jumps in his squad and leaves as I turn to my team. I signal to Nicole to come out. Tears are streaming down her face, and I have to fight to keep myself from dragging her away from all of this and saying fuck the damn bakery.

She buries her head in my chest. I wrap my arms around her as I address my team and her. "Michelle is on her way to the hospital." I hold Nicole closer, knowing she'll collapse as soon as she hears the words I'm about to utter. Jesse and Korie walk up to us. Jesse, sensing something isn't right, puts his arms around Korie. "Her leg is broken. Her face is pretty bruised. And she's got a gash on the side of her head. But she's conscious now."

"What? Who? Nikki? Are you okay?" Korie tries to break free from Jesse, but he pulls her closer.

"Michelle was supposed to be here early," he says quietly.

160

"No..." Korie's knees buckle, but Jesse keeps his grip tight.

"Who did it?" Nicole whispers into my arm as I sway with her.

"Chris, baby. She said Chris."

"And someone else. I don't think she knew who," Dane finishes for me.

Nicole starts shivering. I hold her tightly. "This is all my fault. Completely my fault. I never should have let her go in early by herself." Nicole sobs in my arms.

"We knew the risk. You can't blame yourself. All we can do now is finish this and get her justice," Korie says quietly.

Mark nods in agreement. "She's right, Nic. It's more important than ever now."

"We need more protection on the girls. Jesse needs backup," I command.

"I can sit in the bakery," Zekeih volunteers.

"I like that idea. Someone else in there. The rest of us can be across the street," Dane agrees.

"Chris owns the block. How do we know we won't get sold out and ambushed?" Mark asks.

Dane nods across the street. "Because the owner of that printing shop is like my third cousin or some shit."

I glare at him. "And you didn't think to bring that up?"

"I did think about it, actually. And then decided since the dude is like eighty, it might be best to leave it alone."

I glare again, even though he's right. But glaring right now, since I can't punch anything, makes me feel better.

"So, Zekeih in the bakery," Andrew says.

"Plain view. Sitting at one of the tables," Jesse answers.

"You two don't leave them alone under any circumstances. One of you is with them at all times." I point to both of them.

"Where will you be?" Nicole looks up at me.

I look down at her. "Right across the street, Nikki. I need to get to the precinct to grab my laptop. I intended to get it when we all met there this morning, but that plan is out the window. We're all here. I'll go get it. Quickly. Then we'll have live feed through the hidden cameras Ryan set up for you."

"No! No. Don't leave." She grips my leather jacket in her hands like she's holding me to keep me from disappearing.

"I'll go, Taylor. You should stay here. I don't think Nic will be able to do this without you near," Mark says. I know he's right. My wife might fall apart if I let go of her.

"Please make someone else go." Her eyes are filled with fear. I don't care if my entire team has eyes on me. I lean down to kiss her.

"I'll stay. Okay? I won't go anywhere." She plasters herself to me. I look up at my team. "You guys got your assignments. Get set up."

Everyone scatters as I hold Nicole close to me. Jesse keeps Korie close to him. I briefly question if something is going on. I really don't care if there is. It's their business. Not mine. Jesse is a good guy. He deserves a sweet girl, like Korie, who also won't let him get away with shit. Korie might be as sweet as the pies she makes, but she's tough as hell.

I take Nicole's hands in mine and untangle myself from her surprisingly strong grip. "If you don't want to do this anymore, Nicole, I won't make you. If you want to walk away, I'll let you, and I won't lie, baby, I'd be happy about it. I'm sure the cameras will show him attacking Michelle. I'll have enough to throw him in jail for a little while."

"Not as long as he deserves, though."

"No. You're right, but it's enough."

"It isn't, though." She takes a deep breath and squares her shoulders. "He hurt Michelle. She's my friend. She didn't deserve that. And she wouldn't be in this situation at all if I hadn't -"

I cut her off by kissing her. "Enough. It's not your fault."

"Yes it -"

I kiss her again. "I'm just going to keep doing that."

She smiles and shakes her head. "I don't know what I'll do if Korie gets hurt, too. And I don't know how Jesse will react either. He really likes her."

"I knew it. He's been different lately. He didn't hesitate to hold her when they got here."

"They've gone out a few times. And I think she stayed with him last night."

"Huh. Never thought I'd see the day Jesse fell for anyone." I kiss Nicole's hands. "Are you sure about this?"

"Yes. We need to stop him. Once and for all." She sniffles.

162

I kiss and hug her before I walk with her to her bakery. I don't want her anywhere near this, but Nicole is a strong woman. More than I think she believes. She'll fiercely protect those she cares about. Even if she's scared. She won't give up, and she won't back down. It's just one more thing to love about my perfect wife.

It's not lost on me that I wouldn't be able to nail him to the fucking wall the way that I want to without her. I know he's threatened others. Possibly hurt them. But I have no proof. A lot of these other businesses don't have as good of a security system as Nicole does. They don't have a good camera system.

I guess it's good she's got two billionaire brothers-in-law. I'd never be able to get the amount of evidence I've gotten against him by just interviewing other owners.

I hate that it puts her in danger. That she's scared, but I'm also not stupid. She's got the same sense of justice I do. If I hadn't found out what she was doing, she would've continued on her own. The thought of what could've happened had she continued without me is enough to bring me to my knees. I'd never be able to survive without her.

Chapter Twenty One

✖ Ryan ✖

"I don't know what to tell you, man. You wanted my advice. Looks like Taylor's team is dealing with it, but I don't like the look of what's going on," Rico says.

I sigh. My little gang problem in Chicago seems to have gotten larger. I knew about it. Even before Taylor had given me a heads up. But he'd also said he was dealing with it.

I'm lying flat on my back on my couch. It's been an exhausting day, and I have the worst headache of my life. I do *not* need this. Wednesday's really do suck. Literally. They literally suck the life force from a person.

I hear my front door open and softly close as I massage my temples. "Did you find out how many people are involved in this little gang problem?" I ask into my phone. I close my eyes and continue to rub my temples.

"Six. One leader. The other five are his cronies. Looks to me like he says jump, they ask how high. He's gaining a lot of support."

"I'm not going to Chicago for six fucking people, Rico. Not unless Taylor can't handle it. And I know he can. He's done it numerous times."

"I get that, but I really think -"

"Rico. Done talking. I have shit here that needs to be dealt with. You know that. Keep an eye on the situation. Inform me if Taylor loses control. I'm sure he has a plan. Especially since it's hitting close to home now."

"Yes, sir."

I hang up and toss my phone on the coffee table. I smile and moan softly in contentment when I feel Arianna's fingers in my hair. She rubs and massages my scalp.

"What did you do today that caused this?"

I chuckle softly. "I went to court this morning. That football player got convicted of assault. And then I spent the rest of the day strategizing a plan for Miami's problem and trying to figure out what the fuck is going on in Chicago."

"So, another day in the life of the amazing Ryan Crane."

I reach up and grab her hands, pulling her around the couch to me and opening my eyes. My eyes travel up and down her body.

"Wow. Not often you wear a dress. What's the occasion?"

"Well... I got some news yesterday that I wanted to share in person." She smiles so widely her entire face lights up.

"I love when you're so happy. Your smile lights up the room. You look so beautiful, Aria."

She blushes. "Thank you." She kneels next to her backpack and pulls something out. She hands it to me. I move to my side and pat the couch next to me. She sits.

I start reading. "So... Looks like Juilliard thinks you're incredibly talented. As they should because you are."

"Keep reading..."

I smile up at her and continue reading. "They were impressed with you in all aspects of your interview. Your grades are great. They think you'd be a good fit. And you got a guaranteed spot for fall semester? Baby, that's amazing!"

She beams. I shift and pull her on top of me. I rest my hands on her ass under her dress but on top of her satin panties. We've been exploring what she's comfortable with. This seems to be where she draws the line. Which is fine with me, because I won't go further with her right now anyway.

She wraps her arms around me and lays her head on my chest. "I actually did have plans for tonight, but if you don't feel well, we can do something else."

"Nothing a couple Aspirin and a few kisses from you won't fix."

She giggles as she looks up at me and kisses me. I run my hands up her back and through her hair, pushing her head gently down so I can deepen the kiss. The skirt of her dress is pushed up to her waist leaving her ass exposed.

After a few minutes of kissing her, I finally pull away. "See? Feels better already." I grin. She smiles and kisses me again. "So? What is it you wanted to do?"

"I forgot. I like being like this instead."

I laugh and hold her close and tightly against me. "I have no problem being like this with you."

She kisses my chest, then straddles me as she sits up. "I thought... maybe dinner? Like dinner out, though. To celebrate."

"Okay... Why are you giving me that look?"

"What look?"

"That one. The one that tells me you want something, but you aren't sure I'll go for it."

She looks down at her hands on my stomach, then at me. "Because I don't know if we should go out in public."

"Honey, we've been in public before. I've taken you to dinner. And movies."

"It's kind of different, though. This time, we'd be fighting the need to touch each other."

"There's nothing saying I can't hold your hand." I reach up and tuck her hair behind her ear. "Or touch you." She blushes and leans into my hand. "There's nothing saying I can't kiss you."

She shakes her head. "What about the photographers always following you around?"

I shrug. "What about them? Have you ever seen photographs of me anywhere with you?"

She bites her lip, and I swallow a moan. Damn. That lip. She shakes her head. "No."

"There's a reason for that. Nothing comes out in the media about me or my family that we don't want to. You know who we really are, but

166

them? They see a mafia family with enough power, money, and control to make their lives miserable. They don't fuck with us." She gives me a soft smile as she looks at me. "So? Where would you like to have dinner?"

"Um... Have you ever heard of Bobby Van's Steakhouse?"

"On Park Avenue?"

"Yeah. I've really been wanting to try it."

"I think I can get us in, but they book out weeks in advance."

"I know. So…, I reserved it, but I had to use your name. I hope you don't mind. I wouldn't have been able to get in otherwise."

"Mind? Why would I mind?"

"I don't know." She looks down again.

I pull her back down to me. "If you ever need to use my name for something, do it. It'll open doors for you that you wouldn't have otherwise. And I trust you. I know you won't use it to ruin me."

She shakes her head. "Never."

"And soon, if I have my way, all you'll have to do is use your name and those same doors will open for you."

I feel her stiffen as those words sink in. Very slowly, she looks up at me. "Are you... saying... what I think you are?"

I smile and kiss her. "Yes."

"You want to marry me?"

"Yes." I watch as her smile turns up to megawatt level as she hugs me tightly. "Did you really not think I did?"

"I... didn't really know, I guess. I mean, I've been imagining my wedding since I was like five."

I chuckle. "Why am I not surprised?" I hug her tightly for a few moments and kiss the top of her head. "When is the reservation?"

"Seven."

"Seven, huh?" I tighten my grip a little, enjoying her

"Mmm... Two more weeks."

"Counting down?" I run my hands up and down her back.

"For more than one reason. Not having to stop at just this. Being able to just be with you. Giving myself fully to you. Finally not having to leave home to go to my stupid dad's."

My heart swells at her calling my home hers as well. "I was kind of thinking about doing something with your room."

"My room?"

"Yes. Your room. The one with the piano."

She wiggles on top of me. I groan quietly as my dick immediately responds to her. I sit up and position her so she's straddling me. She smiles as she puts her arms around my neck. "What do you want to do with that room?"

"I was thinking of an office. A place for you to study. Do homework. Practice. Whatever you need."

She leans in and kisses me. I run my hands up her legs as she presses against me and deepens the kiss. "I like that idea."

My dick twitches underneath her. I shift her so she can't feel what she's doing to me. "It's probably a good idea if I get up and get ready, Aria."

"Okay. You're probably right."

"I'm always right."

She gives me another dazzling smile as she stands up and lets me up. I lean down to give her a quick kiss as my phone starts ringing. I glance at it and see it's Taylor. I sigh and pick up my phone. "I'll be back down in a few minutes." I answer my phone and walk up the stairs as Arianna quietly watches me. I give her a wink. "Hey, Taylor."

"Ry. Hey. Look. I'm handling it, but I just want you to know that the gang I was telling you about has somehow taken over quite a bit of your territory."

"I know."

"You know?"

"I got a call from one of my corporate businesses. They'd been approached about using Chris and his gang for security. Security for my business told them they could go fuck themselves. I sent Rico there to assess the situation."

"I almost have them."

"I trust you, Taylor. I trust you'll call me if you need me."

He breathes a sigh of relief. "You're going to be pissed. I haven't been a hundred percent."

I sit down on my bed and rub my temples again. Fucking stress headaches. "What happened?"

"He's after Nicole's bakery. One of her employees got hurt. But hear me out before you start yelling at me."

I tense and narrow my eyes glaring at my wall. "Thirty seconds."

168

"I have a plan. We're using all of the hidden cameras. We have a whole undercover operation going."

"Taylor. Please be careful. They're expanding. More people are joining. They're at six now, but word on the street is they're gaining support. Take care of this before it blows up. I mean it."

"Understood."

"If you want me there, say the word. I'm taking Arianna to dinner tonight. She got accepted to Juilliard. And I would like to be at her graduation this Saturday, but I'll head there instead if that's what you need."

"Be with your girl. I said I can handle it, and I will."

"Keep me informed. Don't let my sister get hurt."

"I won't." Taylor hangs up.

I lay back on my bed. When things settle down, I'm disappearing. I'm taking Arianna on a trip around the world.

And I may contemplate not fucking coming back.

Chapter Twenty Two

☒ Nicole ☒

(One Week Later)

It's been a week since Chris put Michelle in the hospital. We know he's intimidating area businesses from coming into the bakery. I'm so pissed off about it.

He came in to get the second half of his payment and didn't like it that I told him I didn't want his services. He told me that we had a deal. That I owed him the full amount of a thousand dollars by tonight. Sunday night.

Taylor told me not to give it to him. The more and more I think about Chris, the more angry I become. The more angry I become, the more I want to tear Chris apart.

How dare he think he can do this to anyone? How dare he think he can just try and make people bend to his will? And hurt people when they don't comply?

I've had enough. He's fucking done.

Done.

"Do you plan on glaring at that frosting for the rest of the day, or are you going to finish that cake?" Zekeih's voice snaps me out of my dark thoughts.

I growl from deep within. "If I stab him, would you have to throw me in jail?"

He laughs. "I'd wipe the tapes and tell the jury I didn't see shit. You're scary for such a little thing when you're pissed off. I may be a little crazy, but I'm definitely not fucking stupid. I wouldn't go up against you." He grins at me.

I can't help but feel a little bit better. "Thank you. I actually feel slightly in the right frame of mind again." I finish frosting the cake and put it into the fridge so the flowers don't melt. Jesse needs to finish it. I don't do very well with intricate designs, and this cake requires quite a bit of that.

"I don't mean to be a dick, but I kind of have to go to the bathroom. You just about done?"

I can't help but laugh at the pained expression on his face. "Go. I just need to grab some cake batter cookies. I'll be right behind you."

"Not a chance in hell. I have my orders."

I point up to the ceiling. "Taylor's watching. If anything happens, he'll let you know. Just go. This will only take a couple minutes."

He winces. "Are you sure?"

"I'm sure. Really." I shoo him away. Zekeih nearly sprints out to the bathroom in the dining area. I laugh again as I toss a paper towel into a very full garbage can. "Ugh. That needs to go."

I quickly bundle up the trash bag and tie it. I lift it out of the can and walk to the back door. I love Chicago in May. It's not too hot and not too cold. It's perfect. It reminds me of Minnesota a little. Except there's no chill in the air. No frost on the ground in the morning. The afternoons are usually warm and inviting. I even love the smell.

I open the side door and take a deep breath as I walk to the garbage bin to toss the bag in. It's probably not something Taylor would want me to be doing, but I know he and his team are watching. The garbage bins are in our side lot where we park. Which means Taylor should be able to see me.

When I turn around, Chris is standing behind me. With the same two gang members that were fighting in my bakery. All at once, I realize my mistake. Taylor wouldn't be able to see me. There's a wooden fence that encloses the door and the bins. It's locked, but there's enough of a gap between the building and fence on the alley side that someone could slide through and not be seen doing it.

The privacy of walking out the door to the bins is honestly something I fell in love with about this building. I've been meaning to have the gap fixed, but I've been so preoccupied. I know now I should have made it a priority. I don't even think Taylor knows about it. There's more of a chance of Taylor seeing someone trying to jump the fence then there is seeing them slip through that gap.

I fight the panic threatening to take completely over. There's a camera out here. Taylor will see me. I know he will. Maybe he saw them come in. Maybe he's waiting in the shadows to take them out.

I have to stay calm. I have to feed the anger, or I'll collapse in fear at Chris' feet.

"Mrs. Reddick. Where's my money, beautiful?" Chris gives me a grotesque grin.

"I told you I don't want your services. I refuse to be shaken down by a thug and his gang."

"You got a hell of a mouth on you, little girl," one of his cronies says.

"Lots of things I could have you do with that mouth." The other gang member looks me up and down. I nearly vomit.

"Enough. Both of you. We came here for one reason." Chris glares at them. They instantly shut their mouths.

"I'm not paying you anything. I already said no more of your services." I back towards the door, hoping he lets me leave.

Chris chuckles dangerously, and I know instinctively he's not going to let me get away. "See. I don't like that answer." Very suddenly, his hands are on my throat, and he's shoving me against the wall. His grip is tight. I fight to breathe. My hands automatically go to his to try and break free. I struggle and fight, but his grip only tightens. "I didn't want to do this. I really like you, Nicole," he sighs.

"But you didn't seem to learn when we gave you that last warning," one of the two gang members says. My vision is starting to blur around the edges. I can't tell which one is talking.

"Poor Michelle. How is she, by the way?" the other one says.

172

"That window we shattered. Looks like you just boarded it up," Chris says. "Tsk… Tsk… That doesn't look very good for me. This is my district. It has to look nice."

I try to kick at Chris or any of his gang, but I miss. My vision is blurring even more. Chris punches me in the stomach and drops me to the ground.

"No…" I start to cry. Taylor will be here. I know he will. One of the other gang members kicks my leg. The other one kicks my chest. "No… Stop," I beg. I'm weakened. I try to scream, but I can't.

Chris kneels next to me. He slaps me hard, and then slaps me a second time. I try to cover my face, but he grabs my wrists.

"One hour, Nicole. Your band of bodyguards won't be able to help you. Just make it easier on yourself and do what I say." Chris shoves my wrists away and stands. He kicks me in the stomach as he walks away. The other two kick me as well, one of them in my chest, the other in the back of my neck.

I try to get up, but I can't. I feel like every bone in my body is broken. I look around to see if they're still here, but the motion makes me sick to my stomach.

"Taylor…" I whimper. He's coming… I know he is.

I try to crawl back to my door, but my vision darkens further and further.

Eventually, I collapse against the ground and succumb to the darkness.

Taylor

I yawn and stand up to stretch. My eyes haven't left the laptop screen. I've been on edge the entire day. Chris hasn't been seen anywhere since last Sunday when he attacked Michelle. It was almost like he'd disappeared. But I'd been hearing grumblings of him gaining more support. And all in Ryan's territory. I can't figure this guy out. Why Ryan? He has no connections to him.

I glance down at Dane. "Watch that, would you?" I point to my laptop screen. "I'm really unsettled, and I think we need backup."

Dane looks up at me nervously, then at the screen. "I didn't want to say it, but I have the same feeling. Something isn't right. This week has felt off. Despite the shattered window, we haven't heard from him at all. It's fucking not right. Even the outside cameras haven't picked up shit other than the window."

"Yeah. I agree. Get the guys in here."

I have the rest of my team canvassing the area looking for any sign of Chris. I have them asking businesses if they had seen or heard from him. So far, no one has reported back any useful information. Just that they hadn't seen him.

"You thinking of calling Ryan?" Dane asks.

"I don't know if it's necessary right now, but I've never ignored my instincts. I'm not starting now. We've never had someone vanish like this and not be able to track them down. I think we need him."

"Good idea. I think we need him, too." I take out my phone as Dane calls in the team, his eyes glued to the screen.

"Taylor," Ryan says into the phone.

"Ryan. I'm not saying I lost control and can't handle it, but something isn't right. I think it's time for backup."

"What's going on?"

"He's good at disappearing. There are so many things that aren't right about this guy. He's not acting like the typical thugs I deal with. He's completely calm and collected in every interaction I've seen. With the security team at both yours and Chase's buildings. Every interaction with Nikki. And then he vanishes, gains a few more people and does it all over. I don't... know what the hell to make of this guy. He's acting a lot like you."

"Like me?"

"Yeah. I'm not stupid. I'm glad you're on our side because if you weren't, we'd never be able to beat you. This guy isn't as big, but he's got a hell of a set of balls on him."

"I could've told you that. Going after a cop's wife."

"Not just my wife. You. He's going after one of the biggest mob bosses in the world and winning. With six fucking people that I know of. He has to have more in order to have amassed so much power."

"Sometimes, bodies behind you aren't what amasses power. It's brains. Wit. Ruthlessness. Cunning."

"Well, whatever the fuck it is, I think it's time you stepped in."

"You know if I show up the entire operation becomes mine."

"I know."

"You and your team do what I say."

"I got it, Ryan."

He sighs. "Arianna is turning eighteen this week. Her dad has been pretty ruthless with her since she graduated Saturday. I wanted to be close this week in case I needed to step in."

"I wouldn't ask unless I felt it was necessary, Ry. You know that."

"I know. When do you want me there?"

My eyes fall on my laptop screen, and I narrow them as I cock my head to the side. "Hang on, Ry." Nicole has been frosting that cake for quite a while. And I saw her put it in the fridge. "Dane, did Nicole grab another cake to frost?"

"What?" He looks up at me, confused.

"That cake. She never does two of the same kind of cakes. Those cakes are one of a kind."

"Taylor?" I can hear the sudden edge in Ryan's voice.

"I think he found the fucking signal to the live feed," I say just as much on edge as him.

"Look at the screen. Any glitches? Any type of blackened edge or corner?" Ryan asks?

I kneel close to the screen and notice fuzziness. "Fuzziness. Barely. But it's there."

"Get your ass over there. Now! He found it and looped the feed. Don't you fucking hang up!" Ryan has never yelled at me until right now. But he doesn't have to. I'm already sprinting out the door. Dane and my entire team are close behind me. We all run across the street, traffic honking at us. I don't give a shit. All I care about is getting to Nicole.

We all pound into the bakery. My heart drops at what I see. "What the fuck?"

"What the fuck happened?" Dane asks. Jesse and Zekeih are both laying sprawled out and face down on the floor. Korie is crying in the corner. Blood is running down her cheek.

"Where's Nicole?" I ask no one in particular.

175

"Talk to me, Taylor. What's going on?" Ryan asks.

"Zekeih and Jesse are out cold. Korie's got a split lip and gash on her head. I can't find Nicole." I kneel down next to Korie. "Korie? Where's Nicole? Where is she, sweetheart?" She shakes her head and cries harder. "Fuck. Fuck!" I stand up and sprint to the back.

Mark grabs me. "Gun out and with backup. What the fuck, Lieutenant?"

I take a deep breath. He's right. I have to calm down. I take out my gun and let him go first. I follow. "She's not here, Ryan. Not in her office. Not in the back."

I'm panicking. How could I have let this happen? How could I have let this happen to my girl? My wife? My beautiful wife. My entire heart and soul.

"Check outside," Ryan growls.

"Outside? What the hell would she be doing outside?"

"Do it, Taylor!"

I motion for Mark to take the lead again. He kicks open the door and stops dead. "Holy shit." He checks around the door as he moves, then finishes by checking around the garbage cans.

My eyes fall to Nicole. "No." I drop my gun and my phone on the ground as I scoop her in my arms. I have to get her inside. Mark follows, my phone to his ear, and my gun in his hand. I'm shaking as I carry Nicole out to the front of the bakery.

"We found her. Outside. She doesn't look good." Mark is talking to Ryan. "I don't know. She's unconscious. Bruised."

"Come on, baby. Talk to me. Wake up, Nicole." I nuzzle her face and kiss her softly.

"Shit," Dane says shakily when he sees us.

Zekeih is awake and kneels next to me when I slide down the wall holding my girl. I hold Nicole close and turn my furious glare onto him. "I said fucking stay with her. You had one order. Protect her."

"I -"

"You're fired," I growl viciously.

His eyes widen. "What? Taylor, you don't understand!"

"What's to understand? Your orders were to stay with Nicole! I find you out here and her outside! How the fuck does that happen?"

176

Dane puts a hand on my shoulder. "Taylor, calm down. We need to figure out what happened before you start firing people. Which isn't even your call anyway." He looks at Mark and holds out his hand for my phone. Mark gives it to him. "Ryan? It's Dane. Everyone but Nicole is conscious. She's breathing fine, and I have EMS on the way. You need to get your ass here. Now." He pauses. "Good. I'll take care of it."

He hangs up, and I look back at Zekeih. "Suspended. And you're off the team."

Dane shakes his head. "Stop it. Taylor. Enough. Our focus is Nicole. We regroup. We talk to Ryan. We come up with a plan. We take every single one of those fuckers down. No one is fired or fucking suspended."

I look down at Nicole just as she stirs in my arms. I kiss her head, forehead, and eyelids. "Wake up, baby. Please wake up. Come on."

Her eyelids flutter open and she grips my shirt in her fists as she buries her head in my chest. "Taylor... I'm so sorry, Taylor."

"Shh... It's okay, Nikki. I'm here. It's okay."

"I took out the garbage. I'm so stupid," she whispers.

"Stop it, Nicole," I whisper in her ear as dominantly as I can manage even though I'm breaking. "You know better." I hate when she calls herself stupid or talks down on herself. She knows I do.

"It was stupid. So stupid to go by myself." She shutters in my arms.

"Nikki. Enough. Please stop," I beg. I can't hear her talking like this. I'm the one who failed her. This is my fault. Not hers.

She cries into my chest. "I told Zekeih he could go to the bathroom. I was only going to grab cookies, and then be out. But I saw the garbage was full. I didn't think. I took it out and saw Chris with the same two guys that were fighting in here a couple months ago. I'm so sorry. Please don't hate me." She sounds so fucking shattered.

I shake my head. "Baby. I don't hate you. Please don't do this. You've come so far from where you started when we first met. Don't revert back to that. None of us here blame you. None of us are upset with you."

I hold her as close to me as I can without hurting her. Jesse is holding Korie tightly. Zekeih is sitting at a table in the corner by himself with his head in his hands. Dane, Mark, Andrew, and Adam are all standing guard as paramedics show up.

I should've called Ryan in as soon as we figured out Chris and his gang of mindless monkeys were targeting his territory. That he was targeting Nicole. This is no one's fault but my own. It's my fault that Michelle is in the hospital. My fault that Nicole and Korie got hurt. That two of my team members got hurt. My friends.

I look up as the paramedic kneels next to me to check out Nicole. She refuses to let go of me, and I know it makes his job a little harder, but I refuse to make her. Not when I'm what she needs to ground herself.

When he's done checking her, he turns to me. "I think she needs to go in. At least be under observation for a little while. I don't like the look of the gash on her head."

Nicole shakes her head. "I'm fine. What about Korie?"

"She's going in, too," the paramedic says.

"Nikki, we need to go in."

"Taylor -"

"I almost lost you today." I leave no room for argument. The paramedic helps her up. I follow, sticking close, and help get her on the stretcher. I hold her hand as the paramedics wheel her and Korie out.

"Lieutenant." Jesse looks like he's about to cry as he glances at the other ambulance where Korie is being loaded up.

"Go, Jesse."

He gives me a shaky smile, then jumps into the rig after Korie. I climb up in the other one behind Nicole.

So many things are running through my mind as I hold her hand and kiss her on top of the head. One of the things at the forefront, though, is tendering my resignation.

I failed everyone I love today.

I almost lost my wife because of decisions I fucking made.

178

Chapter Twenty Three

⚔ Ryan ⚔

I hang up my phone after finishing my conversation with Dane and throw it across the room. "Fuck!"

Arianna, who is sitting next to me, jumps. "Ryan?" The fear in her voice makes me flinch.

I immediately turn to her and take her hand. "I'm sorry, Aria. I didn't mean to scare you." I kiss her hand, then her.

"What happened?" she asks softly.

"Remember that small gang in Chicago?"

"The one you said Taylor could handle?"

"They went after Nicole. She's on her way to the hospital."

"Oh my God! What?" She covers her mouth with both hands as she starts to cry.

"I need to call my pilot and fly to Chicago."

"Which means… you won't be here this week," she says through her tears.

"Baby, if I could take you with me, you know I would."

"I understand." She nods, but she's breaking my heart. She's trying to put on a brave face, but I can see how scared she is. I know how nervous she is being here without me.

Since she graduated, her dad has been really different with her. He's always been mean, but lately, he yells at her for looking at him the wrong way.

I know there's something else going on, but she isn't telling me. Whatever it is, though, I've been feeling the need to stay close to her in case she needs me.

Like tonight.

She called me and asked if she could come over because her dad was upset she had messed up dinner. Mushroom risotto and roasted duck. He made her cook it by herself from a recipe book, and she'd never cooked it before in her life. Risotto itself isn't easy. It took me years to master it, and I went to school to be a chef. Add in something like roasted duck, and she was set up for failure from the very start.

I take both of her hands in mine and lean forward, pressing a soft kiss to her lips. "Plan hasn't changed. The morning you turn eighteen, leave. You have a key. Come straight here. Turn off your GPS. You'll be safe, but if I am not back, I'll have someone here that you can trust, and who will keep you safe."

She nods, trying to be strong, even though it's obvious she's barely hanging on. "You have to take care of this. Taylor and Nikki need you. Family is important. I would never dream of keeping you from them."

"I'm sorry, baby. I really am. I wish I could take you with me. I don't want to leave you here. I know you need me, too, and you're just as important to me."

"I'll be okay. I'll hide in my room. Maybe go to Renza's."

I squeeze her hands. "I'm sorry, Ari. I wish I could be two places at once."

She wipes her eyes and gives me a brave smile. "Go. I'll call you or text you every day. If you can't respond, I'll know you're busy, and you'll respond when you have time."

I lean in to kiss her again. My heart is torn. Part of me knows she needs me just as much as Taylor and Nicole. I quickly grab my phone and keys, trusting if she needs anything, she'll tell me so I can get her help. I jog out to my car before I have a chance to think anymore. I can call the pilot on the way to the hangar, but if I don't leave now, I might not at all.

✗ ✗ ✗

After the flight, I'm pulling up to Taylor's house even more furious than I was. He never should have let this go on as long as he did. He should've called me a long time ago.

But Taylor has an overwhelming sense of justice. I have it, too, but it's different. Taylor struggles with doing what it takes to get things done if what it takes is anything less than legal. I don't. Taylor does everything he can to stay on the right side of the law. I try, but if I have to cross a line to protect those I love, I'll do it. I have a feeling that he may have just been pushed over the edge, though. It's my job to make sure he doesn't jump.

I knock on the front door. I need to reign in my temper. Taylor doesn't need my wrath right now. He needs my support. And my help. More importantly, he's my brother.

"Hey, Ryan," Breetana says tiredly, even though she smiles.

"Hey, gorgeous." I lean down to kiss her cheek, then pluck Tait from her arms. He smiles and squeals. "I missed you, too, little one." I give him a kiss and tuck him into my arm.

Breetana laughs. "Okay. Obviously, I lost him. Everyone loves Uncle Ryan!"

"Obviously. I'm pretty great." I wink at her as she closes the door. "Where's Taylor and Nikki?"

"They just got home. Taylor is tucking her into bed. Chase and I were just going to put Tait down again. It's been a hard night. For all of us."

Chase walks into the room. "Go easy on him, Ry. He's really having a hard time."

"He should've called me. Why the hell has this gone on for so long?"

"You know Taylor. He doesn't like to get you involved unless he has to. He really thought he had this under control. He's fucking talking about resigning and everything."

My eyes widen in shock. "Resigning? Come on. He loves his job."

181

Chase nods. "This shook him, Ry. I haven't seen him like this since he killed his dad. Even though I still argue that he wasn't the one who pulled the trigger, but I digress."

This is way worse than I thought. I may be pissed that he didn't call me in sooner, but I won't let him withdraw into himself. Not again. I didn't know him when he killed his dad. I know about it. I know how he was, and I'd seen it after we first met. He blamed himself for all of the deaths of the cops who showed up for that arms deal gone wrong call that he was on. He really blamed himself for the death of his partner.

I never want to see him go back to that. He's too good.

"Damn." I hand Tait back to Breetana. "Is he upstairs?"

Chase nods. "In their room. He's really shaken. So is Nicole. It might be a good idea to deal with this tomorrow."

"You're probably right. I'll just let him know I'm here."

"Chase and I were going to stay here tonight. To help with the baby," Breetana informs me.

"Good idea. I think I might, too. I don't want to drive across town to my penthouse, but I think he might need me around tonight."

"I think he'd feel better with you here," Chase agrees.

I smile and head up the stairs to Taylor's room. I quietly knock on the door. After a few moments, Taylor opens it. I'm taken aback. He looks like he hasn't slept in weeks.

"I can't handle a lecture, Ryan. I'm already beating myself up. What do you want?"

"I just want you to know that I'm here. I'll be down the hall. We'll talk in the morning, okay?"

"Fine." He turns and closes the door. He could barely stand straight. It was like he had the entire weight of the world sitting on his shoulders, and he was about to crack under the pressure.

I sigh as I head to a guest room and close the door behind me. I know Taylor is good at what he does. He rarely needs me to help. But he needs to learn to ask me before everything blows up on him. I'll need to talk to him about that.

As well as this resignation bullshit. That isn't fucking happening. Not on my watch.

XXX

Taylor

I haven't slept. I've spent the entire night watching Nicole sleep. I held her in my arms all while feeling like the worst husband in the world.

After she crashed, I sat up and typed out my resignation. I love my job. My family and my job are the most important things in my life. But how the fuck do I expect to be good at my job and protect the citizens of Chicago when I can't even protect my own fucking family?

I let her down. I missed a lot of shit. I assured her she would be safe. I fucking failed.

I kiss Nicole softly on the forehead, then get up and grab my resignation. Ryan is here. So is Chase. Nicole and Tait will be protected until I get back. I need to just do this now. Get it over with. It's very rare I cry, but as I walk down the stairs, I feel tears sting my eyes.

As I turn the corner into my living room, Ryan is sitting on my couch. I should've known that I wouldn't be able to sneak out without him seeing me.

Fuck.

"I'm out, Ryan. I'm done. Take over. Fix everything. You won't have to worry about me fucking things up for you anymore."

"Enough. Sit down."

"I'm not a fucking child! I love you, but I'm not letting you treat me like someone who just falls to your every command. And I've made up my mind. I'm resigning from the department. This whole thing is yours. It should've been in the first place."

"Taylor. I'm not in the mood. Either sit down or I'll make you."

Ryan's cool as a fucking cucumber demeanor infuriates me. "Fuck you." I turn and head for the door.

"Taylor!" The tone of his voice stops me in my tracks. I turn and growl dangerously. Ryan is standing now and glaring at me. "I left Arianna by herself a week before her eighteenth birthday when all of my instincts are screaming at me that I shouldn't have. When everything in me is saying her dad is going to do something that is going to change both mine and her

183

lives forever. I don't know what. But I do know this situation is volatile. Yet, I'm here because you're also family to me, and you need me."

I've never seen Ryan vulnerable.

Looking closer at him, I can see the stress all over his face. The tension in his body. Like me, it doesn't look like he's slept in weeks.

"I feel like I'm being torn in two different directions, Taylor. I'm between my family and the woman I love. And I have a responsibility to both of you. Do you have any idea what this is doing to me? Not being able to be there for her and seeing you beating yourself up for something that you didn't do?"

"It's my fault it happened, Ryan. My wife is laying upstairs bruised and sore as fuck because I thought I could handle something I obviously couldn't."

"The last time I saw you like this was when you watched your partner die. What did I tell you then?"

I close my eyes and give in. I sink into the couch across from where he was sitting. "It's not the same thing."

"Maybe not the same situation, but the advice still stands. Do you remember what I said to you?"

I lean back against the couch and open my eyes. Ryan is sitting now. "You said that it doesn't matter what happened out there. It doesn't make me or break me. It doesn't define me."

"You're a good cop, Taylor. You're too good of a cop to let a career you've worked so fucking hard for just drop down the drain."

"I'm only good because of you. Your tips. Your guidance and help."

"Bullshit. How many cases have I actually helped you with?"

"I've lost count."

"I haven't. I may have given you countless tips. But you're the one who took them down. I've helped you three times. In twelve fucking years. You got where you are today because of yourself, Taylor."

I close my eyes again, tears once again stinging my eyes. "I don't want to give it up, Ry. But how can I possibly be trusted to protect the people in my city when I can't even protect my wife?"

"Taylor. Look at me." He waits until I give in and look at him. "Not even I expected him to be smart enough to find that live feed. I never thought he'd go after Nicole or anyone else in broad fucking daylight. We aren't dealing with normal with this guy. He's cunning. Smart. I absolutely understand why you didn't come to me, Taylor. He isn't that big. He's smaller than a lot of gangs you've gone after on your own. And things have been busy for me. I get you didn't want to interfere. But you can't do that. If you need help, Taylor, I'll help you. That's what family does," His voice cracks. I take a deep breath and nod. "Don't do this again. Tell me if you need me."

I nod again, and he holds out his hand. I look at him quizzically. "What?"

"The resignation. Hand it over." I laugh and hand it to him. "You aren't resigning." I watch as he tears it up.

I sigh, the grin dropping instantly. "So, what's the plan?"

"I have word he's gained a few more people. And that they're all staying in a warehouse he's refurbished into a headquarters."

"It's a block down from Nic's bakery."

"Yes. He's up to around twenty in his gang now."

"What? He was at six yesterday!"

"Last night. They had an initiation party."

I look at him incredulously, then shake my head. I don't know how he does what he does and knows what he knows, but I'm grateful every day that he's on my side. "So, what do we do? What's the plan?"

"I need to check in with Arianna. I wasn't kidding about my bad feeling. I want both you and Nicole to rest today. Just be a family. Do something together. Hang out with Tait. I don't care what you do. Just do it together. Forget about all of this. Regroup. Tomorrow morning, we'll call in both your team and mine. The plan is to spend a bit of time observing him. Watching him. A day. Maybe two. And then we go in with an army and take him the fuck out."

"Why can't we do that now? We know where his HQ is."

"Because if we go in guns blazing without some kind of an idea of what their habits are, we may miss a few people. We don't know if they have another hideout, Taylor. Think like a SWAT officer. I know most of the time they take the lead on your takedowns. They tell your team where to be and what to do. That's their job, right? That's why you work so well together."

"Yeah, I guess. They usually have a meeting I'm not involved in at the same time I'm briefing my team."

185

"It's to prep. We need prep time. I need to call a few people in. I'll send some of them to observe today and tonight. We'll brief in the morning. Right here." He points to the floor. I take another deep, calming breath and nod again. "Feel better?"

"Surprisingly. I guess I just needed my ass kicked a bit."

Ryan stands and pats me on the back. "I have to call Arianna. I need to know she's okay."

He starts walking to the stairs. I look up at him. "Hey, Ry?"

He stops and turns around. "Yeah?"

"Nikki and I were talking last night. We think it would be a good idea to have you, Chase, and Tana all here. Under one roof. I know you have your own place here, but..." I trail off and shrug.

"If that's what you guys want, then I'll be happy to."

I nod as he smiles and jogs up the stairs to his room. I feel more confident after our talk. It's not surprising. Chase and Ryan are two of the very few people in this world who can get me out of my head.

I get up and walk back up to my room. I quietly shed my clothes and crawl back into bed with Nicole. She sighs in her sleep and curls into my arms.

"I love you," she whispers against my chest.

"I love you, too." I kiss her forehead and fall into a deep, relaxed sleep a few minutes later.

Chapter Twenty Four

⚔ Ryan ⚔

I sit down on the edge of my bed and take out my phone. I hated leaving my girl last night when I knew she needed me. Arianna is having such a hard time. I know she isn't telling me everything going on, but I also know it's because she's scared. Every time she shows up at home, the fear in her eyes is more and more prevalent.

It usually takes me a couple of hours to bring back her smile, and it instantly disappears as soon as she has to leave. She's trying to be brave and stay strong until she can leave her dad's, but I know how hard that is getting for her.

I take a deep breath and call her. She doesn't pick up until just before her voicemail would. "Hello?" Her voice is quiet, and I can tell she's been crying.

"Baby, what's wrong?" I fight off the crack my voice wants to let out. She's quiet for a long moment. "Aria. Come on, sweet girl. Talk to me. What happened?"

"I just miss you, Ryan. That's all."

I can tell that isn't all. "I miss you, too. But I know that's not why you're crying."

"It's just that... Renza is out of town. Her and Robby went on a road trip before college starts. I forgot they were going. So, I'm stuck at my dad's. And my dad? He's been so mean."

I drop my head in my hand. "What happened? What did he do?"

"It's hard to explain."

"Try, baby. Please?"

She takes a deep breath and lets it out slowly. "He took away my car. I'm stuck here. And he's..." She pauses, and my heart stops beating.

"What, baby? Please?" I'm not used to begging. I've never had to. If I can't strike a deal, I've always just taken what I want. But Arianna? She brings me to my knees.

"It's like he's trying to... domesticate me? I don't even know how to explain it, Ryan."

I do. And the protective, possessive instinct in me rears up. I know exactly what he's trying to do. I swallow and take a deep breath. "What is he making you do, Aria?" I can't keep the edge out of my voice, no matter how hard I try. I know she hears it, and I know it scares her.

"U-um... H-he's been making me cook. Which y-you knew…" She inhales sharply, and my anger grows. "Like... intricate, h-hard stuff. The stuff y-you cook, Ryan. He t-told me I'm cooking f-filet mignon tonight. W-with garlic p-potatoes and as-asparagus." She starts crying. My heart clenches in my chest. "If I m-mess up, I do-don't know wh-what he'll d-do!"

"Okay. Baby, it's okay. Listen to me. Shh..."

I wait for her sobs to subside. She takes several deep breaths and hiccups a few times as she forces herself to calm down. I keep whispering to her, comforting her in any possible way I can think of.

She sniffles and takes another deep breath. "He gave me a menu for the whole week," she whispers. "He said if I mess up, there will be consequences. He took my car because after dinner yesterday, I snuck out." She sounds so defeated.

I fist the blanket under me in my hand as I close my eyes to steady myself. "Send me the menu, baby. I'll give you tips to make everything easier. Okay?"

She sniffles a few more times. "Really?"

"Yes. Really. Tonight for the filet mignon… How does he eat his steak? Do you know?"

"Um... Like you do. And so does the guy he has over for dinner."

I swallow. Hard. "You're going to cook it rare. The trick to a good filet mignon is timing. I'll send you directions on how to cook it, ingredients and everything. But keep in mind that you have to leave the steaks out. Keep them packaged, but leave them out for twenty minutes. They have to rest. Are they already thawed?"

"Yes." Some of her confidence is starting to come back.

"Good. So, take them out twenty minutes before you're going to cook. They won't take long to actually cook, so use that time they are out for other stuff. You'll only need to cook the filets for a couple of minutes in a pan, then you'll put them in the oven for no more than five minutes."

"Are you sure?" she asks hesitantly. "That seems… so… short."

"I promise you, baby. Do you trust me?"

"Of course I do."

"Then just follow my directions. Keep a close eye on your times." I hear her take another deep breath. "What else, baby?"

"He's making me work with our housekeeper. Doing dishes. Making the beds. Vacuuming. Dusting. I don't mind doing chores. Really. But he intentionally messes something up, then lets the housekeeper yell at me for not doing it right because she doesn't see him messing it up."

"Christ, Aria." I massage my temples. "Okay. Here's what we're going to do. If things get too bad, if he touches you, Aria, leave. Go either home or to Jason's. If he forces anyone on you, get away. Call Jason or Nick or Rico right away so they can get to you. Them first. Then me. Understand?"

"Yes, but what do you mean by forcing anyone on me?"

I don't want to scare her more than she already is, and I don't know if my instinct is right, or not. At the end of the mini argument I have with myself, I decide not to say anything. "Just... be careful, baby. I have a pretty good feeling of what he's trying to do, but I don't know. All I can tell you is I won't let anything happen to you. So, if things get out of hand, run."

"I can't just leave until I'm eighteen. You could get in trouble."

"Baby, you're right. I *could* get in trouble for taking you away right now, but that isn't why I won't. I wouldn't put it past him to immediately call in whatever lowlife cops he bought off. But I'd be out of jail within hours. It doesn't matter, though, because that's all the time he needs to go after you, Arianna. I don't give a fuck that he'd go after me and try to get me in trouble. I'm not willing to risk what he'd do to you. If things do get that bad, though, I'll do whatever I have to do to keep you safe. Consequences to me be damned because I can fix whatever the fuck he'd try with me."

"He's just being really mean right now."

"I know, baby. If all he does is yell and scream, then try and deal with it the best you can. Call me. Text me. Whatever you need. But if he escalates it, baby, just run. Don't worry about me. I'll figure something out." I wish I could reach through the phone and hug her. She sighs. "Arianna. I mean it. Don't try and protect me. I can protect myself. You know that. My priority is you. Just run."

"Okay." She shutters a sob. I force myself to keep breathing as my phone pings with a text. "I just sent you the menu."

I open her text and scan it. "You won't have to make Beef Wellington. I can't believe he's making you cook something like that on your fucking birthday."

"That was the one I was most concerned with."

"Don't worry about it. I'll send you tips and recipes for everything else. Do you know how to make stroganoff?"

"Not the sauce."

"That's fine. It's not too hard, and I'll make it easy for you." I smile when I hear her chuckle. "There's my girl."

"Thank you, Ryan." She sounds far less scared, and I'm glad I was able to ease some of her fears.

"You're welcome."

"I should probably go. I'm supposed to check in with Renz. She was really worried."

"Okay. I'm only a call away, baby. Don't overthink and not call just because you think I'm busy. I'm never too busy for you."

"I promise." She kisses the phone.

I chuckle. "I'll see you soon, baby."

"And talk to me later?"

"Of course."

"Can't wait."

We say goodbye. I immediately text her the directions for the mignon. I'm sick to my stomach. I'm being torn apart, and I have no idea what to do. My responsibility has always been to my family. I've never been in love, so I've never had to choose. If my family needed me, they came first. It wasn't really even a choice. It's always simply been the way I operated.

I know he's going to try and force this guy he's been inviting to dinner on her. That's why he's trying to domesticate her. To make her into a perfect cook and perfect housewife. Mafia wife.

In the mafia, that's what women are used for. Sex, drug transportation, and whatever else their mates can dream up. Women are used. They aren't respected in the slightest. Unless they belong to someone, their safety is always at risk. If the person isn't high in the ranks, there's a chance their woman will get shared with other members within

190

the mafia. Specifically those who are higher up. They're considered property. A play thing for bored men.

They're used as prostitutes. Decoys for drug deals or arms deals. They're used to gain the trust of other women who are then brought into the mafia and either sold to the sex trade or used just as the woman who brought them in is. It's sickening. It's so fucked up that thinking about it makes my blood boil.

One of the first serious missions I'd been on with my father before I took over the Crane Mafia was that of a drug dealer selling in our territory. While we were looking for him, we came across a woman in the basement of the house we believed him to be in. We uncovered one of the biggest sex trafficking rings in the entire state of New York. We found out it was being run by another large mafia in the area. The cops couldn't do much of anything because the connection wasn't big enough to give them a solid case. They took down a couple key players, but not the kingpins. That's when we stepped in.

Back then, we weren't legal like we are now. My dad ran things a lot differently than I chose to when I took over, but one of the things we've always agreed on is that certain lines just aren't crossed. We've never let our mafia treat women with disrespect. We've always honored them and treated them with the respect they deserve. And we've made sure that if we ever came across a woman being mistreated, we did whatever we could to help. If it was one of our guys…, well, they were swiftly dealt with. They became friends with the dirt.

I guess I can't speak for every mafia. I know a few that treat women like they should be treated. My best friend, Alex, and his twin brother, Josh, had gone legit as soon as Josh took over the reins. I consider them both as much brothers as I do my own. Alex isn't the leader of their mafia.. He didn't want it, even though he was bred to take over. Just like I was. But he still helps out if he's needed. Both to me and Josh. No one in their mafia disrespects their significant others. Just like with mine, they would answer to Alex or Josh. And become very intimate with Hell.

I won't let Arianna be forced into that life. Even if I hadn't been the one she'd chosen, I would do everything I could to get her the fuck away from him. She's far too good for me, let alone that life. The idea that she's being forced to marry either another leader of another mafia or someone important enough and high enough ranked to create an alliance between the

Massena Mafia and theirs is not something I'll ever let happen. I know how the Massena Mafia works. Arianna has always been protected by her father. It's the one thing I can actually respect him for. He may be an asshole to her, but he's never let anyone else touch her. Until recently…

I shake my head with a low growl. I have to trust in my girl. I have to trust that she'll listen to me and run if she needs to. I have to trust my brothers and Rico to help her if she calls them for help. I have no choice because right now, Taylor and Nicole need me. I couldn't abandon them anymore then I could Arianna. I only hope that nothing implodes on me. The foundation I'm standing on is shaky. Every move I make is highly calculated so as not to tip the balance. If anything happens to either Arianna or my family and I'm not there for them, I'll lose it.

No.

I have to trust in my family. I have to trust my girl. If I can't control my racing mind and keep it on the task at hand, I could lose Taylor or my men in the takedown I'm planning. I have to focus. I have no other option.

✕✕✕

Nicole

The next morning, after spending the previous day as a family and having a picnic, I open the door as the doorbell rings for what seems to be the hundredth time. All of Ryan's fifteen mafia members had already arrived. So had most of Taylor's team. We're waiting on Jesse and a couple other people I'd never met. I smile and immediately hug Michelle when I see her on the other side of my door. She's with two police officers. Reed I know. The other one I don't recall meeting. Maybe I've seen him before, though.

"Hey, Nicole. I'm Mike Kane," the one I don't know says.

"And you know me," Reed says with a huge smile. He's taller than Mike and sticking really close to Michelle. I smile widely.

"Taylor had them on bodyguard duty," Michelle says, with a blush as Reed puts his arm around her waist.

I let them in and carefully pull Michelle to the other room with me after Reed reluctantly lets her go to join the others. "How are you? Are you okay?"

"I'm actually really good. Still kind of hurting, but I'm healing. The guys are really good about getting me whatever I need." She smiles shyly.

My smile gets impossibly bigger. "You finally landed the hot SWAT cop?"

She shushes me as her eyes go wide. She looks directly at Taylor, who comes around the corner, grinning. He folds his arms over his chest and eyes Michelle. "You and Reed, huh? He seems your type." Michelle turns bright red but can't hide it behind her hands because of her being forced to hold her crutches. "Don't worry. He's not going to get in any trouble. I'm not that kind of boss. Who am I to stand in the way of love?" He puts an arm around my waist and tenderly kisses my cheek. I smile as he gently pats my ass and walks into the living room to join everyone else.

"So, I know you're okay. But how is Korie?" Michelle asks softly.

"She said she's coming with Jesse. She just wants girl time."

"I can't blame her. So do I."

"I think we all need it." I see Reed eyeing Michelle protectively, and I smile at her.

"I think Reed would feel a little better with you close."

She looks over at him. He smiles sweetly. "He hasn't left my side since the hospital released me. That night at home, he slept on the floor in my bedroom. The second night, he had planned on doing the same thing, but I felt so bad. So I told him he could sleep in the bed. We started out on separate sides, but somewhere during the night, I curled up next to him. And that's kind of where he's kept me ever since."

"Oh my Gosh, Michelle. I love that. So much." I'm so happy to see her happy that I can't help but hug her again.

"How are *you*? Reed told me what happened after he was filled in. Are you okay?"

I nod into her shoulder. "Sore. But I'm okay. It could've been a lot worse." We hug each other for a moment, both needing the comfort. When I let go, I help her over to the chair Reed confiscated. He smiles widely at her as she puts her crutches against the wall and sits in his lap. I share a look with Taylor as the doorbell rings again. I turn and head to answer it.

"Hey, sweetheart." Jesse leans down to kiss me on the head.

"How are you feeling?" Korie asks.

"I'm okay. What about you?"

"Just a headache. He didn't bother that much with me. Just shoved me away from Jesse."

"She fell and hit her lip against a chair and her head against the floor." Jesse says.

"And you?" I ask him, eying him for injuries.

"Pistol whipped me. But I came around pretty quickly. He was gone by that time, and Taylor and the rest of the team were already there."

I hug them both. When I pull back, Jesse kisses Korie softly before joining the rest of the guys. I smile. They're so cute together.

"Jesse said you were making snacks for everyone. Do you need help?" Korie asks.

"Actually, I made breakfast. I hope I made enough. I've never cooked for this many people. My sister is in the kitchen right now keeping an eye on everything. It should be almost done. Want to help?"

"Sure? What do you need?"

"Chase should be back any minute. I made him go get those heavy duty disposable plastic plates and silverware. I only have enough for eight people. When he gets back, can you help set everything up buffet style in the dining room?"

"Of course!"

The two of us walk to the kitchen. Breetana is sitting at the kitchen bar and Ryan is pulling everything out of the oven. I raise an eyebrow.

"Remind me the next time you have any kind of party involving food, to make the food for it myself," he teases.

I stick a finger in his chest as he sets the last pan down and turns to me. "I'll have you know, I'm an excellent cook, thank you very much."

Ryan laughs. "Are you sure about that?" He eyes my dishes suspiciously. "What the hell is it? Quiche?"

"Nope. It's scrambled eggs with bacon bits and cheese." I smile up at him and bat my eyelashes.

He shakes his head. "Stick to baking. Get out of the kitchen. All of you. I need to fix this. I need these guys on their game. And no one is going to be able to do that on an empty stomach."

I laugh. "No one would have an empty stomach." I gesture sassily to the spread in front of him.

He grins arrogantly. "No one is eating this. Out."

I put my arms around his neck and stand on my tip toes as I pull him down to kiss his cheek. "Not everyone can be a world class chef."

"Not world class. Good enough to not kill people. Now, get out, you brat."

I laugh, and we leave the kitchen. Korie makes a beeline for Jesse and follows Michelle's lead. She sits in Jesse's lap. I smile as I sit on the arm of the couch next to Taylor. He slips an arm around my waist and gently guides me into his lap.

"I love how you're so incredibly gentle with me." I say it quietly and turn my head to meet his lips. I close my eyes as he sweetly kisses me.

"Anything you need." He kisses my shoulder as everyone around us talks about different things. Chase walks in, and Breetana beams at him. She immediately kisses him, then helps him set everything up in the dining room.

Tait coos happily in the middle of the room, delighted at all of the attention he's randomly getting by so many people.

"We have a very social child," Taylor says, quietly.

"He certainly loves the attention, doesn't he?"

"I think we might be doing a good job."

"Of course we are. We're awesome."

Taylor laughs. "We do kind of have this parent thing down."

"It may help a little that Chase and Tana help us so much."

"Maybe just a little." He kisses my shoulder again as everyone takes turns cooing at Tait and passing him around.

"Listen up!" Ryan's powerful and commanding voice cuts easily through the loud din of the house. "Breakfast is buffet style in the dining room. Be orderly, or you face me. You all know the mood I'm in not being able to be close to Arianna right now, so don't test me."

Everyone, including Taylor's team, follows Ryan's orders, and I'm in complete awe. Even Tait has stopped cooing and just stares at his uncle. Someone hands him to Ryan when Ryan reaches out for him.

"Amazing," I say in awe.

"I know." Taylor chuckles as he watches.

"Is that where you get it from?"

"The commanding voice? Probably. But mine isn't quite as good. Ryan can strike the fear of God into anyone."

"You can, too."

He smiles at me as I stand up. It's amazing to see how many people constantly support us. How many people come together when one of us is in trouble.

I hold Taylor's hand as Ryan stays in the background and snuggles Tait. Ryan is constantly the one who brings everyone together. He's everyone's protection.

But I can see the worry all over his face. The fear he tries so hard to hide is very evident in his eyes. I think when all of this is over, we all may need to come together for him.

Chapter Twenty Five

✗ Taylor ✗

After breakfast, Nicole takes Tait and the rest of the girls to another room so they could all talk and decompress. I haven't told my team who Ryan is yet, and I'm not looking forward to it. We don't keep secrets from each other.

I take a deep breath and stand, preparing to address my team. Everyone silences without me saying a word.

"Alright. My team. You're probably wondering who all of these people are standing here. And who the hell that guy is that everyone here listens so closely to." I nod to Ryan. He stands.

"That's Ryan Crane," Adam announces.

"Most powerful mafia boss in the world," Mark continues.

"Has most of Chicago under his control," Andrew says.

"Works closely with law enforcement to clean cities with crime problems up." Jesse shrugs.

I look at them all incredulously. Dane is looking at them in open-mouthed shock. I glance at Ryan, who looks just as surprised as I am.

Zekeih gives us all a cocky smile. "What, Lieutenant? Didn't think we knew?"

"I didn't know," Mike says.

Reed shakes his head. "Me either." I clear my throat, glancing back at Ryan.

"Listen," Mark begins. "We figured out who he was after the incident at the bakery. We also figured there was a reason you didn't tell us. And we trust you."

"Well, then you know Ryan and his team are the good guys here," Chase interrupts. "They've helped you guys out more than you know."

I meet Chase's eyes, grateful for his help. I clear my throat again and look at Reed and Mike. "I know you two don't work with me often, but Ryan really is on our side. Trust me when I say that if he wasn't, we wouldn't stand a chance against him."

Mike nods. "Lieutenant. I trust you. I see the work you've done, and I'm not blind. I see what you're doing now to protect your family. If you say we can trust him, I'm with you."

"Couldn't have said it better myself," Reed says. "I've worked with you a few times. I know your rep. I'll follow your lead."

"Good. There's a few things you need to know. All of you. Ryan works with Law Enforcement agencies all around the world. But he stays anonymous. He only works with a few people. His identity needs to be a secret and remain that way. If it doesn't, he can't do the work he does. Think Batman." I wink at him. Ryan snorts, and I smile.

"From this moment on, Ryan Crane is the new Taylor Reddick. You listen to him. Follow his commands," Dane says.

I nod in agreement. "He's your commanding officer. What he says goes."

Ryan stands and gestures to his team. "This is your new team. We aren't two teams out there. We need to work together if we want to take these assholes down." He glances at me, Reed, and Jesse. "They hurt loved ones. You guys don't know much about me, but when it comes to family, that's where I draw the line. No one fucks with family. Nicole is my little sister." He points to Jesse and Reed. "Michelle and Korie are your significant others, right?"

"Yes, sir," Jesse says without question.

"Absolutely, sir." Reed nods.

"What I'm about to ask is a personal, but important question. It changes everything depending on your answer. Have you gotten to the point where you'd do anything for them?"

They don't hesitate, and I'm proud as hell.

"Absolutely, sir," Jesse nods.

Reed doesn't break eye contact. "Without a moment's hesitation, Mr. Crane."

"Good. Had you said anything different, I would have left your asses here. So here's the deal." Ryan focuses his attention on everyone. "We're going after a ruthless, vindictive fucker. He's smart. And he's cunning. But he's also arrogant. He's been able to elude an elite taskforce literally designed to take assholes like him down. Arrogance will be this guy's downfall."

"We need to observe. As much as I know we'd all love to just go in there and take him down, we can't do that. We have to be smart." I cross my arms over my chest.

"We're breaking off into three teams. Each team will have eight people," Dane explains.

"If any of you are questioning the math on that after looking around this room, you should be. That leaves two extra people." Ryan looks at Rico and Chase. "Chase, I know Taylor has trained you, and when it comes to defense, you're second to none. You've been trained by one of the best. I want the girls and Tait under one roof. I don't want them split. I don't want either of my sister's by themselves, and I don't want Michelle or Korie on their own."

Jesse sighs, relieved. "I'm completely for that."

"Damn, me too. Makes me feel a lot better about leaving Michelle." Reed looks a little less stressed.

Ryan smiles. "Glad you both agree. I want everyone here. This is where Tait is comfortable. All of his stuff is here, and I don't want his life disrupted at all. Chase. You stay with the girls. Taylor has an extra Glock. I'll get you an AR-15. Rico. Your job is to be Chase's back-up. You know the rules. No one in this house or out of it except me, Taylor, Jesse, Dane, or Reed without my explicit consent." He pauses and glances at everyone else in the room. "It's not that we don't trust the rest of you. But until this entire fiasco is over, access has to be restricted. If we allow twenty-six people in or out, it's far easier for security to be compromised. Questions so far?" There's a murmur of no's and a chorus of head shakes throughout the room. "Good. Your three leaders will be me, Dane, and Taylor. Like I said. You will be divided by eight. When you hear your name, divide up. Team One by the fireplace. Team Two by the window. Team Three by the stairs." Ryan starts calling off names until everyone is divided up.

"Team One. Your leader will be me," Dane says. "Our assignment is to observe the warehouse. I want a perimeter set up. Our job is to document and photograph everyone going in and out. Pictures. Typical surveillance. Starting as soon as this briefing is over."

Team One nods.

I step forward. "Team Two. Lead by me. Our job is to get close to the building and see what we can see inside. That's why I have Reed and why I took Miguel from Ryan's team. Both have SWAT experience. We're dividing up into two teams. The first four will be led by me, and I'll need Miguel. We need to get close, maybe get in. At least see through the windows. Get a feel of inside. We'll be the day team. Reed, I need you leading the second team. Same deal, and I apologize, but night shift."

"Not a problem, Lieutenant," Reed agrees.

I nod, feeling a little guilty. "Good. I know you probably want to be with Michelle tonight."

"Really. It's not a problem. She'll be here, so I know she'll be safe." He gives me a reassuring smile, and I nod.

"Team Three. You're with me," Ryan says. "We're Team One's relief. Observe. Typical surveillance. Documentation of everything. We'll be going in at 10PM and leaving tomorrow morning at 10AM. I don't know that it's necessary for more than one day of observation but Teams One and Two, be prepared to be called back out if I want more documentation. For now, the plan is to reconvene here tomorrow evening to figure out the rest of the plan."

"Ryan will be calling in a fourth team of eight people tomorrow to continue surveillance if we aren't there," I continue.

"They will be reporting directly to Ryan," Dane says.

"If I feel there's relevant information to pass along, I'll do it. But their job is to make sure no one disappears. If Chris adds more people, they'll know," Ryan finishes.

"Questions about your assignments?" I ask. Another collective chorus of no's and head shakes fill the room.

"Comments or concerns?" Dane asks. More no's.

"Anyone from any team have an issue with who your leader is?" Ryan follows up. More no's.

I breathe a sigh of relief. I had a bit of apprehension about both mine and Ryan's teams taking orders from different people. "Good. Team One. Move out. Team Two A. I need to say goodbye to my wife and kid. Give me ten minutes. We'll head out. Team Two B. Check in with Ryan and Team Three since you'll be working with him. I expect you to follow Reed's orders. He'll be getting them directly from Ryan and me."

"Team Three and Two B. Hang tight here until everyone is gone, and I'll brief you on where to meet and when," Ryan commands.

"Everyone grab a radio from the table in front of you," Dane says. "We're using SWAT channel four. They should already be programmed to channel four. Please don't touch the channel. I don't need our shit broadcast to the entire world."

"We have intel that Chris and his band of losers listens to our main police channel," I inform everyone.

"We have no intel that they listen to any of the other channels," Ryan continues.

Dane rubs his head like it's painful for him to say what he's about to. "Don't give away your position either way. We won't be using street names. We'll be using sectors."

"We won't be on the radio unless it's necessary for us to be," I say.

"Team One. Let's go. I'll give you your sector's outside. All teams. One more thing. Two people together at all times," Dane says.

I nod in agreement. "For safety."

Dane leaves with his team, and mine heads for the door. I signal Chase and Rico to follow me. They do, and I lead them to Nicole's favorite room. The sun room that overlooks the lake behind our house. The girls all look up as we walk in.

I smile at Nicole and lean down to kiss her. "Chase and Rico will be here at all times. I'm heading out with my team right now, but Ry will be here until tonight."

"Jesse is on Ryan's team and Reed is on Taylor's, but he's leading Team B so both of them will be here with us until later," Chase says to Korie and Michelle.

"And Taylor will be back tonight. So you'll always have me and Chase here. Taylor later," Rico finishes.

The girls all breathe a collective sigh of relief as I grab Tait and lead Nicole out of the room. In the semi-privacy of the hallway, I kiss my son and snuggle him close for a moment.

Nicole snuggles into my arms as well, and I kiss the top of her head. "Promise to be careful."

"Always, baby. I promise."

"It's so dangerous to do this in broad daylight."

"I know, Nic, but it has to be done. In order to fix this mess and get back to normal, this is necessary."

"Doesn't mean I have to like it."

I hug her tightly, then tilt her chin up to meet my lips. Tait tugs her hair while I kiss her.

This.

This is what I'm doing this for.

These two beautiful human beings.

My entire life.

Chapter Twenty Six

☒ Ryan ☒

(Four Days Later)

It's Thursday morning, and I wake from an unsettled sleep to an insistent knocking on my door. I look at the clock and groan. Four in the morning. I decided my own team can deal with surveillance. I need everyone else on their game. We're going in to take out Chris tonight.

"Ryan! Please wake up!"

"What, Nicole?" I call.

The door bursts open as I'm sitting up in bed. Nicole flings herself at me. I barely have time to catch her and steady myself, keeping her from hitting her head on the nightstand. We both tumble backwards into the bed.

"They burned it!" She sobs into my arms. I look up at Taylor as he walks in. I'm completely confused.

"Burned what? What's happening?" I hug Nicole as she starts babbling incoherently.

"We got a call from the alarm company. There was a fire alarm."

This causes Nicole to burst into a wave of fresh sobs. "I have to go. I have to!" She tries to break away, but I hold her tighter to me.

"She wants to go to the bakery, but I don't want her out of the house. I'm not taking Tait out there. I'm not leaving him here without me, and I'm not letting Nicole go alone. I don't think he knows where we live, but I am not taking chances."

I sigh as Nicole cries harder. "Give me five minutes, Nicole. You can go with me."

"Like hell," Taylor growls. "Did you not hear what I just said? I do *not* want her out of the house." Taylor glares at me.

I return it. "Taylor, I get it. I understand exactly where your protective instincts are coming from. But you have two choices. You take her, and I stay here, or I take her and you do. Either way, keeping her from something she's worked so fucking hard on is wrong. Make your choice, Reddick."

He looks between Nicole and me completely torn before finally taking a deep, shaky breath. "Fuck, you're right. Take her. I feel better if she's with you."

"Five minutes, Nicole. I'll meet you downstairs," I tell her.

She runs out of my room. Taylor slowly trudges after her as I throw on a pair of jeans and a sweater. I grab my phone, keys, and wallet and hurry after her, still having no idea what exactly is fucking happening.

✕✕✕

By the time we arrive, Nicole's bakery is fully engulfed, and there's nothing that can be done. As soon as I stop my vehicle, she's out of the door before I even have time to react.

"Nicole! Dammit!" I jump out of the vehicle and catch her before she's able to cross the barricade. "What in the hell are you trying to do?"

"It's gone. Everything is gone! Everything I worked so hard for. Gone! Gone! Gone!" She collapses against me as her customized sign falls to the ground. All I can do is hug her. "What do I do?" She looks up at me as I sway side to side with her. "What do I do now, Ryan? It's the same thing as Silver Bay all over again! The bullying. The targeting!" She sobs into my chest.

"Rebuild, sweetheart. Let me fix this issue with Chris. Then I'll get you on track to rebuild."

"I worked so hard to build my reputation here. Now, I have to start all over." She cries as she watches her bakery crumble to the ground. Everything she's built is engulfed in flames and crashing down in epic fashion.

And all she can do is watch as she grips my leather jacket like her life will be taken from her if she lets go.

"Chase and I will help with getting all of this cleaned up and rebuilt. Right here. Same location. Stronger than before."

She takes a deep breath as she watches the flames. It takes her a long time, but she stands a little straighter. "Stronger than before?"

I smile, still hugging her. "Just like someone else I know." The tension in her body slightly releases, so I keep talking. "My brother, Jason, owns a real estate company. He's got businesses all over the world. Jessa, his wife, is one of his project managers. I can have both of them help and expedite this. Just say the word, Nikki."

"How long would it take to rebuild?"

"Maybe a few months? We'd start from scratch. If I enlisted Jason's and Jessa's help, we could probably have you back by the end of the summer."

Nicole pulls away and stands tall looking into the flames with her own fire in her eyes. There's my little sister. That passion and fire. That's Nicole.

She nods resolutely. "Let's do it. I want to send a message to everyone. I'm here to stay. No one can beat me. This isn't Silver Bay. This is different. This is my home."

She continues to stare down the fire, her fists clenched at her sides. When she looks like that, I know no one can hold her down. No one can beat her.

✕✕✕

Later that night, I'm standing in Taylor's living room as everyone straps on weapons and protective gear. Tonight is the night. Nicole's bakery burning down gave everyone an entirely new determination for this mission. No one is talking. Everyone is in their own world. My mind is on Arianna, but I force it clear and concentrate on the mission ahead.

I take a deep breath before beginning my speech. "Everyone listen up." Everyone in the room looks at me. "Tonight is the night. I know Nicole's bakery being set on fire has given all you guys a newfound determination for this mission for one reason or another. But we still need to stick to the plan." I look at everyone. "My team makes all the necessary kills. Our job is to protect Chicago PD and your jobs out there. No one touches the scene when we're done except our team. Chicago PD does nothing except what I say."

"If anyone calls 9-1-1, our dispatch knows, as usual, what they need to know about our mission. To them, we're training. We all have silencers, but we need to take precautions," Taylor says.

"With all due respect, I don't think any of us are afraid to get our hands dirty," Jesse says, glaring at the wall.

Dane smiles and shakes his head. "But you won't unless it's to protect your life or someone else's. We follow the same rules we always do."

"If you need to make a kill, you abide by department protocol. Same as any other mission we've ever been on," Taylor says.

"Only difference is our goal isn't to arrest the leader or any of his officers," Dane says.

"Chris and his two cohorts belong to me and my team," I say.

"Who are the two cohorts?" Reed asks.

"I'm glad you asked." Taylor passes out eight by ten photocopies of Chris and the two gang members that attacked Nicole. "These three are not to be touched by us. Ryan and his team are under direct orders from me to deal with them on their own. This is to protect us. We don't have enough evidence to put these three away for life. They'd get out after maybe five years for the assault on Nicole and the girls as well as Jesse and Zekeih. The extortion of anyone else would be swept under the rug because we can't prove it's been happening to any of them other than Nicole."

"I'm not willing to take that risk and neither is Taylor. I know none of you are either," Dane continues.

I nod. "So, they won't be walking out of there alive. Everyone else, you'll be arresting them."

"We have enough evidence from Ryan's team to link them to gang activity. They won't be behind bars for a long time, but without the leadership, they'll have no place to go back to either," Taylor says. "Same shit as every other day."

"We aren't concerned about the underlings," Dane says. "The main goal is Chris and his two officers."

"Contact between all of us is the same as before. Except with these earpieces. We're still using the same SWAT channel. We aren't dividing up. We're going in there with everything we got. Weapons are outside in the back of the SUV's," I explain.

"My guys," Taylor begins. "Ryan's SUV's are unmarked and untraceable. Me and Ryan will be in the lead SUV. Everyone else, pair up. Two of my guys in the rest of the SUV's. No one takes their own vehicles or department vehicles."

"I left a surveillance team in place," I say. "They'll be looking out for us. Get armed and suited up. Say your 'see you laters' to your loved ones. We leave in exactly five minutes." I grab my earpiece and head out to my SUV. Mine and Taylor's weapons are already loaded up, so I get in and wait for him.

A few minutes later, he gets in. "Man. Nikki is pissed the hell off at you."

"Wouldn't be the first time a woman wants to kill me."

"You didn't say see you later to her."

I glance at him. "I'm not trying to be a dick, Taylor. I'm just having a hard time."

He smiles supportingly. "How's Arianna?"

"I want her the fuck out of there. Now."

"She turns eighteen tomorrow, right?"

"Yeah. But her dad is going more and more off the deep end."

"More than making her cook intricate five-star chef level dinners?"

"He's making her dress a certain way. She sent me a picture yesterday of the outfit he forced her to wear." I pull up the picture and show it to him. She's dressed in a short skirt and a shirt you can practically see through. "Scroll through. There's three of them."

Taylor scrolls through the images and gives a pained look. There's one of her in shorts that show off her ass cheeks with a tank top that shows off her tits. There's another with a short black skirt that definitely would show off her ass if she bent over. "Knowing her, she has to be extremely uncomfortable in those outfits."

"You have no idea. There's one guard there that's been looking out a little bit for her. But he isn't there all the time. He's not one of her dad's main guards. He's the one who she asked to take those pictures."

Taylor hands me my phone as it starts ringing. "Arianna."

"Put it on speaker so we can get this shit done." He does as I pull out of his driveway. "Hey, sweetheart."

"Hi." As per usual, she sounds like she's been crying. I look at the clock on the dashboard. Midnight here. One in the morning there. She's eighteen now.

"Happy birthday, baby, but it's one in the morning in Manhattan. What are you doing awake?"

"My dad is having a really loud party. I tried to sneak out now, but he has guards at all of the doors because of the party. I can't get around them. I was still wearing that stupid outfit from earlier, and he accused me of being a slut and trying to seduce all of his gross friends."

I glance at Taylor. His mouth has fallen open in horror. "Arianna. Sorry to interrupt, sweetheart. It's Taylor."

"Oh. Um. I-it's okay."

"Listen, can you get out your window? I can call one of my contacts in Manhattan and have him meet you a block away from your house. He can bring you to Ryan's."

Arianna bursts into tears. "H-he put an alarm on my w-window so I c-can't get o-out."

I feel like I've been stabbed in the chest. "Fuck."

"Hey, it's okay, Arianna. How do things look during the day? When do you get up?" Taylor asks.

"He m-makes me make breakfast, too, s-so I have to be u-up and have breakfast on the t-table by n-nine."

Seeing where Taylor is going with this, I take a deep breath. "Baby, remember when I told you to be really observant?"

"And t-tell you about the g-guards?"

"How many are there in the morning?"

"F-four. Sometimes five. If the one who h-has been helping is h-here." She's starting to calm down.

"How often is he there, sweetheart?" Taylor asks.

"He's b-been here the past t-three days. He said h-he'd be here tomorrow. H-he knows about my relationship with y-you."

208

Taylor and I look at each other. "Baby, what? How?"

"He was ordered to f-ollow me last weekend. H-he didn't report the truth to my father. He said I was with R-enza."

I breathe a sigh of relief, but I'm even further on edge now. I don't know what to make of this guy. I don't know who he is, and I don't like it.

"Sweetheart, what's this guy's name?" Taylor asks.

"Luke."

"Do you know his last name?"

"Ambrosio." She sniffles.

"I'll start a check right now," Taylor says.

"Baby, listen to me. Don't bother taking anything with you. It's too dangerous. Just get out as soon as you can."

"Arianna, I'll have a squad meet you, okay? It'll be someone I trust, so you know you can. As soon as you're out, get as far away as you can, and then call me or Ryan."

"I d-don't have your number. R-Ryan o-only put a f-few people here in my phone w-who could h-help."

"I'll text it to you, sweetie. I mean to put it in there. I'm sorry I forgot to," I say as I pull up to our rendezvous location. I shut the SUV off as everyone else pulls behind or next to me. "Baby, I'm really sorry, but I just got to the warehouse. Mission is about to go down, and as much as I hate to, I have to let you go."

"I understand. It's o-okay. I'll t-talk to you in the m-morning."

I close my eyes and lean my head against the headrest. "If you need me, just call. Okay?"

"I love you, Ryan." It's barely above a whisper, but it hits me hard. I've felt it for a long time, but I never let myself say it out loud.

"I love you, too, Aria."

Taylor hangs up my phone, and I force myself to open my eyes and look at him. I expect a knowing smirk, but all I get is the same level of concern I feel written all over his face.

"First time with the 'I love you?'"

I give him a half-hearted smile. "Yeah."

"We need to get her the fuck out."

"You're telling me. Run the check on Luke Ambrosio. I want to know everything about this guy, and why he's so protective of Arianna."

We both step out of the SUV. Taylor already has his phone to his ear to start a check. I force my mind to the mission at hand. As soon as this is taken care of, I'm flying Arianna out of Manhattan. I don't care where we go as long as she's with me.

✗✗✗

Taylor

I'm standing at the back of Ryan's SUV strapping on my gun belt. I check my Glock and put it in its holster. I strap on my thigh holster and put my backup weapon in it. I grab an AR-15 and strap it to my back.

"Lieutenant, are we doing flash bangs?" Reed asks as he comes up next to me.

I nod. "Flash bangs. Smoke bombs."

"Tear gas," Ryan continues. "We throw flash bangs first. Followed by smoke. When we enter, we throw the tear gas." He closes his eyes and rubs the worn, leather band tied around his wrist.

Not many know that he does that before every single mission he's on. It was given to him by his grandfather, who told him it always brought him luck before battles. He told Ryan it brought him the confidence he needed to go in and come out alive. The man died peacefully in his sleep, so it must have worked for him.

Dane steps in. "Lethal force is authorized if you need to protect yourself or one of your partners."

"Reed, I want you with Ryan's team on entry," I say. "He needs your SWAT experience. You've got more than Miguel."

"Yes, sir."

"Everyone else, I've got the okay from my team to go." Ryan addresses the others as they gather around us. "Everyone is inside the warehouse. There are twenty people, and they're initiating ten more. That's why you see an extra fifteen people here. We need to overpower. Show our numbers. They won't know what hit them."

"Everyone suited up?" Dane asks. Everyone says yes or nods, and we all move out.

Soon, we're all outside the warehouse behind the ten people we have on the entry team.

Ryan's voice comes over all of our earpieces. "Masks down. Entry team. Enter in five... four... three... two... one... Enter!"

The entry team busts through the door and immediately throws flash bangs. Instant chaos inside the warehouse ensues.

"Smoke!" Ryan commands.

The entry team throws the smoke bombs, shielding us all as we enter.

"Exit team. No one gets out until I give the all clear!" Ryan says.

We enter the warehouse, surrounding everyone by staying close to the walls. As the smoke starts to clear, we all start to move in closer.

"Tear gas. Now!" Ryan yells.

The entry team throws the tear gas. The room is filled with the potent chemical, and the unsuspecting gang members start coughing. Some fall to their knees.

"Kill team. On me!" Six people immediately break off and follow Ryan.

"Everyone else! Take everyone into custody!" I command.

Everyone is surrounded, and most surrender without a fight. Before long, everyone is in custody with no shots fired. I look around for Ryan. He has Chris and his officers surrounded at gunpoint.

He meets my eyes. "Everyone out. Take the twenty-seven you've arrested to booking and clear the scene. You should have enough room in the SUVs."

"Yes, sir. You've all heard him. Herd the cattle out!" I command.

We all usher out the arrested gang members and load them into the SUVs, leaving Ryan to deal with the assholes who've caused my wife so much trouble and heartache.

I finally enter my house after what seems like days later. Everyone had been booked. I'd been congratulated by my Captain for taking so many dangerous people off the streets.

I'm barely in the house when Nicole jumps on me, wrapping her legs around my waist and nearly smothering me with kisses. The fatigue disappears. So does everyone else in the room until all I see is her.

Behind me, Korie jumps into Jesse's arms and wraps her legs around his waist. Just as Nicole had done to me. Reed gently but tightly lifts Michelle off the ground. They share the same type of long kiss that Jesse and Korie are.

"I don't care what any of you guys do. Take a guest bedroom. Fuck on the couch. The kitchen counter. The floor. Have at it. Just leave me and Nic alone." My lips don't leave her mouth as I carry her upstairs to our bedroom. I kick the door closed behind me and drop her on the bed. We both tear our clothes off at near record speed. I lay down on top of her, holding myself off her slightly so I don't completely crush her.

"I missed you." She kisses me.

"I missed you, too." I kiss her.

"I'm glad you're okay." She kisses me again. I don't break the contact, but I do reach down between her legs and run a finger along her entrance to her hot and wanting center. I slowly slide it inside her. "Mmm... Taylor..." She murmurs against my lips as she arches into me.

"So wet for me already. So ready."

"I'm always ready."

I remove my finger and replace it with my hard cock as I put my finger in my mouth. "You always taste so sweet."

Nicole wraps her legs around my waist and her arms around my neck. After she gets used to my size, I start slowly moving, thrusting hard.

Our tongues twine together, and I wrap my arms around her, pulling her close to me. Her hips meet mine in a slow but steady rhythm.

I bury my head in her hair and kiss her neck. I lightly bite it and then run my tongue across the mark. She arches her body into me again and again and sighs on a shaky breath as she closes her eyes. I keep thrusting into her pouring all of my love into each one. If my girl wants me to make love to her, I'll do exactly that.

"I love you, Taylor," she whispers it in my ear as she kisses my neck and shoulder. Her legs tighten around me.

"I love you, Nicole."

I feel her pussy constrict and clench around me. I give her a couple of hard, deep thrusts, hitting every one of her pleasure spots.

She digs her nails into my shoulders and throws her head back against the pillows. "Ahh…," she moans.

She tightens and pulses erratically as her orgasm hits. It's like she pulls me deeper inside and doesn't let go. Her tightness sends me so far over the edge, I know I'll never be able to come back. My dick thickens, and I fill her pussy with all of me.

After a few moments of catching our breaths, I roll off her and pull her close to my side. I kiss her forehead.

"We'll rebuild the bakery, baby."

"Bigger and stronger than ever." She kisses my chest.

"I'm so glad this is over and we can move on."

"Me, too." She pulls herself closer to me. "Taylor?"

"Yeah, beautiful?"

"I think Ryan is really going to need us soon. All of us."

I think back to Arianna's phone call earlier and sigh. "I think you're right."

And we will be. Ryan has never turned any of us down when we needed him. No matter what he has going on in his life, he has always dropped it all for all of us.

It's about time we show him that he has that same level of support from everyone in his family.

Chapter Twenty Seven

⚔ Arianna ⚔

I nearly cry as I shut my alarm off. I'm happy I'm about to get out of this house, but I'm panicking, as well. I'm so scared. I'm scared that I'm not going to be able to get out of here. That my dad is going to figure out my plan and keep me from leaving.

He's already taken my car keys. I have no way to drive out of here because I don't know where he hid my key or any of the keys to any of the other cars.

I'm also scared because there's something I have been keeping from Ryan. Something huge. I've told him about being bullied. And he did exactly what I knew he would and didn't want him to. He stormed in in true Ryan Crane fashion and fixed it with a couple threats and a lot of intimidation.

But if he did that with Chad, the true bully, the true intimidator, the true instigator, it would start a war. Ryan is always at war with someone trying to take over his territory or someone trying to take him down. I don't want him to be at war over me. And if I had allowed him to go after Chad, that's exactly what would've happened.

My hope is that by keeping him out of it and enduring everything with Chad, I'll have kept him from another war with another mafia.

What I haven't told him, though, is that my father has invited Chad to our house. Ever since we graduated, Chad has been living with us. I've tried to stay away from him as much as possible, but I'm forced to be around him every night for dinner. I'm forced to wear skimpy outfits that I'm uncomfortable in because my father wants me to look sexy for Chad. I'm forced to clean the house in skimpy outfits. I do everything I can not to bend over because I know it shows my panties when I do.

I drag myself out of bed and hurry to get dressed. My dad laid out another stupidly sexy outfit for me, but I don't touch it. I throw on a pair of jeans and a hoodie. Ryan's hoodie. One that I sleep with to feel closer to him.

I grab my house keys for Ryan's house, I keep them separate from my car keys. I find my cellphone. I shut my GPS off like Ryan taught me. Both my keys and my cellphone go into my back pockets.

I steel myself and quietly walk out of my room. I make my way down the stairs and stop dead in my tracks.

"Where do you think you're going dressed like that?" My heart stops beating. Chad is sitting on the couch with my father. They've never been sitting there together this early in the morning. Ever. My heart sinks. I know something really bad is about to happen.

"Where's the outfit I laid out for you, Arianna? Go change immediately. Stop embarrassing me in front of your future husband," my father says.

"My w-what?" I can't breathe. I start to get dizzy.

"I told you I'd have you one way or another," Chad sneers. "You've been promised to me since you were born, little girl." The sickening smirk on his face makes me ill. I start to hyperventilate, but the anger within me bubbles to the surface.

I level an icy glare on my father. "How dare you? How could you do this to me? Do you know what he's done to me? He's tried to sexually assault me!" I scream at him. My voice is barely recognizable even to my own ears.

My father's face reddens. "You will speak to me respectfully!" The tone of his voice shuts me up immediately. Tears immediately start falling as the fear overtakes the anger. I watch Chad stand and start stalking towards me. "You can't be sexually assaulted by your husband. And that's what he has been to you since you were born. Papers or law be damned. You will marry Chad. Our mafias will become aligned. And we will finally be powerful enough to take down Ryan Crane. We will have control over Manhattan and New York."

My father's plan suddenly becomes crystal clear. I shouldn't have kept this from Ryan. I should've told him. My effort to keep him out of another war falls completely at the wayside with those simple words.

Chad reaches my frozen body, and he roughly grabs my chin in his hand. "See, baby? I told you we'd be together eventually."

"I'll never marry you. Never," I growl.

"You will."

"Tonight," my father smirks.

The tears are streaming down my cheeks. "What? You c-can't do this! You can't f-force me to m-marry anyone!"

Chad shrugs arrogantly. "It's too late for arguments. You're going to marry me, and we're going to live happily ever after. And if you don't, I'll chain you up in my basement."

I shove him away from me and run for the door. He catches me and slams me against a wall. "Get o-off me! Get a-away from m-me!" I knee him in the groin and run again. He grabs my hair and throws me onto the stairs. "Ow! Ow..." I cry harder and try to scramble up, but Chad pins me down. He grabs my wrists and slams me into the stairs. The air leaves my lungs. I fight to get it back.

Chad leans down really close to my ear. "No use fighting this. You're mine."

"You *will* be married tonight, Arianna. Stop resisting it. Chad *will* be your husband."

"No!" I scream and bite Chad's neck as hard as I can until I taste blood.

"Fuck! You fucking bitch!" He instantly lets me go and grabs his neck as he scrambles backwards and off of me. He looks at his blood covered hand. "She fucking bit me! You stupid fucking bitch!"

I get up as quickly as I can and start running, but my dad grabs my hair and yanks me back to him.

I scream. "Let me go!"

"What the fuck are you doing? What have you done?" He tugs my hair so far back my body is arched.

I grab my keys out of my pocket and twist around so I'm facing my father, even though the pain he's causing by pulling my hair is excruciating. I fight through it and plunge my keys in his neck. He screams in agony as I take my keys out. He releases my hair as he grabs his neck. I spit in his face and scramble away. Then I do exactly what Ryan told me to.

I run.

"Guards! Stop her!" he gurgles.

I yank open the front door and sprint as fast as I can away from him. I duck behind houses and stay away from streets until I can't run anymore. I collapse to my knees in a fit of coughs and take out my phone to call Ryan.

"I've been waiting for your call. Are you out?"

"Ryan." I cough as I cry.

"Baby? What the fuck is happening? What's wrong?" He sounds panicked. I try to calm down, but I can't. Not with him as panicked as me.

"I'm out. I'm -" I start coughing again. Ryan calls for Taylor. I take deep breaths, trying to calm down enough to talk.

"Arianna? Sweetheart. It's Taylor. Tell me where you are. I have my guy waiting for you."

"I don't know. I ran. I just r-ran," I sob.

"Give me a cross street. Can you do that for me? I need you to be strong for me, sweetheart." His calming voice gives me the strength to pull myself up. I need that. I need the calm. The commands. I force myself to walk. "Arianna, you need to keep talking to me. Ryan is freaking out. You have to be the strong one for me, honey."

I wipe my eyes uselessly. The tears keep falling. I have to be strong for Ryan. "I'm walking. I'm t-trying to find a cross street, but I'm scared I was followed. I don't want them to find me."

"When you left your house, did you leave from the front?"

"Y-yes." I choke on another sob.

"Breathe for me, honey. Take a deep breath," he says calmly. I do as I'm told. The cool air fills my lungs and calms me slightly. "I know you're scared, but you gotta trust me, okay?"

"Okay."

"Which way did you run?"

"I ran to the left. Towards the city."

"Good girl. Stay with me, okay? Find me a cross street. I'm getting a squad out to you."

"Okay." I continue to weave through houses until I can see a street as Taylor barks orders to someone. "Taylor?"

"I'm right here, honey."

"Whitney Avenue and Clove Road."

"Okay. Listen to me. I want you to hide, but hide somewhere you can see the road. When you see a squad car pull up and stop, that's your ride. The cop will be in uniform. He'll get out, and he'll put his hands on his roof. Like he's looking for something. His name is Jeff Reigns. The number on his license plate is 7651."

"O-okay."

"He's under orders to take you straight to Jason's office."

"Okay." I'm hiding behind the corner of the house, praying that no one sees me. "Is R-Ryan okay?"

"He's okay, honey. I'll give him back to you as soon as you're in that squad car."

"I see no-one coming. I can't quite see the p-plate."

"Just hang tight, honey. Don't move until I say." I hear him talking to someone else before his voice comes back on the line to me. "What's that squad doing right now?"

"He's stopping. On the corner. I can see the number. It's 7651."

"Good girl. Just stay where you are. Keep telling me what he's doing."

"He's getting out. He's in uniform. Like you said. He's... um.... He put his hands on the roof, and he's looking around."

"Okay. That's the signal. Walk to him. Don't run. Get in the front passenger seat. He'll get in afterwards. I'll give Ryan back to you after he introduces himself."

"O-okay." I stand up and slowly walk to the car. I don't say anything as I slide into the passenger seat. The officer gets in after me.

"Arianna? I'm Lieutenant Jeff Reigns. I'm a friend of Taylor's. You ready to get the hell out of here?"

I nod as the tears fall again. "Yes. Please. So ready."

"Baby? Are you okay?" Ryan asks. His voice is so much calmer.

"I am now. I promise," I say quietly.

"What happened, Aria?"

"My father. He t-tried to force me into a marriage. I was supposed to marry h-him tonight."

"Baby. I'm so sorry. I should've just said fuck it and taken you with me."

I shake my head. "It d-doesn't matter now. He w-wants your territory. He th-thinks if he m-marries me off that h-he'll have enough p-people between the t-two mafias to take you down."

"None of that will ever happen. Ever, Arianna."

"I just w-want to get out of here. Please d-don't m-make me stay here." I start to cry harder, completely breaking down as all of the adrenaline wears off.

"Baby, you're not staying there. Get to Jason's office. He'll know what to do."

"I'm a-almost there. I th-think."

"I'm so sorry, Ari. I never should've left you."

"Don't. Don't d-do this, Ryan. Please? I c-can't be the st-strong one anymore. I'm f-falling apart. I'm s-scared. Please d-don't."

"Okay. Okay, baby."

"We're p-pulling up to J-Jason's office."

"Okay. Nick will be waiting for you."

Jeff escorts me inside and doesn't leave my side until Nick takes his place. "N-Nick is w-with me now," I say to Ryan, wiping my eyes.

"I love you, Aria."

"I love you." I hang up as the elevator doors close. Tears continue to fall, and Nick holds me close to him.

"Shh... You're safe now, Arianna." All I can do is nod as he strokes my hair.

Jason is waiting for us. I run to him as the elevator doors open. He completely envelops me. "I got you, honey. You're safe."

"Jessa is in a meeting. Then Jason has a few. As soon as Jess is done, I'm going to escort you both to Jason's house so you can get changed and cleaned up. And then you and I are jumping on Jas's plane and flying to Chicago," Nick says.

"I d-don't have any other cl-clothes. I have m-my phone and keys."

"Ryan said you have some things there," Jason says. "I don't mean to alarm you, but you have blood all over. It's in your hair; on your clothes. You need to clean up, honey."

"What the fuck happened, Arianna?" Nick asks.

I snuggle closer to Jason. Just his size makes me feel protected. Safe. "I g-got away. I f-fought. I s-survived.."

XXX

Later that day, I'm settling into Jason's plane with Nick. As the plane takes off and Manhattan becomes smaller and smaller outside the plane window, I start to relax.

The closer I get to Chicago and Ryan, the less stressed I feel.

But I still feel like someone is following me, and I'm so scared.

I don't know what the future holds, but I do know that my father won't let me go until he's no longer breathing.

The End

Next In The Crane Family Series

The dark and sexy Crane Family Series continues with *Dangerously Forbidden Love*.

Being the leader of the largest and most powerful mafia in the entire world didn't leave me time to fall in love.

Unfortunately for me, the Goddess of Love doesn't give a damn about schedules or how much free time I have. She strikes when she wants to. She does it furiously, without prejudice, and comes in the form of the exotically beautiful and completely forbidden Arianna Massena, daughter of a rival mafia.

I do everything I can to stay away from her, but when her father tries marrying her off to the son of another mafia, I'm forced to take action. I won't lose my girl to anyone else, and there's no way I'll ever let her be treated like nothing more than property or a bargaining chip.

I've never been afraid to do what needs to be done to protect my family. Everyone knows I'm ruthless.

But no one dared dream of the dangerous lengths I'll go to protect the woman I love…

~ This book is a steamy Age-gap/Mafia Romance that has dark and violent themes, and strong language that may not be suitable for all readers. ~

Order *Dangerously Forbidden Love* Today!

The Crane Family Series

Available Now

The Reluctant Mafia King
Sweet Lies
Billion Dollar Love Story
Be Mine
Protecting Her
Dangerously Forbidden Love
His Heart
Love In The Dark

Box Sets Available

The Crane Family Series

Other Books By Melony Ann
The Beautiful Dream Series

Available Now

Loving You
My Love, My Heart
Softening Lyric
Undercover Temptations
Captain Charming
Breaking Boundaries
Crashing Into You
Tactical Inferno
Ravishing Our Queen
Cherished By The Texan
Unveiling Our Passions

Box Sets Available

The Beautiful Dream Series: Box Set: Part 1
The Beautiful Dream Series: Box Set: Part 2

The Deimos Trilogy

Available Now

Connor's Legacy
Aryan's Alpha
Kade's Redemption

Box Sets Available

The Deimos Trilogy

The Forbidden Temptation Series

Available Now

The Detective's Forbidden Temptation
The Running Back's Forbidden Temptation

The Lucinio Family Series

Available Now

Rising From The Ashes
The Player's Rebel
Encrypting My Heart

Multi Author Series
Piper Falls: Firehouse 49

Available Now

Ignite My Fire by Melony Ann
Regain My Fire by Kindra White
Playing With My Fire by D.L. Howe
Fight My Fire by Darley Collins
Against My Fire by Anneke Boshoff
Relight My Fire by Louise Murchie
Harness My Fire by Ayana Lisbet
Quench My Fire by Havana Wilder

Let's Be Friends

Follow me on

Bookbub

Facebook

Goodreads

Instagram

Tik Tok

Visit my website
www.melonyannauthor.com

Subscribe to my newsletter and get a FREE never-seen-before NOVELLA
just for subscribers!
https://www.melonyannauthor.com/exclusive-content

Join my Facebook Reader Group!
Jason's and Melony's Sizzling Book Nook

The official Crane Family Series Playlist on YouTube
https://youtube.com/playlist?list=PLGEiD5wbQmDc78K7gNeODh-
janqmIFiie

Dedication

You'll always be our protection; the shield that keeps evil and danger away from us.

Acknowledgements

Brad - I love you more and more every day.

Laura - They say love doesn't strike twice. That once you've found your true love, you'll never find another. We prove them wrong every day. We've shown that love comes in many forms. That it doesn't matter where it starts. All that matters is that it is. Without you and your love and heart, I would never be able to get through my day. I love you.

Jay - Your love makes my world keep turning, and I'll never stop loving you.

Ayana - It's been an honor being under your loving wing. I look forward to many more years.

Anneke - You're my real life superhero. I look up to you and aspire to be like you each day. Love you, girlie.

Jason - Have I mentioned recently how amazing you are? No? Well, you're amazing.

To the Bookstagram Community.

To my family.

To all of those who believe in me and support me.

To all of those who don't.

Cover by: Carter Cover Designs

Edited by: Alyssa Skaggs

About Melony Ann

Melony Ann began writing short stories and poetry as a child. She continued honing her craft over the years until she took the plunge and began publishing her work, despite having severe anxiety.

Melony writes contemporary romance stories that are full of suspense and a lot of steam.

When she isn't writing, she is loving her family and working to make her life something she deserves.

Melony believes that if her writing can inspire just one person, then all of her hard work is worth it.

Her hope is that her writing allows each and every one of her readers to escape for a little while. To dive into a different world one book at a time.